Tapestry

A Lowcountry Rapunzel

SOPHIA ALEXANDER

ONALEX BOOKS

Savannah, GA

<u>The Silk Trilogy</u>

Silk: Caroline's Story
Tapestry: A Lowcountry Rapunzel
Homespun

℘

To those who have begun to grasp the extent of life's intricacies,
yet still aim to make the best of it.
And for Michael, in particular.

ISBN: 978-1-955444-26-2
Library of Congress Control Number: 2021921867

Tapestry: A Lowcountry Rapunzel is a work of fiction. Where real-life figures or locations appear, the situations, incidents, and dialogues concerning those persons or places are fictional and are not intended to depict actual events or to change the fictional nature of the work. The names, characters, places and events portrayed in this book are the products of the author's imagination or are used fictitiously.

This book contains an excerpt from *Homespun* by Sophia Alexander. This excerpt may not reflect the final content of the forthcoming edition from Onalex Books.

CONTENTS

1• Gaynelle's Time

January 1918, Greeleyville, SC

WHEN GAYNELLE SNATCHED HER TOES from the hard, freezing floor, her breath caught—not so much from the cold as from the bed's squeak of protest. Shivering, she fished out a scratchy woolen sock from under the mound of covers. Socks were like cats, always wandering off at night.

"No, please no…" the lumpy mound whined. "It's so cold."

A few clumsy pats revealed that the quilts had shifted off of the ice blocks that were her sister's feet. The second stray was curled up next to them.

"Sorry," Gaynelle whispered, putting the quilts back in place.

Padding into the kitchen, she blew the cookstove embers and lit the kerosene lamp, taking care not to smudge her sleeves with soot.

After layering a coat, hat, and boots over her nightgown, she hurried into the bracing chill of the early morning air, thrilled to be free for at least a little while. When her boot slid on the porch, she gave a short, elated gasp. Her exhalation was a cloudy puff in the swinging lamplight.

As usual, Gaynelle was the first to rise. No matter the weather, this was her favorite time of day, when the world belonged to her alone. Mama generally stayed up at night until she was sure everyone was asleep in their beds, so earlier and earlier bedtimes had led to the discovery of this hour or so for herself. It was so peaceful that she could hardly believe a war was going on across the ocean, a Great War that didn't have a blessed thing to do with her, seeing as how her daddy was too old to have to register for the draft.

Crunching across icy grass to the stable, Gaynelle let herself into Julep's stall. He nuzzled her hand.

"Just a minute." She reached into a burlap sack for a handful of oats. His lips tickled her palm. She hugged him close, enveloped by his warm horse breath. She patted his sleek chestnut coat.

After feeding Julep and the mules, Gaynelle climbed up a narrow wooden ladder to her perch in Julep's stall, where she hung the lantern on its hook; its orange light illuminated the small space and part of the stall with a tangerine glow, leaving the other half in shadow.

Daddy had built the perch for her after he found her reading in the straw on the floor of Julep's stall. Novels upset Mama even more than schoolbooks, so he'd fashioned a cubbyhole under the seat that allowed her to stow her books where Mama wouldn't see them. Since Mama didn't much like Julep either, Gaynelle imagined she might not even know about this spot. Each morning, after the family clattered awake, Gaynelle would stow her book and complete the outside morning chores.

For now, though, she settled onto her perch and pulled out *Rebecca of Sunnybrook Farm*, a gift from Aunt Anna. Gaynelle seldom saw their old family friend, but Daddy would sometimes stop by her place when he took his produce into Kingstree to sell. Occasionally he brought back presents from her for his girls—usually novels or new clothes. Daddy would stash the rectangular packages that meant books directly in her cubbyhole.

When Gaynelle finished a story, she'd see if Vivian wanted to read it. If not—and it had been a while since Vivian had shown any interest in reading—she'd send it with Daddy back to Aunt Anna's for safekeeping, where big oak bookshelves waited like a far-off horde of hidden treasure.

Mama didn't approve of books and clutter. In fact, Mama didn't approve of much anything Gaynelle liked. She'd find fault with whatever caught her attention. Even the stable was resented for being sturdier than their house—never mind that Daddy could only do but one thing at a time, and the stable had been built long after the old house. It was true, maybe, that if it weren't for the kitchen cookstove, the stable would be warmer than the house during the winter. Even now, the animals' body heat kept the stable almost cozy. But Mama's resentment would no doubt multiply if she took the trouble to discover Gaynelle's perch, a hardwood construction sanded perfectly smooth with such obvious care.

Shaking her head, Gaynelle shifted, trying to get comfortable on her cushion. She'd sewn it herself from one of her prettiest outgrown dresses—one that Aunt Anna had given her. Lace and buttons had been salvaged from the dress to decorate the cushion, and it was stuffed with leftover cotton from the field; she'd picked the neps from the bolls by hand. If she had to do it over again, however, she might leave off the buttons—not because Mama was right in her scorn for unnecessary ornamentation, but because they poked her bottom. It was like sitting on rocks, almost.

Gaynelle's favorite clothes used to come straight from Aunt Anna, but they hadn't received anything new in a long time. Now her best dresses were hand-me-downs from Vivian. If Mama bought Gaynelle anything, it was certain to be ugly. Serviceable, Mama called it. She'd always been more indulgent towards the strong-willed older daughter—or previously strong-willed, since Vivian was only a pale reflection of her exuberant self these days.

To drown such thoughts, Gaynelle sniffed at the ink-print of her book. It smelled heavenly, though the story wasn't as thrilling as her last read, *The Turn of the Screw*. Still, Gaynelle identified with poor, plain Rebecca. She could imagine leaving their meager conditions at home to stay with her aunt—only living with Aunt Anna would be worlds better, as Aunt Anna wasn't much like the spinster aunts in the story. In fact, she wasn't even technically their aunt. She'd been the best friend of their birth mother, Caroline.

A widowed fashion designer, Aunt Anna was not only successful, but she'd married into money. She used to visit them on occasion—until Mama told her not to. It wasn't fair, but Daddy always insisted that they do whatever Mama wanted. He wouldn't tolerate complaints, cutting his girls short every time, saying they'd have been lost without Jessie—and that Gaynelle owed her respect and obedience. He knew how unfair it was, though—Gaynelle was certain of it.

She sometimes wondered what Caroline had been like, what her own life would have been like if Caroline hadn't died. Even Vivian didn't remember her.

Daddy rarely mentioned his first wife, but he once told Gaynelle that she had Caroline's blond, curly hair. That suggestion had burrowed into Gaynelle's consciousness like a wood-tick under her skin—or at least Mama would deem it just that pernicious. Mama preferred Vivian's smooth, dark tresses.

Even though Vivian was pretty much already a grown woman—and had recently begun wearing her hair up like one—Mama had taken to brushing it every night. Vivian just let her.

Mama didn't brush Gaynelle's unruly locks in that same gentle way. If Gaynelle didn't fix her own hair in the morning, Mama would yank the brush through unmercifully. Braids were safest. Gaynelle had asked Daddy how Caroline wore her hair, but he didn't want to talk about it.

Hair was only one small way that Mama preferred sixteen-year-old Vivian. The best Gaynelle could manage was to do her chores and stay out from underfoot. She wished it were just the staying-out-from-underfoot part, because then she'd sit and read all day long, but all too soon the stable door was creaking open.

Daddy's voice called out, "Mornin', Gaynelle. Time to get to it."

Gaynelle flicked the book's ribbon into place and slid it into the cubby. Out of the stall in seconds, she caught up with him before he'd headed too far towards the new field—a field he'd been steadily clearing for the past month. She tackled him from behind, wrapping her arms around him. He laughed and spun around, sending her hat flying. She screamed with mock indignation. Early morning was not only *her* special time, it was *their* special time, if only for a few moments. It had been for a couple of years now.

When her feet were again safely on the still-crunchy grass, she snatched up her hat and took off for the chicken coop, calling back over her shoulder, "The chickens are waitin'!"

Indeed, Ivanhoe and Old Dom were crowing majestically as she headed over to let them out of their coop. "Here, chick, chick, chick," she piped in the cheery, high-pitched voice she reserved for critters. Ivanhoe, the handsome young rooster, was always the first one out; he strutted confidently, lifting his bright red comb high in the air and showing off well-preened feathers. Old Dom, the patriarch of the black-and-white-barred flock, stayed with the hens, more concerned with keeping order. Gaynelle threw down scratch-feed for them, then lugged some firewood into the house.

After depositing the wood, she began to pull off her coat but immediately realized the house was practically an icebox. Vivian was sitting by the inert wood stove, rubbing her arms as Mama tucked a blanket around her. Gaynelle bit her lip. *I forgot to get the stove goin' this mornin'. Again.*

Mama scowled at her. "Well, it's about time. Your sister's gonna catch her death. Don't dawdle. You need to fix breakfast, too. I swear, child."

"Sorry, Mama." Gaynelle stoked the fire, equal shares of guilt and resentment igniting at once. With a sigh, she snapped up the kettle to fill at the pump. When she returned, she set it on the stove with a small clatter. As she prepared the breakfast, she periodically cast her mama a glance that said, *You could do it yourself.*

Finally, Mama's steely hand seized her arm. "I've had 'bout enough outta you. You're this close to a lickin'."

Gaynelle stumbled over her own feet as she was hauled to Vivian's side.

Mama's short fingernails bit into her flesh. When she let go, it was to clamp Vivian's pale hand against the nape of Gaynelle's neck. "Feel this. You jus' feel this."

Gaynelle gave an icy shudder.

"Don't give a second thought to your sister, do you? Only thinkin' 'bout yourself, but you ain't cold like her."

The hand wasn't growing any warmer. The cold seemed to sting Vivian with a ferocity that evaded the rest of them. Her lips were tinged blue, her extremities those of an ice maiden.

Gaynelle peered anxiously into Vivian's pale, drawn face. A disinterested glance flicked upwards; then the glazed, empty stare found its way back out the kitchen window, unsettling Gaynelle more than anything Mama could say. With a queasy stomach, Gaynelle regarded the dark hollows surrounding Vivian's blue eyes—hollows which bespoke sadness, dark winter, and disquieted, tormented thoughts. A chill that had nothing to do with the icy hand on her neck trickled down Gaynelle's spine. When the tea kettle whistled, breaking the spell, she shook herself. *Too many ghost stories.*

Mama poured the steaming water over a cotton drawstring bag that contained a mixture of dried herbs and roots. Handing the ceramic cup to Vivian, she murmured, "Hold this to warm your hands first, then drink all of it."

As Gaynelle inhaled the aroma of mint, she imagined the warmth thawing Vivian's hands. Her own body began to slump with relief.

Nodding absently, Vivian obeyed Mama's instructions. This had been the routine for some time, ever since the weather had grown cold.

Ain't nothin' to worry about. She's not in any real danger if she can pull herself together like that. Despite the vacant stare, Vivian had at least been tidy as usual this morning, hair pinned neatly back.

Gaynelle poured some hot water in a pitcher for her own morning wash. Taking it to their bedroom, she stood on the rag rug and scrubbed beneath her nightgown as fast as she could. Peeking back out at Vivian, she dried off, reassured. Her sister looked perfectly normal sipping on her tea. Gaynelle had just sighed with relief when she noticed Mama slipping Vivian's boot onto her foot.

As Mama tied it for her, Gaynelle froze, stunned at the sight of Vivian being dressed. Swallowing the lump in her throat, Gaynelle knew that she would have to leave for school alone, once again. Vivian hadn't felt well enough to attend school nor church for some time, but Gaynelle hadn't been overly concerned until now. After all, she could practically still hear Mama's clear voice repeating those words she'd said so often these past months—"Vivian already has 'bout as much learnin' as a girl could want."

At this rate, Gaynelle hoped she was right.

2• Rosa's Secret

CLAMBERING DOWN FROM THE SCHOOL WAGON, Gaynelle could hardly feel the rough wooden side planks, her fingers were so numb. She hurried into the Greeleyville schoolhouse, where it was blessedly warm, and slid into her seat next to Rosa Pack.

Gaynelle straightened with pride, ignoring the sharp prickles as her fingers began to thaw. Carefully she set her books and slate on the shared table. Sultry, voluptuous Rosa was allowing her the privilege of sitting there during Vivian's absence. Gaynelle glanced admiringly at Rosa's thick red shawl draped over one shoulder and drooping to the opposite elbow.

"Hey," Gaynelle murmured shyly, putting her hands under the table to stretch and clench the tingling away.

Rosa drum-rolled her own fingers as she cast dark, frustrated eyes her way. "Isn't Vivian ever comin' back to school?"

"I dunno. Maybe not." Lengthening her back to seem as tall as possible, Gaynelle asked, "Whatcha itchin' so bad to tell her 'bout?"

Rosa pursed full lips, considering the earnest face before her. "I ever tell you that you look like the girl on the Jell-o ad, only without the big blue hair bow?"

"I'll wear one tomorrow." Gaynelle tossed a braid, elation fluttering in her chest. "You know, *I* can tell Vivian whatever it is you wanna tell her."

Rosa regarded Gaynelle for a long moment. "You hafta keep it a secret. You can only tell Vivian."

Gaynelle's heart pattered with excitement. She bent close. Rosa smelled like fig preserves.

"I went to a party with my ma at Rennie's place," Rosa whispered with relish. "You remember my sis and her husband, Zingle, right?"

Holding her breath, Gaynelle nodded, though she only remembered hearing their names.

"Well… while Ma and Rennie were busy dancin' and showin' off, I started talkin' with Henry." Her dark-brown eyes glowed. "He ain't never even looked my way before, but this time he shared his drink with me. I was pretty much walkin' on a slant by the time we made out behind the barn." Her voice rose to a squeak, and she cupped her hand over her mouth.

Eyes round as marbles, Gaynelle gasped, "Henry Timmons?"

"What? No!" Rosa cast a horrified glance at their classmate, then replied in a whisper, "No, silly. I'm not dilly-dallyin' with little boys. Henry is Zingle's brother. *My* Henry is a man." She batted her eyelashes. "A full-grown man. One old enough to get married."

"Or go off to war," Gaynelle said flatly. "Bet he had to register for the draft."

Her eyes flashed. "Better not. Figures I'd finally meet someone and him be sent off straight-away to die. So much for Wilson keepin' us outta the war."

"That liar," Gaynelle agreed. Waving a dismissive hand, she leaned in closer, wanting to hear more. Pretty much anything Rosa chose to do was instantly fascinating, even if all the boys Gaynelle knew were imbeciles. In a whisper, she asked, "Did you really kiss him?"

Rosa's frown softened into a smirk. "Ain't you ever kissed no one?"

Heat rose in Gaynelle's cheeks. "Not a big grown man. Not like that."

Rosa tossed her head. "Every fella is different. Henry knows what he's doin'. He don't flail about like no drownin' fish." She bit her lip as if to stop from saying too much. Turning back to her slate, she murmured with a sideways glance, "I'm gonna tell Vivian the rest myself."

Her heart full, Gaynelle gazed at the older girl. Rosa Pack was, for sure, the wildest friend they had. It was her Injun blood, that Injun blood they weren't supposed to talk about. Rosa's ma had a reputation for throwing parties and dancing, and everyone chalked her behavior up to the fact that she was part-Injun—just in whispers, of course. Rosa's pa was off hunting or out of town with his sales business half the time, leaving his family to their own devices. The rest of the time he was there, joining in.

Turning to her own slate, Gaynelle started to copy sums from the board until Rosa breathed in her ear, "We been meetin' on the sly, and not even my ma knows."

Gaynelle looked up into eyes twinkling with mischief. "Would she be mad?"

Rosa's lips curled. "Prob'ly not, but it wouldn't be so much fun, then, now would it? 'Sides, Ma's always stealin' my thunder. Talks Henry's head off whenever she's 'round him. Don't give a chicken's gizzard that she's takin' his attention from *me*."

Gaynelle nodded sympathetically.

"Anyhow, could be we get married. Then if they make him register for the draft, he can try for an exemption."

"Would they give it jus' cuz he's married?"

"Maybe… 'specially if we have a baby."

"A baby?" Gaynelle gasped.

Rosa laughed, preening under the girl's gaze. She might be only three years older than Gaynelle Bell, but anyone with two eyes could see that she was a woman ready for a family, worlds different than the pinafored child seated next to her. Rosa wore a ladies' two-piece dress, and her black hair was coiled into a large bun. Not to mention all her feminine accomplishments. Her jelly rolls were now in demand at each and every church function, and her singing voice was near loud enough to drown out the pump organ she played tolerably well. No one had had to teach it to her, neither. Her pa had just brought it home one day. He was so proud of her for learning to play it that he'd toted it around ever since, wherever they moved—and they moved fairly often. Some folks had to depend on sheet music, but Rosa played by ear and didn't need it. She patted her bun, sublimely self-satisfied.

Just then, the morning bell rang. The schoolteacher rapped on her desk for their attention, and they stood for the pledge of allegiance, reciting by rote, "I pledge allegiance to my flag and to the republic for which it stands, one nation, indivisible, with liberty and justice for all."

Gaynelle touched her own hair self-consciously. Maybe she'd wear a bow tomorrow, but it wouldn't help her seem any older—and she'd never given much thought to actual boys at all, much less grown men. Gaynelle frowned. She was excited to be included by the older girl, but she wouldn't officially turn into a teenager for another half-year, and she'd really still rather think about animals and books than boys. *Even earthworms are more interestin' than the boys around here*—at least, that's what she and the rest of the girls told each other at recess, where the boys stuck with the boys and the girls with the girls. That had always worked for Gaynelle until now, but if she was going to be Rosa's friend, then the few older students would expect her to start behaving more like them.

Sliding a hand down her still-relatively-flat chest, Gaynelle reminded herself that Vivian was nowhere near as voluptuous as Rosa, either. Nor was Vivian even talking much about boys yet, for all that she had been fascinated by that scandal about Mata Hari and was getting near old enough to marry.

The thought struck Gaynelle like a mule-kick. Bad enough that Vivian was so sickly. If she got better, romance could then steal her away, assuming Rosa's shenanigans were anything to go by. Gaynelle thought about it a moment longer, then sadly shook her head. *Vivian can't meet no one while she's sick at home. That's the last thing I have to worry about—and marriage to some draft dodger ain't the worst thing that could happen to her, not by far.*

3 • Jessie's Flower Garden

W ITH INFINITE CARE, Jessie patted the crumbly, cool earth around the newly-planted bulb. Red camellias bloomed nearby. The scraggly remnants of mint so recently crushed underfoot invigorated the air with an aromatic scent. Between patches of green, the dry ground was uniformly barren in shades of brown—the blackish-brown of the earth, the dull brown of the grass and dead stems, and the copper-brown of pine straw heaped over flower beds. Twining, thorny rose briars, overdue for a pruning, haphazardly graced the fence.

During the past several years, Jessie had developed this herb and flower garden in front of the clapboard house, looking forward most especially to seeing the lilies rise in the spring. Comfrey, mint, and chamomile all had their set places in the garden, but Vivian's disarmingly lovely attendants, the lilies-of-the-valley, had spread with relatively little assistance—their rhizomes ever finding new, fertile soil in which to propagate, long before Jessie had any inkling she would have such need of them.

Vivian was lying down for a rest in the house as Jessie weeded the garden and mulled over the young woman's dosage. Vivian was again refusing her food. *Perhaps I'll give her less for a spell*, Jessie decided, though she normally waited until Vivian took to complaining about her vision before reducing her measure of the *Convallaria* tea.

Her skin was cold as death this mornin', Jessie fretted. *S'pose I'll just have to substitute plain mint again for a while. No point keepin' the child safe at home if she dies on me*, she determined grudgingly. She pulled up a briar growing under the camellia, wincing as a thorn pricked her hand. Her job was difficult and thankless, but as Vivian grew older, it was imperative to protect her from the dangers presented by society in general and one man in particular.

Jessie still shuddered at the memory of Dr. Stephen Connor approaching them nearly a year ago. She'd always fretted about the ongoing presence of the Kingstree family physician, Vivian's blood father, and time had eventually proven her right. He'd left them alone for so long, though, not bothering them once in all the years since Caroline's death. Then out of the clear blue, he'd startled them with that audacious offer.

Clayton had actually been enthused; he'd been *excited* at the suggestion that Vivian be sent off to live at some secondary school for young women far away from them in the big city of Charleston. He'd dismissed Jessie's arguments like so much hot air. To tell the truth, her faith in Clayton's devotion to his family had been undermined that day. *How could he? How could he consider sendin' Vivian away?* Of course he preferred his own flesh-and-blood daughter, Gaynelle, but Jessie had never expected him to send away her own favorite. *Thinks I'm ignorant to the fact that Vivian isn't his blood-child, no matter that she looks so much like Dr. Connor—but that jus' makes it all the more shameful that he's set on sendin' her away.* Stabbing her spade into the earth, Jessie pried at an invading root.

Clayton had referred to Vivian as *nearly a grown woman* and *independent.* Maybe he'd been right on those counts, but Jessie had swiftly taken care of that independent streak and had done so ever since with the assistance of her flowering helpers. Vivian would stay home where she belonged. No conniving, manipulative man was going to take her away from her loving mama's arms. Dr. Connor had certainly not raised the girl, and Jessie had spent far more time tending to the child than Clayton had. She clenched her lips together, vowing, *Vivian is my very own soul child, given into my keepin' by the Lord Almighty himself, and no one on earth will tear us asunder.*

Nevertheless, a few days of vibrant health would hardly persuade anyone that Vivian was well enough even to return to her local school, no matter how much Clayton might wish it. Jessie smiled slightly and patted another bulb. *If they do insist, well, my faithful lily attendants will swirl and steep to perform their sacred duty, as always.*

4 • Vivian Seizes an Opportunity

GAYNELLE FELT LIKE AN ICE-CREAM CONE that might melt before she could share Rosa's delicious gossip with Vivian. Every time she began to tell it, Mama appeared like a fly drawn to sweet, milky drops. Gaynelle would then have to clamp her lips shut to wait for a better time. She tried to stay up at night until Mama finished stalking through the house, but she could never quite manage to stay awake that long. When she attempted to wake Vivian in the pre-dawn morning, her sister would growl and pull the covers over her head.

Rosa cornered Gaynelle on a Thursday morning at school. She'd demanded Vivian's responses to her news a number of times already, but Gaynelle would only shake her head and bend low over her schoolwork as if the teacher were walking by.

Now, however, the buxom teenager took her delinquent courier by the shoulders. "Look here, Gaynelle, it just ain't right that I'm 'bout ready to marry a fella and my best friend don't even know 'bout us. Maybe I should come see her myself."

"I'll tell her tonight," Gaynelle gasped, clutching at the older girl's hand imploringly. The prospect of Rosa visiting their house made Gaynelle forget to breathe. Mama wasn't normally a jolly person, but she loathed Rosa something fierce—and Rosa could not have forgotten the one and only time that she'd been to their house, when Jessie had slammed the door in her face. Gaynelle didn't understand just why Mama hated Rosa, but a visit from Vivian's friend would only cause trouble at home, that much was certain.

As Gaynelle rode home on the school wagon that afternoon, she fretted to herself about how to get Rosa's news to Vivian. Her reverie was broken, however, when she spotted the new yellow house that now signified she was almost home—it was small, little more than a hastily-thrown-up shack for another family of sharecroppers that hadn't been there very long at all. An ebony-skinned teenage girl chased an equally-dark youth about the front yard, splashing a bucket of water on him. He shouted out a protest, the front of his shirt now plastered to him. The girl's laughter brimmed with infectious joy. Gaynelle giggled and wondered if she might dare to say hello. Then she noticed the pale, almost ghostly figure strolling down the lane to meet her and promptly put any notion of greeting the new neighbors out of her head.

"You feelin' better?" Gaynelle asked as she clambered down.

Vivian smoothed back her dark hair. "Well, maybe not completely. But I did eat a whole plateful at dinnertime. Don't know where that appetite came from. Ain't it a beautiful day?" She flashed a broad smile, and Gaynelle marveled at it. It seemed like she hadn't seen that smile for months.

Bouncing on her toes, Gaynelle started with her back down the lane, urging, "Come with me while I do my chores."

"I don't feel *that* well." Touching her forehead, Vivian threw back her head.

Gaynelle laughed and drew to a halt. "Then, real quick. I gotta tell you about Rosa and her fella while I have the chance."

"Mama's waitin' for us. I had to talk her into lettin' me come meet you, and if we don't head straight back you know she'll get mad as a yellow jacket we done stepped on."

Gaynelle closed her mouth and nodded, frightened at the notion of Mama appearing out of nowhere like she sometimes did—with stinging words and perhaps a stinging belt.

"Best if you just come sit with me when you're done. I been crochetin' some on the porch. Remember that scarf I started months ago? There's still a little light left."

Gaynelle rushed through her chores as though Rosa were watching from on high. All the while, Vivian looked perfectly normal again. The rocker creaked back and forth as she focused on her yarnwork. Their orange cat rubbed against her skirt, gladdening Gaynelle's heart.

By the time her chores were finished, she was chiding herself for having possibly missed her chance once again. She'd also meant to ask her sister if she knew anything about the new family at that little yellow shack, but first she had to complete her mission for Rosa. Glancing around dutifully to make sure Mama wasn't lurking nearby, she said in a low voice, "I gotta tell you about Rosa now."

Vivian's eyes widened with interest at hearing the news. "Oh my gracious," she breathed. "Rosa kissed that nincompoop Bubba Browder in the coat-room once, but she ain't never said nothin' about a real grown-up man."

"And she ain't even as old as you," Gaynelle taunted with delight, making smooching noises at her sister. She leaned closer, thrilled to have Vivian back. "And that's not all—Rosa said she might just hitch up with him. Her mama don't even know."

Vivian's jaw dropped. "Are they really in love, you think?"

Gaynelle set back on her heels. "Well, her eyes sure are all sparkly when she talks about him. Maybe she is. And she seems downright convinced it'd help keep him from havin' to go off to war. They're meetin' up tomorrow mornin' behind our church."

"To get married?" Vivian's eyes were wide.

"No, silly. He's bringin' a picnic for them."

Vivian sat up straighter. "Down the road here? Maybe I can go, too."

"No way Mama's gonna let you."

"She's takin' some stuff over to Granny and Uncle Simms' place early in the morning. I've gotta go. Think you could saddle up Julep for me? Tomorrow mornin'?" At Gaynelle's dismayed stare, she waved her crochet hook. "I haven't felt this good in ages. Every time I start feelin' better, I fall sick again. If I don't go now, I might never see Rosa again."

Gaynelle sobered at the thought. "But Mama'd get mad."

"Then wait 'til after Mama's gone, dingbat."

The uncommonly rosy color in her sister's cheeks was marvelous—Vivian was bright-eyed and flushed, animated and energetic, alert as a chickadee. Gaynelle threw her arms around Vivian's neck. "I'll have to saddle Julep up real early cuz o' school. Mama might get mad, but I don't care. They're gonna be right here. It'd be a shame for you to miss 'em."

"And there's nothin' really wrong with a mornin' outin', anyway." Vivian pried her sister's arm off her neck and went back to crocheting.

"Besides," Gaynelle said, convinced she'd just come up with the best reason of all, "when's the last time you rode Julep?"

5• The Picnic Revelry

ROSA RUBBED A BIT OF TALLOW on her lips as she stood behind the church, waiting for Henry. Dreamily, she put the small tin back in her pocket and began to stroll across the graveyard, reflecting on their time together over the past few weeks. Henry was by leaps and bounds the most amazing man she'd ever met. Tall, forceful, strong, domineering, experienced—there weren't enough wonderful words to describe him, and besides all that, his warm, full lips felt absolutely right against her own. She couldn't believe that he was interested in her, a small-town girl—no, a small-town woman—with practically no worldly experience.

Life was going to be exciting with Henry. In their long hours together, he'd told her stories he hadn't dared share with their families. She knew the intimate details of his world travels. Everyone else thought he'd just gone off to work on the railroad for the past couple of years, but she knew the fantastic truth—that he'd taken to the seas on an international cargo ship not long after the Lusitania was sunk by the Germans.

In that short time, he'd had adventures to last a lifetime. His ship had narrowly missed being torpedoed by the Germans. After rerouting, they'd had to fight hand-to-hand with bonafide pirates on the Canary Islands. Then he'd served as acting captain of the cargo ship while the real captain recovered from his wounds.

Not long after they made port in Morocco, he'd bumped into none other than Teddy Roosevelt in a tavern. The former president was chafing for war so bad that he'd gone to Africa to hunt for big game to distract himself. Excited to meet the famous former president, Henry bandied about with him for a while, but Teddy kept trying to wrangle him into his war plans. Too smart to sign his own death warrant, Henry instead signed up for a big camel race in the Sahara just for an excuse to get away from him but ended up passed out from the heat only yards from the finish line, toppling into the desert sand like a rag doll.

Rosa clicked her tongue. Poor Henry had absolutely nothing to be embarrassed about. Not that time, at least—unlike in war-weary England, where he'd had to creep out of the country like a cat-burglar smack in the midst of one of the air raids.

Rosa shook her head. It was too bad it had come to that. Henry had actually been a hero of sorts after rescuing a stolen Rolls-Royce for that British duke. The duke had been shouting and pointing, so on impulse Henry had pushed a cart in front of the fleeing car. The driver had slammed on the brakes. Then Henry had dragged the thief from the car. He'd started pummeling when it looked like the fellow might be reaching for a weapon, all the while spouting curses about 'bloody Germans'.

Rattled, Henry had relinquished the criminal to guards in tall, furry hats. The duke had been so grateful that he gave him five thousand pounds, then offered his daughter's noble hand in marriage. Full of grand ideas about becoming part of the Saxe-Coburg family, Henry had stayed in their palace that night.

The next day, just as he was preparing to accept the proposal, an explosion rocked the palace. They ran outside. The sky was surreal, like some sort of floating carnival. Huge zeppelins were dropping bombs on them, on all of London.

In that moment, Henry realized he didn't want to become such a target. An Austrian prince's murder had started the whole war, after all, and the English hated the German blood that reeked to high heaven in their royals' veins. So Henry regretfully declined, telling the duke that what he really wanted was an American girl, a solid Southern girl who could sing and play the piano—and who could cook and garden and shoot anyone that needed shooting. The duke nodded so understandingly that Henry went on to suggest that maybe the royal family should change their name to something not German. At this, the duke grew very still, then excused himself to speak to a guard.

In sudden fear for his life, Henry didn't even wait for nightfall. He stole away as bombs continued to rain on London, berating himself for insulting the royal family. As far as he knew, though, his reward money still sat right there in an English bank. Perhaps one day they would go back for it.

Rosa shivered with excitement and pulled her shawl around her shoulders more closely. She hadn't really believed his tales until she saw headlines that the royal family actually had changed their name to Windsor. Stunned that his confidences had been true all along, she resolved not to make the mistake of doubting him again.

Henry was twenty-two years old but smart enough to tell everyone he was only nineteen so as to avoid the draft. He'd already seen the world and had sown his wild oats. Maybe some fellas had never left Greeleyville and were dying to go off to war, but Henry was past all that and was ready to settle down.

Rosa bit her lip and drew to a halt. It was just too bad he'd gotten mixed up with Julia after he came home. Julia was Henry's biggest mistake—Rosa knew this because she'd overheard Henry telling Zingle about her. They'd been sitting around the campfire, months ago, before Henry had ever looked twice at Rosa. 'Easy to bed, but crazy as hell'—that's what he'd said about Julia. The words kept repeating in her head. Julia was with that other fellow now, though, and somehow they already had a baby—a little baby boy. Rosa sent a rock skittering with her boot, then another one.

Henry was going to forget all about Julia and harem girls and royal suitors, though. Hadn't he told her that she was more beautiful than any of them? That he'd embrace a penniless existence just to stay with her? He wanted to live out the rest of his life on a modest farm, safe in a rural existence near a small town. Well, that was fine for now, but one day when the war was over, she'd convince him to go back to Britain to retrieve his fortune.

Rosa hugged herself at the thought, wishing she could tell her best friend about Henry and his fortune and, well, all of his dashing deeds of derring-do. And about Julia, too. It was hard keeping it all to herself.

A low whistle made Rosa look up. Hastily, she pinched her cheeks, hoping to put some color into them. As Henry sauntered around the corner of the church, she laughed.

A large grin was plastered across his face. Mindless of the chilly weather in just his shirtsleeves, he wagged a large food satchel at her—and a bottle of what she guessed was moonshine. "Look what I managed to dig up, Rosa-girl. We can have a party, just us two, and that be the best kinda partyin' I know."

"No foolin'. But Ma'll run you off like a bat outta hell if you bring me home smellin' like a distillery. She thinks I'm at school." Rosa's grin belied the words she belted back at him. She was delighted with Henry's antics, and his smirk showed that he knew it.

"Well then, maybe I just won't take you home at all, Rosa-girl. I'd ruther keep you with me anyhow." Henry drew Rosa into his arms, bussing her lips before drawing her towards the church's picnic table. "These vittles should still be warm. Ma cooked 'em up just 'fore I headed over here."

As Henry spread the food out on the picnic table, the soft thump of approaching hoofbeats made them look up.

Vivian was sitting astride Julep, jauntily waving mittened hands. She called for them to help her dismount and didn't bother to secure Julep before hugging her friend.

"Oh, Rosa… I just had to come and see you. When Gaynelle told me you were meetin' over here with your beau this mornin', why, I couldn't bear to just sit at home like a ninny and miss you." Turning towards Rosa's companion, she breathlessly added, "You must be Henry Caddell. Rennie's brother-in-law, right? I'm Vivian Bell."

Henry gave another whistle as his eyes raked her slim figure. "Well, you are right welcome to join us here, you pretty thing. It is a *real* pleasure to meet you."

At this, Rosa smacked his arm, but she laughed, "Never mind him, Vivian—he's incorrigible."

Some women would take offense, Rosa sighed to herself, directing Vivian towards the picnic table. *Henry's never had any qualms about sweet-talkin' the girls, that's for sure. But what's important is that he chose me. If he really wanted Vivian, he'd go after her instead. He's a man who gets what he wants, and he wants me.* With this satisfactory conclusion, Rosa took her seat next to Henry, placing a possessive hand on his low back. *There's somethin' real refreshin' and honest about a man who makes no secret of his thoughts and wishes. Rather, it makes his choosin' me extra-special. He's not blind or stupid or shy or settlin'…* Her heart swelled with pride as she reflected once more that he had chosen her, Rosa Pack, above all the other women in the whole world, but Vivian's smile was now rather obviously forced.

"How you feelin'?" Rosa asked with sudden concern. "Thought I might never see you again. Can't believe you made it out here today."

"Oh, I'm havin' a few good days, finally." Vivian tried to relax her shoulders. "Always so cattywampus. No tellin' how I'll feel tomorrow, so when Gaynelle said y'all was meetin' out here, I found the gumption to come see you and your fellow." Vivian shot a glance towards Henry, indicating she wasn't quite so glad to see *him*.

"What'd you bring for the picnic?" Henry asked.

"I—I didn't actually—"

"Then what's this?" His face puckered with exaggerated confusion as he leaned towards her, reaching to brush behind her ear. He brandished a biscuit on his palm as he withdrew his hand. "Well, look at that."

"Pay no mind to his tomfoolery." Rosa laughed and pushed the biscuit towards Vivian. "Eat up. Henry brought it all. I only brought my usual school dinner this time, cuz I haven't told Ma about us yet, y'know. Isn't Henry thoughtful?"

Vivian nodded, slipping off her mittens to butter the biscuit.

"He almost married royalty when he was in England." Rosa glared at Henry, daring him to protest her sharing this privileged information.

"Oh, really?" Vivian's brow arched. "Maybe that's why he likes you, too."

"No comparison." Henry squeezed Rosa's shoulder. "Way better than some hoity-toity princess."

"Rosa comes from one o' them English kings, too," Vivian insisted.

"Oh, for heaven's sake!" Rosa scowled at her but laughed at Henry's look of surprise. "You ain't heard my pa go on about it? He'll talk your ear off. Just ask him when he's been drinkin' sometime."

"Nah, you tell me."

"I dunno, really. His great-great-granddaddy was s'posed to be the son of some duke or somethin'. The king gave him a bunch of land where Paxville is, but I bet it was just to get rid o' him."

"Dang, I didn't know Paxville was named for your family," Henry enthused. "Which king was that?"

"The one durin' the Revolution—that's why I think he musta been tryin' to get rid o' my ancestor, else why else would Joseph Pack go off and fight for the patriots?"

"You sure 'bout that?"

"Yessir. Pure American."

"Your mama's got more right to call herself that than some son of a British duke," Henry snorted.

Rosa pelted him with the crumbs in her hand.

Henry put up his arms as if to block an assault. "Just kiddin'!"

"Quit bein' ugly."

"Zingle teases Rennie about bein' an Injun all the time, and she don't seem to mind."

"Well, I do."

"But I ain't never heard you talk about bein' royal. Ain't that somethin'? Say, you ever heard this?" Henry's eyes were bright as he broke out in hearty song to the tune of 'My Country, 'Tis of Thee'. "God bless our noble king, God save great George our king…"

"I like our words better," Vivian muttered when he finished. Raising an eyebrow, she asked, "You sing that to the king while you were there?"

"Didn't get the chance. He missed out on a real treat."

Rosa laughed. "You really are too big for your britches."

"Y'all know they're antiquated, right?" Vivian leaned forward. "The Brits don't let their monarchs rule any more than we do. They vote on everythin', just like us except *way* better. Even women can vote there now."

"How do you know this stuff?" Rosa's brows knitted.

"Aunt Anna told my daddy. He said she was all excited about women gettin' the vote *there*. She has friends in Charleston who are part o' the Equal Suffrage League, and they tell her all that sorta thing."

"You one o' them suffragettes?" Henry made a face. "Aw, I don't give a heck about the Brits, really. I like my women more exotic, like

Rosa-girl here. That's why I didn't hang around to marry that duke's daughter." As Rosa scowled at him again, he took her hand and plied it with a kiss. "I know exactly who I wanna be with, sweetheart. I'd ruther be with a duke's great-great-great-granddaughter."

Vivian shook her head, grudgingly more at ease with Rosa's beau. *He's outspoken, coarse, and probably full o' hogwash, but at least he's friendly and fun.*

Henry slipped from the table to kneel on the cold ground, blinking up at Rosa. "Will you marry me?"

"I already told you I would," Rosa laughed, looking up to see Vivian's mouth gaping open wide as a canning jar's.

"You're—you're gonna get married? For real?" Vivian gasped.

Rosa laughed again. "It just makes sense. I mean, maybe then he won't get drafted. They might give him an exemption if he has a family to support here."

"My brother Zingle is married to her sister," Henry put in. "They have a little boy, and he ain't had to go yet."

"I've met Rennie, and she's a sight older than Rosa." Vivian plucked at her friend's sleeve. "No way your pa's gonna even consider lettin' you get married at your age."

"Then maybe he ain't gotta know." Rosa turned to study Henry's face for a long moment. At his encouraging nod, she stood up, a hand pressed to her chest. "Y'all, my heart just skipped a beat."

"Darlin'…" Henry said warmly, leaning against her.

"What is it?" Vivian asked.

Taking a deep breath, Rosa announced, "We're gonna elope!"

Vivian screamed, jumping up to hug her friend. Her reservations about Henry fell away like so many shucks from an ear of corn.

Not to be outdone, Henry sprang up and climbed on top of the table. Hooting and hollering, he danced in circles before jumping back down to lock arms with Rosa. They skipped around in a sort of square dance. Then he held out a hand to Vivian and repeated the pattern— after which she collapsed onto the bench in exhaustion. Still, she dissolved into hysterical laughter with the ribald couple and began to discuss their elopement plans as Henry toasted them with moonshine.

Vivian took a sip of the drink waving in her face. Coughing, she asked, "So, you can go to the county courthouse anytime and get married? Just like that?"

Rosa nodded. "Accordin' to Ethel, I just have to say I'm eighteen, and we're golden as that ring Henry still needs to buy me." She cast him a look. "That's what she and Cecil ended up doin'. They had to go to Sumter because they ran into so many people she knew at the Kingstree courthouse. I'm just 'bout ready to head on over there for our own nuptials." She grinned at Henry, and he threw his arm around her shoulders. Then Rosa's grin faded, replaced with a worried pucker as she gazed past Vivian's shoulder.

A sinking dread stole over Vivian. She slowly turned around.

Standing stock-still next to the church, Jessie stared at them. Her face was flushed a dark red, and her eyes narrowed. Anger radiated from her, palpable even at that distance. Like a goaded bull, Jessie began striding towards them.

Turning to her friends, Vivian felt her throat trying to close up. "Oh, God… she heard us. Mama's not gonna let this go. You'll hafta tell your ma and pa. I'm so sorry."

Rosa shook her head. "That would ruin everythin'."

"I can't wait that long…" Henry pleaded, as if Vivian could do something about it.

She caught her breath. Maybe she could. Grabbing both their hands in hers, she urged, "If you two wanna get married, for real, you'd best go do it right now, before she can stop you."

"You think?" Rosa breathed.

"It's your only chance." Vivian spoke rapidly, squeezing her fingers. "Otherwise you'll have to wait years. And who knows if you'll even be able to marry then? Like you said, Henry might get drafted 'fore you can get married. Take Julep. He's fast enough. You don't have enough hours left in the day to get to Sumter, but you might still be able to make it to Manning this afternoon." A lifetime of dealing with Jessie had taught Vivian that the only things that got past her mama were those that she hadn't had time to catch. Spontaneity had long been Vivian's only hope for any sort of willful, independent action.

A hand clamped tightly around Vivian's wrist. Jessie had reached the revelers at last. "You're comin' home, right now."

Heart pounding, Vivian nodded. "I was just 'bout to anyway. Let me give Rosa a hug good-bye."

Reluctantly, Jessie released her hold on Vivian's arm.

Circling the table, Vivian embraced her friend and whispered, "Go now. Climb on Julep and git."

As Vivian drew back, she screwed up her face, glaring at Jessie.

"I'll never go home!" she shouted. Springing backwards, she took off at a run towards the rear corner of the church, Jessie right on her heels.

Meanwhile, the astonished lovers mounted Julep and set off for the Clarendon County Courthouse.

Only a half-hour or so earlier, Jessie had dutifully dropped off the rutabagas, mustard greens, and dried beans that Clayton had sent his mother.

Amarintha had lived with them for a full year after their marriage. Though it had been crowded, she and Jessie had gotten along well enough at first. Jessie held an inexplicable tolerance for Clayton's mother, but eventually she'd gotten tired of everything she owned reeking of stale tobacco. She put her foot down, demanding that Amarintha stop smoking her corncob pipe in the house. To the older woman's dismay, Clayton had sided with Jessie on the issue. There was nothing else for Amarintha to do but to move out in a tobacco-laden huff to live with her brother Simms, who'd long run a moonshine still behind his old cabin and grew enough tobacco for them both. There she smoked and drank to her heart's content—secure from fussy daughters-in-law and that Prohibition, which just kept getting worse. She never thought state prohibition would last, but now they told her that Congress had just approved an actual nationwide Prohibition amendment to the Federal Constitution. Nevertheless, she was doing her darnedest to ignore how uptight the whole world was getting.

Jessie knew all this by rote, given how many times Amarintha had told her. Their visits rarely went entirely smoothly. Jessie might still keep her cool with Amarintha better than with almost anyone else, but on this particular day, Amarintha had been even worse than usual.

She'd been sitting on the porch, puffing on her corncob pipe. As Jessie climbed down from the wagon brimming with food for *her*, Amarintha had offered, "I'da been jus' dandy with smokin' on da porch, y'know. Dat's what I did when Carrie was alive. Didn't mind doin' it fer her."

She often lumped Clayton's two wives, which didn't much suit Jessie, but for her to express a preference for Caroline was almost more than Jessie could bear. Pursing her lips, Jessie stared at her in the way that shut most people up.

Amarintha cackled. "Don't you never blink? Dunno how my respec'able brudder lived wid dem lizard eyes o' your'n starin' at 'im fer so long." Shrugging, she tapped the pipe upside down against the arm of her chair to shake out the ash. "Reckon I jus' gotta chalk it up to his soft spot fer younguns."

Even this didn't truly provoke Jessie. Still, she set down the bushel-baskets with a thud. Such remarks reminded her of how grateful she was that Clayton's mother didn't live with them anymore.

"Too bad *you* ain't got a soft spot fer younguns."

Sucking in her breath, Jessie swiftly unloaded the other baskets, telling herself how nice it was that she didn't have to put up with the old woman's nasty habits anymore, how much better it was to have Clayton to herself. Delivering vegetables was well worth not having to live with her, so Jessie was willing to put up with this extra chore, give the requisite hugs, and make tedious small talk. She'd thought today would be a good day for it—she could have reassured Amarintha that Vivian was better, and that no, she didn't think the girl needed to see a doctor, not even that root doctor the old woman so persistently recommended. But Jessie didn't feel like having that conversation anymore. Instead of suffering through it all, she spun on her heel and left without another word.

As she drove back home, she stewed. Even Clayton had taken to wondering if they should seek medical help for Vivian, but at least she knew how to clam him up. She had only to start fretting about Dr. Stephen Connor and his peculiar interest in Vivian. Might as well use Clayton's efforts to keep things from her to her own advantage.

Such thoughts swirled in various derivations along with the dust clouds being kicked up by their mule, dust clouds that coated the rickety wagon and irritated her eyes as she tried to peer down the dirt road. She closed them, giving Button full rein.

Amarintha hadn't been wrong about her stares, Jessie knew—and she purposely unnerved folks with them at times. But that wasn't generally why she stared. It was her calling to remain vigilant, especially when mysterious goings-on were afoot. Through the years, she'd learned that the ignorance of others had inevitably been their downfall—though she envied their carefree lives, she scorned their simpleminded, self-centered views of the world. People were, by and large, a gullible, rash lot. Even the clever ones were so wrapped up in their own personal dramas that they could miss a freight train barreling straight for them. *Well, not me. Gonna make sure I'm not blindsided by any such devilry. No one will be makin' a fool o'...*

Just then, unexpected hoots and laughter demanded her attention, irreverent sounds drifting from Clayton's family's graveyard.

She turned to see a little gathering behind the Mount Hope Baptist Church. A fellow was jumping on the picnic table, actually jumping on it. *Young hooligans*, she thought, spying a moonshine bottle. Determinedly, she pulled her wagon to the side of the road, securing the mule to the picket fence bordering the property.

Jessie blinked as she recognized her daughter, then froze for a long moment. The world began to waver and dim before her. Finally, she gasped in a painful breath, and the unwelcome sight returned. It would have been better to be struck senseless. *How? The child has not so much as stepped foot outside her own yard in months. We've skipped her lily dosage for less than a week. And yet here she is with that Injun-child... and some lecherous man with liquor. At our church!*

Snatches of their conversation drifted towards her. Marriage? Courthouse? Her wrath began to rise. *She's nowhere near marriageable age, and that other girl is even younger than her. I let up for even a moment, and my child is determined to leave home. Next she'll be prostitutin' herself on the streets. I cannot afford, can never afford to be so lax again. It's for her own good.* Eyes narrowing at Vivian's unsavory companions, she stepped out of the shadow of the church.

When Vivian yelled that she wouldn't go home, Jessie was sure the devil had possessed her child. She ran after her charge, confusion and outrage coursing through her like wildfire.

Within moments, Jessie overtook her. The girl had tired quickly, though Jessie wouldn't have expected her to be able to run at all, not yet. Wordlessly, Jessie grabbed her arm and dragged her towards the mule wagon. Half-blinded with angry tears, Jessie drove to their house in silence.

Vivian sat flushed, adrenaline streaming through her body. She didn't speak but felt more alive than she could remember feeling in ages. *Rosa's gettin' married—this very afternoon. And Mama don't even know. But even if she did, who cares? None o' her business nohow.*

As Jessie pulled into the yard, she turned distraught eyes upon her daughter. As she met Vivian's impenitent gaze, however, new fury broke forth. *I been too givin', too kind. Kindness is weakness. Costs too dearly. Children don't need parents to befriend and indulge 'em. What they need is a firm hand. I won't fail again.*

Hauling Vivian into the house, Jessie thrust her into a chair. Struggling to regain her composure, she filled a tea kettle at the pump. Vivian waited docilely, her energy spent.

Several minutes later, Jessie turned towards the young woman, transformed. She was breathing evenly, a patient smile on her lips. Self-control had always been her strong suit. "Now, Vivian, I'm sure I don't know what all that was about."

Vivian's eyes flashed once more. As the girl leaned forward to speak, Jessie realized she'd made a mistake in even addressing her. Ignoring the retort passing her daughter's lips, Jessie thrust the cup of hot tea into her hands. The child's over-excited thoughts needed to be quenched as soon as possible. Talking would only refuel her mutinous urges, and Jessie needed Vivian to cool down, to forget such rebellious thoughts. "Hush now. You're gonna make yourself ill again. Drink your tea and calm yourself. We can discuss this later."

6 • Consequences

A s Gaynelle burst through the front door that afternoon, Jessie shushed her. "Vivian's sleepin'. Had another one o' her bouts. You just go on and get those chores done."

Reluctantly heading back outside, Gaynelle began to sweep the porch, distracted with impatient thoughts. *Did Vivian make it to Rosa's rendezvous? Did she get to meet Henry?* She'd waited all day to find out, but Rosa had never shown up to school. Gaynelle wasn't just excited to hear the gossip—she'd also been worried about Vivian getting into trouble.

Before long, the screen door banged open. Vivian stumbled past, clutching her stomach, heading in the direction of the outhouse.

"You okay?" Gaynelle called out.

Vivian disappeared into the structure. Emerging only after several minutes, she halted when Gaynelle spoke to her again but seemed not to comprehend her. Then she spun around, darting back into the privy.

When she finally left the outhouse some time later, her face was even paler than usual and her gait irregular. Gaynelle's questions died on her lips as, for the first time, she was struck with the notion that her sister might not make it to the house without assistance. Grasping Vivian's elbow, she helped her up the stairs and directed her into the rocking chair on the porch.

"You gonna be alright?" Gaynelle asked uncertainly, touching her sister's shoulder in concern. She almost didn't expect an answer.

Sighing, Vivian wiped her clammy forehead with her shirtsleeve. "I guess so… Feelin' somethin' awful—but I held out long enough to see Rosa today." A delighted grin arose, large and aberrant on her peaked countenance.

Encouraged by the smile, Gaynelle asked, "What happened? What did you think o' Henry?"

Eyes brightening, Vivian leaned towards her. "He swaggers. Trouble, no doubt, but that makes him a match for Rosa, right?" She sat back as though already tired from the effort of their conversation. "Oh, by the way, they have Julep."

"What do you mean?" Gaynelle's interest morphed to alarm.

"They borrowed Julep to go elope." Vivian leaned back in her seat, pale and weak but pleased with herself. "Don't tell anyone."

Gaynelle gasped in outrage. "You loaned him to a troublemakin' stranger? So Rosa can run away and get married? How stupid is that?"

Vivian shrugged. "I'm glad I did it. Someone needs a life around here."

Gaynelle glared at the older girl then made an unprecedented decision. Rising decisively, she strode into the house to get her mama. Vivian had clearly lost her senses, and Mama could put a stop to it if anyone could.

To Gaynelle's dismay, Mama looked neither surprised nor angry. She merely nodded as Gaynelle listed her sister's transgressions—and then told Gaynelle 'not to worry about it.' Instead of scolding Vivian, she just started making her another cup of tea, humming all the while.

I should have known, stormed Gaynelle. She ran back outside, intentionally bumping into Vivian's chair as she ran past her on the porch. *I shoulda known. Vivian can do no wrong in Mama's eyes, and this just proves it!*

Ignoring her chores, Gaynelle ran to Julep's empty stall and threw herself onto the straw bedding. Worry about Julep and helpless anger overcame the girl in subsequent waves. She sobbed fitfully until her daddy found her there when he returned from the fields at suppertime.

Clayton held her as she related what had happened to Julep, her tale interrupted by occasional hiccoughs. He reassured her that he'd make sure Julep was returned safely—the only thing he could think to say. Then he brushed the straw out of her hair and carried her into the house, all the while shaking his head and wondering how on earth to deal with this houseful of such very complicated females.

Gaynelle moped as she finally set the table. Trying to make up for it, Jessie chatted more than usual during supper. She talked about Granny, Uncle Simms, and their new tomcat. Clayton took her cue and recounted his plans for toting winter crops to sell in town the next day. When they were done eating, however, Jessie heaved a breath and related what had transpired with Vivian, who remained silent, eyes downcast, still toying with her food.

"Think I'll have a look for Julep soon as I get back from Kingstree tomorrow—check 'round here some, leastways. Have to wait 'til the next day to head towards Manning if I can't find 'im," Clayton resolved. Glancing around the table at the three morose faces, he finally asked in frustration, "What on God's green earth were you thinkin', Vivian?"

She looked up at him with a dazed expression.

"Why would you loan Julep like that, without our permission?"

"Julep?" Vivian seemed mystified.

Clayton raised his voice. "Pay attention. I expect a straight answer from you, young lady!"

Her brow creased, and her unfocused eyes searched the table as if looking for an answer.

Raptly attentive, Gaynelle regarded her sister with dismay, her desire for justice falling away like so much ash. "Vivian?" She spoke her sister's name softly.

The older girl continued to look baffled.

Gaynelle reached out to touch her cheek, gingerly turning Vivian's face towards her own.

Vivian's distraught expression melted to one of relief as she made out the younger girl's visage. Sudden tears flowed down her face in rivulets as she choked out, "Mommy!" and fell into Gaynelle's arms.

Rising to her feet, Jessie grabbed Vivian's arm and pulled her from the frightened girl, demanding angrily, "What's the matter with you?"

Without so much as turning her head towards Jessie, Vivian emitted an ear-piercing shriek. She yanked her arm from the solid grip, screaming, "No! I want Mommy!"

Vivian scrambled away from Jessie, fear plastered across her face. When Jessie renewed her hold, Vivian fought like a wildcat until she was free, then ran out of the house into the dark of night.

Clayton dashed after her, catching her just as she stumbled off the porch. He enveloped her in a secure embrace.

She crumpled against him, tears streaming. Her head burrowed into his chest, drenching his shirt with its second dowsing that evening.

Gaynelle followed them onto the porch and tentatively touched Vivian's arm. The older girl blinked at her as Gaynelle uttered in a small, scared voice, "I'm Gaynelle. Remember?"

Vivian nodded and wiped her eyes. She pulled away from their father, sniffling but starting to regain her composure.

Clayton and Gaynelle followed Vivian closely as she took hesitant steps back into the house.

There she was confronted by Jessie, who stood hands on hips.

As she met the older woman's unflinching eyes, Vivian fainted dead away.

7• Night Emergency

CLAYTON CAUGHT VIVIAN AS SHE FELL. He lifted the unconscious girl, tersely instructing Jessie, "Grab me a blanket."

As soon as he wrapped her in it, Clayton strode from the house, nabbing his overcoat from its peg. He slowed as he approached the wagon, wondering where he'd set Vivian. The wagon bed was piled with winter crops. Gaynelle appeared at his elbow, struggling into her winter coat. "Put those collards on the turnips," he ordered, his voice gruff.

As he waited for her to move the vegetables, Jessie tried to reason with him. "What do you think you're doin', Clay? It's dark out. This is no time to be drivin' all over creation. It can wait 'til mornin'."

He shook his head angrily, settling Vivian into the cleared space. "Get the new mule, Gaynelle. Damn, wish we had Julep."

"You don't need to go right now," Jessie insisted.

After tucking the quilt around Vivian, he turned to face his wife. He rubbed his brow. "The girl could be dead by mornin', for all we know. Hell, Jessie, somethin' is sore wrong with the child, and we been negligent in not attendin' to her all this time. I'll never forgive myself if my laziness and goddamned fearfulness hurt her."

"It's not up to you. God bestows health and illness as he sees fit. We are just his vessels. You can't take the blame nor the credit for God's choices," remonstrated Jessie.

His jaw hardened. "I'm not fit to be called her father if I don't do what I can for her, right this minute. Now, get outta my way. I know how you feel about this, but I gotta follow my conscience right now."

As Gaynelle led the mule up to them, Jessie turned on her, red-faced. "Go put that creature back, you little nothin'!"

"Like hell she will. Maybe you'll understand what it feels like to be a parent when you've birthed one o' your own, but 'til then, get outta my goddamned way!" Clayton seized the mule's reins and furiously began to hitch him to the wagon.

Abashed, Gaynelle clambered inside the wagon bed with her still-unconscious sister. She lifted Vivian's head to cradle in her lap and avoided looking at Jessie, who hissed a curse at Clayton and turned on her heel to head back into the house. Gaynelle couldn't believe her daddy had said that to Mama, but then, she couldn't believe Vivian was lying in her arms as though she were dead, either.

At eleven o'clock at night, a creaky wagon holding three passengers pulled up in front of Dr. Connor's office building. Flickering gas streetlights revealed the stairwell next to the office, which led up to the small apartment where Stephen Connor had lived for the past twenty years.

They rang the bell, and after several moments, Stephen appeared in his dressing gown. Astonishment flickered across his face when he saw who was standing behind Gaynelle. He ran his hand through his dark, wavy hair in consternation. "What's going on, Clay?"

"We need your help, Dr. Connor. Vivian needs your help." Clayton's voice was cracked and hoarse, pleading not only for help but for forgiveness.

As her daddy spoke, Gaynelle stepped to the side, allowing Stephen to better see Vivian. Dr. Connor's gasp of concern didn't seem odd to her. Anyone should be so affected by the sight of her sister lying there helpless.

ᏸ 35 ଓ

Collecting himself, Stephen unhooked the key to his office from his wall. Moments later, he was ushering them inside, waving Clayton into the treatment room. There he methodically began checking Vivian's pulse and listening for her breaths, his ear to her mouth.

With effort, he subdued the surge of panic that had rioted through his veins when his gaze first landed on his daughter's gray, lifeless face. Years of experience in dealing with trauma and emergency had honed his ability to block out debilitating emotional reactions. Still, the sight of his own unconscious child had threatened to incapacitate him for a moment.

Gaynelle held her breath and watched anxiously as Dr. Connor opened a small glass vial and waved it under her sister's nose.

After a moment, Vivian gagged and began to cough, her eyes fluttering open at the noxious fumes.

"Thank God," Clayton murmured.

"I'm Dr. Connor," Stephen said to his confused patient. The corners of his eyes crinkled as he smiled. "I'm so glad to meet you again."

Vivian blinked at him and coughed once more, raising her hand to her mouth.

"Ah, it's these smelling salts. Irritatin', but they do the job. Would you like a drink to soothe your throat?"

Nodding, Vivian glanced around the room in bewilderment, then gratefully gulped the glass of water. Rubbing bleary eyes, she asked, "What's goin' on?"

Clayton stepped forward. "Well, you fell sick again, so I brought you to see Dr. Connor. You can trust him."

Stephen's eyes flickered with surprise, and he cast a bemused smile. "We go way back. But now that you're awake, I'd like to take care of a few things before we start catchin' up, see if we can figure out what's making you ill. I'm going to perform an examination, and you can keep your dad or your sister or both of them in the room, if you'd be more comfortable."

Vivian nodded and murmured, "Yes, please."

With a reassuring pat on her arm, he pulled out a bell-shaped tube.

"Is that an ear trumpet?" Gaynelle asked curiously.

He laughed. "Yes, for all intents and purposes, it's exactly the same thing as an ear trumpet. I'm all set if I ever start to go deaf. This kind is called a stethoscope, though. I need it to auscultate her heart and lungs—to listen to them."

"I've never seen one before, but I was readin'—"

"Hush now," Clayton interrupted. "Let the doctor perform his exam."

Stephen's smile faded as he listened to Vivian's slow, irregular heartbeat. Clayton and Gaynelle were forgotten as he proceeded systematically, noting his patient's dilated pupils, cold extremities, and red skin rash. Hives covered her ankles and lower legs.

Lips in a thin line, he went to the sink and washed his hands. Gripping the towel, he turned to Clayton. "Mr. Bell, it looks like Vivian is havin' some sorta reaction. It may be a severe allergic condition—I just don't know. Has this been goin' on long?"

"Nigh on a year now," Clayton admitted. "We kept hopin' she'd get better, and she'd have short spells where she seemed just fine, but I ain't never seen her pass out cold before."

Gaynelle piped up. "Daddy, tell him about how she was just 'fore that."

Stephen tilted his head expectantly.

"Yeah." Clayton frowned. "She done got all confused and hysterical. Doggone if she didn't think Gaynelle here was Carrie for just a moment. I didn't even know she remembered Carrie."

Turning towards the younger girl, Stephen pondered her for a moment, then smiled. "Well, there's certainly Caroline's spark about her—and that hair, of course. But that's your chin."

Gaynelle held her breath and rose to her tiptoes, waiting for more.

Clayton laughed. "Look at those saucer-eyes. Ain't she somethin'?"

"It's too late for y'all to be out. Why don't you and the girls spend the night?" Stephen proposed as he put away his medical instruments. "I'd like to keep Vivian for observation a while, anyway, and I'm sure she'd be more comfortable with you here. She can sleep on my couch, and I can make a pallet on the floor for you two. I apologize for not havin' better accommodations."

"I imagine you're not in the habit of hostin' unexpected patients," Clayton said. "I'm grateful for your help, Dr. Connor, and I'd be much obliged to spend the night on your floor. I'll admit I'm wore slap out."

Clayton excused himself to tend his mule and secure the wagon while Stephen moved Vivian up to the apartment. She seemed to be drifting in and out of consciousness. At her small nod of acquiescence, Stephen lifted her gingerly, pausing a moment for her to settle against his chest. Her thin, wan face struck him as markedly peaceful as it rested on him. Dark strands of hair splayed haphazardly over his arm and her face. Recalling a distant memory of her asleep as a toddler, Stephen tightened his grip, realizing with a pang that he was holding her in his arms for the first time—and likely the last. He carried her up to the sofa and reluctantly placed her onto its cushions, draping her with a cotton sheet and his old blue coverlet.

To his amusement, Gaynelle hovered near him, carefully re-tucking the blanket more snugly under her sister's heels, explaining, "Her feet get cold."

He piled his remaining blankets for Gaynelle and Clayton on the Persian rug, in front of the woodstove. "I hope you're comfortable enough here."

"Oh, I think it's lovely," she reassured him. She sank down on the floor and plunged her fingers into the thick pile of the rug.

Chuckling, Stephen stoked the woodstove and then headed towards his own bed, allowing Gaynelle to situate herself before Clayton returned.

What a day he's had, Stephen reminded himself, struggling to subdue the envy ever-so-slightly squeezing his heart.

Gaynelle slept fitfully, occasionally waking to see Clayton and sometimes Dr. Connor checking on Vivian. Maybe they were ensuring that her breathing was still regular—Gaynelle knew *she* had been worried about it, back in the rear of the wagon. At one point during the night, Gaynelle awoke to hear Vivian coughing and gagging. Smelling salts cloyed the air again, but it wasn't long before they were all settling back to sleep.

While their breakfast cooked, Stephen waved Gaynelle over to the corner of the room, where a phonograph sat on a small cabinet. "I just happen to have here a phonograph cylinder of the theme from Beethoven's famous Fifth Symphony. He used an ear trumpet kind of like my stethoscope to hear the orchestra. Would you like to play it?"

She nodded eagerly, and Stephen showed her how to turn the crank.

Clayton was filling his plate as the recording began, and his eyes grew wide. "Like havin' your own concert every mornin' when you sit down to breakfast."

"This mornin', anyhow. Don't often eat and tend to the crank at the same time." Stephen followed Clayton to the table as Gaynelle pumped the phonograph. He didn't start eating, however. Instead, he leaned close to say in a hushed tone, "You know, some folks think that Beethoven died from poisoning. No one figured it out at the time, but lead-poisoning was later indicated. Unintentional, of course—a side-effect of unrelated medical treatments."

"You don't say?" Clayton's brow furrowed.

"Sometimes these things happen. Slow, chronic poisonin'. It can be insidious, and the deaths seem unremarkable, blamed on chronic illness. There are more and more chemicals all around us, but sometimes it can be as simple as a case o' lead in the pipes or mistaken wild mushrooms." He threw up his hands. "Some people just keep eatin' poke sallet too late in the season."

Clayton shuddered. "That'll sure make you sick, but that's not it. We ain't that poor." He hesitated. "But you think maybe… some people, even in our town, could be, umm, accidentally poisoned? Like maybe Vivian?" He glanced her way, and a look of relief crossed his face. "She's awake."

"Must have been the music." Stephen hurried over to check on her, and soon she was sitting propped on the couch, listlessly drinking a glass of water. When he returned to the table, he said, "Looks like she's already feelin' some better. What I'm gettin' at is that it's possible she may be reactin' to something at home."

As Clayton took a deep breath, Stephen continued in a flat, matter-of-fact tone. "Clay, I'd like to keep Vivian here with me for observation. I'll look after her, and there's a chance she'll improve simply by avoiding whatever might be causin' this—if it's a reaction to a toxin."

"And you think it might be?"

"We can hope that's all it is. If so, I'll be happy to make good on my offer to send her to school. That way she can steer clear of it."

Clayton glanced across the room at his eldest child. A pained expression crossed his face. The doctor seemed braced for an argument, but Clayton just closed his eyes. "Yeah, I think that might be for the best."

Stephen blinked, trying to hide his surprise.

Shifting uncomfortably, Clayton added, "I haven't told her, you know. I haven't explained about you. Don't intend to, neither."

"I'll honor that." Stephen met the larger man's eyes to convey his sincerity. After a pause, however, he broke eye contact and started examining his hands. "Look here, Clay... I don't know if I'll remember to say this later, so I want to mention that if this does turn out to be something she's reacting to at home, stay vigilant. You'd want to notice right away if it starts happenin' again." At these words, Stephen gestured towards Gaynelle. "Same mother, and she's an absolute treasure."

Clayton's brow furrowed, and he shot to his feet. He sensed the doctor's good intentions, but he was overwhelmed already, unsettled about leaving Vivian behind. He was eager just to be done with the unpleasant task, now that he had agreed to it. Gathering his things, he gruffly instructed Gaynelle to put on her coat.

Before leaving, he sat down on the chair next to Vivian, who now seemed at least lucid, if subdued. He took her hand, and she met his eyes.

"Vivian," Clayton slowly began, "there's somethin' I need to tell you. Dr. Connor says somethin' at home might be makin' you sick. We think it best, given your health, if you try stayin' here with him for a time instead."

"But that's crazy, Daddy!" Gaynelle broke in, one arm in her coat sleeve. Although she was standing across the room, she had heard every word. "You can't just leave her here."

"We've got a special relationship with Dr. Connor that goes way back," Clayton continued, glancing at Gaynelle. "And I know y'all don't know him, but believe me when I say we can trust him. And Aunt Anna, too. She ain't far off at all. Remember that."

"Alright," Vivian agreed. It was the first word she'd said all morning.

"Can I stay here with her, then? I can take care of her while Dr. Connor works. Somebody's gotta." Desperation edged Gaynelle's voice as the drab reality of an existence without her older sister presented itself.

Clayton laughed and jostled her hair. "Oh, you're a piece o' work. No, I have a feelin' Vivian will get better soon enough, with the right medical attention, and 'fore long she'll be helpin' Dr. Connor out to earn her keep. Right, Vivian?" Soothed at his older daughter's nod of acknowledgment, he turned to Gaynelle. "Mama needs *you* at our home to help out."

Ignoring Gaynelle's grumbles, the farmer stood and turned to leave, feeling woefully inadequate and forlorn. He'd explained the situation as clearly as he knew how and was anxious to go.

Vivian caught his hand. "I'll miss you, Daddy."

Struggling to remain stoic, Clayton leaned in to give her a hug. "I'll be missin' you, too. But I'll come by with my next load o' winter crops, alright?"

"Yes, sir." Vivian cast him a gentle smile, as if she were the one trying to soothe.

With a nod, Clayton abruptly headed towards the stairs, calling behind him, "You have just a minute, Gaynelle. Come on down when I ring the doorbell."

Once he was out of earshot, Gaynelle got right in Vivian's face, whispering vehemently, "What are you thinkin', Vivian? You can't live here with some strange man. I don't care if he *is* a doctor. Mama says we're never, ever supposed to be alone with strange men. Can't believe Daddy would even—"

"Can you keep a secret?" Vivian's head tilted slightly.

"What is it?" The younger girl glanced around to make sure the doctor wasn't nearby.

"I think, maybe, that I'm somehow… well, maybe, his daughter." Vivian's eyebrows raised speculatively.

"What?" Gaynelle stared.

"Well, I just heard Daddy and Dr. Connor talkin', and some of what they said sounded strange. Like sayin' that you and I have the same mother."

"We do. You're not makin' any sense."

"And Daddy said they hadn't told me somethin' about him, and the doctor said he'd honor that."

Gaynelle pursed her lips. "Could be anythin'. Prob'ly dropped you on your head when you were a baby. Maybe he feels like he owes us."

"You know how I sometimes come into town with Daddy to deliver his crops? Not even very often, but still folks have come up to me a couple different times to ask if I'm related to Dr. Connor." Vivian's sunken eyes held a faint glimmer of enthusiasm.

"So? That don't mean nothin'. Lots of folks look like lots of other folks." Gaynelle shook her head.

"Right. But one time when I visited Aunt Anna, she was playin' with my hair and said it looked just like my father's. I said Daddy's hair ain't even close this color, and she got real tight-lipped." Vivian gave a peaked grin at the recollection. "She knows her colors if anyone does."

"Maybe she was thinkin' of her own father." Gaynelle shrugged.

"Alright, then, you tell me. Why would Daddy leave me here?"

"I don't know. How about cuz you're sick and he's a doctor?" Gaynelle's eyes were rolling in their sockets when the doorbell rang.

Vivian shoved her pillow in her sister's face, laughing with exasperation. "Your eyes are gonna get stuck like that. Go on, then. Get outta here!"

Snatching the pillow, Gaynelle bopped Vivian's head with it. "Love ya!" she called as she raced down the stairs.

8• Soap & Marshmallows

WHITE, STEAMY MISTS OF BREATH DISPERSED in the morning air as Clayton waited for Gaynelle to climb into the wagon. He figured he'd best appreciate breathing while he still could. Jessie was a right scary woman when she was crossed, and his harsh words to her the night before were unforgivable, even by his own standards.

She'd been praying for a babe of her own since the day they'd wed, and she was devastated that she'd been unable to bring a baby to term. He'd done wrong by throwing her barrenness in her face, and some words were impossible to take back.

I don't even wanna think about what she's gonna say about Vivian. Clayton clenched the reins, uncertain as to why he'd left the girl with the doctor. It just seemed like the right thing to do. Vivian wasn't thriving at home, and it had always seemed to him that Stephen deserved his chance to do something for the child. *He might just be right about what's happened to her. I wish we'd sent her to school last year when he suggested it. Maybe if she'd gone then, she wouldn't have fallen so sick.*

But what the dickens did Dr. Connor mean by all that poisonin' talk? Vivian eats the same food and drinks the same water as the rest of us, and we're all just dandy. Ain't a thing different except that now she has to take those teas Jessie fixes up for her. But that's only cuz she's sick, and it always smells so nice, all minty and refreshin'.

Doctor was talkin' 'bout chemicals, but we don't use nothin' except... Clayton shifted, suddenly recalling the paint chipping in the girls' room. It'd been that way for a couple of years now, and he'd seen Vivian flaking it off. She always stopped as soon as he walked in the room. *Damn it, I hope she ain't been eatin' paint chips. Some folks get weird hankerings. Shoulda listened when Jessie asked me to re-paint their room. She frets and worries about that child to no end, always checkin' on her and tuckin' her in and brushin' her hair. She's like to lose her mind when I get home without her.*

Lost in his confused worries, Clayton guided the mule to the nearby grocery store only by habit. His nerves were on edge, but at least he had something practical to do with himself. Thank goodness a load of vegetables needed to be delivered to the market. They'd made it through the night unmolested, covered with a thick cotton tarp. Truthfully, at this point he was glad for any excuse to even temporarily prolong his trip to Kingstree.

Gaynelle was quiet as a pin next to him, her head whirling. *Mama has dark hair, so it seems only natural for Vivian's to be dark, too, but since Daddy and Caroline actually both had blond hair like me, Vivian's right that it's strange...* Gaynelle shook her head and sighed. The idea was getting to her, for sure. Deep down, she always believed Vivian was right about everything. *But I shouldn't listen to the nonsense of a sick girl, even if she is my big sister.*

Jumping down from the wagon, Gaynelle entered the grocer's and began wandering the store, perusing the aisles while the store owner settled accounts with her daddy. She rarely came into town, and the sheer variety of goods distracted her from thinking about Vivian nearly as well as a new novel would—maybe better, since she knew she didn't have long to look. Few patrons were frequenting the store at the moment, and she was happy not to be in anyone's way as she browsed all the things she'd never heard of and couldn't afford, like the Franco-American canned spaghetti. She picked up a can and inspected the label. It looked as though it might taste like some sort of fancy rice with stewed tomatoes.

Setting it back on the shelf, Gaynelle wandered down the aisle and started up the next. She came to an abrupt halt, however, as she recognized the dark-skinned neighbor girl. She was taller than Gaynelle, and Gaynelle realized now that she was older, too—probably as old as Rosa. Her hair was braided in narrow cornrows that angled away from her face. The young woman was holding one of the oval sweet soaps.

Gaynelle took a deep breath, then boldly stepped up next to her. She picked up one of the oval soaps as well. Its wrapper depicted a little girl with blond ringlets. She sniffed the bar. "It's Fairy Soap," she said, attempting to make conversation.

"Dey have da prettiest packagin'," the girl sighed.

"Smell nice, too," Gaynelle said. "This one's lavender."

"Must be a sight nicer to use dan Ma's homemade lye soap." The girl placed the bar back on the shelf.

"We don't get 'em, neither." Gaynelle hastily set back the bar she was holding, too. "But my sister is gonna be livin' with the doctor in town here now. I bet she gets soap like this."

The girl was rifling through her basket, not paying much attention to Gaynelle.

"You've seen my sister, right?" Gaynelle prompted.

The girl looked up at her, frowning.

"She's not gonna be at home anymore, but I'll still be there. Maybe I can come over to see y'all sometimes," Gaynelle said hopefully.

The girl's brows drew together. She looked perplexed.

"We live right down the lane from y'all," Gaynelle added, her heart sinking. She felt invisible—or maybe she'd gotten the wrong person.

Just then, however, comprehension dawned on the girl's face. "Oh! I have seen ya. I jus' didn't recognize ya here."

"I'm Gaynelle."

A broad smile suddenly lit up the teenager's face. "I'm Shirley. You not 'bout to leave, are ya?"

"I don't think so."

"Wait here, I'm gonna pay out and go get Barney. He's jus' outside. He'll wanna meet ya, too."

As Shirley dashed off, Gaynelle slowly wound her way to the colorful display of candy treats. She was ogling the bright gumdrops and chocolate cigars when a pleasant-sounding male voice startled her.

"Hey, Bell-girl, you ever ate a marshmallow before?"

A thin young man was smiling at her. The fair-haired youth wore a dark-green apron, and his warm brown eyes twinkled. His hands held a tinful of blobs of white dough.

"No, sir," Gaynelle answered, unsure what to make of either the youth or the blobs.

"Wanna try one? You can have one. Uncle Joel always lets new kids try a marshmallow so we can see 'em taste it for the first time. Here you go." The young man speared a marshmallow on a toothpick and held it out to her.

She eyed it suspiciously. "Don't you need to cook it 'fore you eat it?"

The young man laughed and shook his head. "Nope, it's sweet like sugar. Go on, try it. Not a scaredy-cat, are you?"

Gaynelle shook her head. "Can my neighbors have one, too? They'll be right back here in a second."

"Sure thing."

Gaynelle reached for the marshmallow. Biting into it, she closed her eyes at the sweet softness.

The young man was still grinning broadly when Shirley and Barney appeared at Gaynelle's side. At the overt tilt of her head towards them, Joel's eyes grew wide, but he speared another marshmallow and held it out. "Wanna try a marshmallow?"

"Oh, yessir," Shirley replied enthusiastically, and both siblings reached for it.

Just then Clayton set down a bushel basket of potatoes next to Gaynelle. She eyed the siblings sharing bites of their marshmallow, then thrust the treat towards her father. "Try this!"

Clayton took the marshmallow from her, and Gaynelle turned towards her neighbors, eyes bright and expectant. She was waiting for their reaction to the marshmallow, hoping they'd make instant friends, but when Barney finally noticed her, he wouldn't even meet her eyes.

He just nodded in her direction and spoke in a low, soft voice. "Shirley said we had ta come in here to say hello, but our pa's waitin' on us out there. Nice ta meet you, though, li'l miss."

"Ain't gotta be in such a hurry," Shirley huffed as Barney dragged her out of the store.

"Nice to meet you, too." Gaynelle's voice faltered as the siblings disappeared through the door.

Moments later, Clayton said to the grocer, "Little Joel, wrap me up a tin o' these, why don'tcha?"

"Yes, sir," the youth replied.

Turning to Gaynelle, Clayton nodded his head in the direction of the door. "Who were them folks?"

"Our neighbors. The ones who live in the little yellow house."

"Were they now?" Clayton rubbed his chin thoughtfully, then turned back to Gaynelle. "While we're here, why don'tcha pick out somethin' for yourself, darlin'? I'm in the mood to treat you."

Grinning, Gaynelle promptly retrieved an oval cake of Fairy soap.

Clayton blinked. "Soap?"

Her enthusiastic nod prompted him to laugh out loud. No hour was too dark, so long as his youngest daughter was there to cheer him with her innocent, refreshing ways.

As Clayton finished with their purchases, Gaynelle wandered out onto the sidewalk, but she saw no more sign of their neighbors. She'd been standing there long enough for the chill to creep through the pavement into her feet when the idle young grocer followed her outside. He leaned against the rough brick wall then pointed at the looming memorial in the intersection circle. "You know about that statue?"

Gaynelle shook her head.

"Craziest thing. The ladies' organization ordered that monument to the Confederate veterans, but the sculptor carved a Yankee instead."

"How come?"

"Seems he was Italian and didn't know no better—just made an American soldier from the Civil War. Guess he didn't understand the whole idea o' the war. Can't believe they left it up there, no matter how much—"

Just then, a strident, sing-song voice pronounced, "No money, no gitty!"

Gaynelle turned to see a bronze-skinned man in a white apron pointing out towards the street.

A kerchiefed woman in a worn dress argued, "But Mr. Chang, please! I'll bring the money tomorrow!"

The launderer crossed his arms. "No money, no gitty!"

"That Injun's mean," Gaynelle protested as Mr. Chang disappeared into a building with the words 'Hand Laundry' brightly painted on a window.

"Shh! You don't wanna get on his bad side. There was this one time—"

Reappearing with a laundry stick, Mr. Chang began striding their way.

Joel grabbed Gaynelle's arm and tugged. "Run!"

Gaynelle took to her heels, right behind Joel. They'd circled halfway round the block when Joel slowed down, glancing behind them to make sure the coast was clear. He stopped, leaning against another brick wall to catch his breath. A moment later, he explained, "That ain't no Injun back there. That's Billy Chang. I done learnt my lesson the hard way, too, when I was 'bout your age. I was with a bunch of fellas, and we were chantin' some foolishness at him, but that China-man threw an iron straight out the door of his laundry at us. Near to killed me."

"For real?"

"Well," Joel admitted, "maybe it just grazed my head. Ain't none of us teased Mr. Chang ever again. He's pretty durned touchy, as you mighta noticed." Scrutinizing the tousle-headed child, he asked, "What's your name, Bell-girl?"

"Gaynelle. What's yours?"

"Joel Hammond. I work for my Uncle Joel at his grocery store sometimes, and I've spoken with your daddy there loads o' times, but it's the first time I've seen you around."

"We live out in Greeleyville. Mama don't like to come into town much, so Daddy generally comes by hisself. But my sister's gonna be livin' here now, leastways for a while."

"Well, I hope she's got better sense than both you and me."

"Someone better tell her about Mr. Chang, cuz her tongue's sharper than a bobcat's claw—so long as she's feelin' okay."

Just then, Clayton rounded the corner. He waved for Gaynelle to join him. "Whatcha doin' way over here? Let's get goin'. We still have a lot to do." With a dismissive glance at Joel, Clayton turned on his heel and headed back towards the wagon.

"Be right there, Daddy!" Gaynelle called after him. She turned towards Joel and cast him an imploring look. "My sister's stayin' with Dr. Connor for a while. Her name's Vivian. She don't know no one here yet—she hardly knows Dr. Connor, even—and she ain't never tried a marshmallow, neither."

Joel gave her a thoughtful nod. "Alright, I'll keep an eye out for her, so long as I'm still here. Hafta register for the draft soon. I turn twenty-one later this year." His chest puffed out, and he stood a bit taller. "It's been fun meetin' you, Gaynelle. See you next time you're in town."

"Okay! Stay safe!" Gaynelle spun on her heel and ran to meet her daddy at the wagon. With any luck, they were headed to see Aunt Anna and her bookshelf.

9 • Aunt Anna's Tapestry

"IS THAT AUNT ANNA'S HOUSE?"

"Sure is. She says it's a Queen Anne-style."

Gaynelle laughed with excitement. Here they were, at last. Daddy had assured her there was plenty of time to come by, and it seems he'd been right—though she wished they'd come here first. They could have grabbed a book for her before swinging by that huge courthouse with its grand columns to 'say hello' to the sheriff. *'Say hello' my foot*, Gaynelle had fumed, staring at 'Wanted' posters until she was sure she'd know any of them by sight. They'd taken so long catching up that she'd almost given up hope of seeing Aunt Anna, sure that it was growing too late for them to visit.

As they waited on the front porch with laden bushel baskets, Gaynelle's nose pressed against the frosted glass of the door. "What if she's not here?"

"Give her a moment." Clayton sighed. "Sure hope she's here. I could use some womanly advice on how to tell your mama about all this."

"She's comin'!" Gaynelle jumped back and hid behind Clayton.

A radiant smile lit Anne's face as she greeted Clayton. "I wasn't expectin' a visit, but I'm glad you stopped by. How are you?"

"I suddenly had a whole lot to do down here in Kingstree outta the clear blue, so I thought I'd swing by." Clayton gestured towards his wagon. "Done sold my harvest this mornin', 'cept this whole mess o' vegetables we saved for you."

"You didn't need to do that, but it's awfully sweet of you. How's the family?" Anne motioned for him to come inside the house, and as he did so, she spied Gaynelle behind him. She laughed warmly. "Oh, I didn't see you there. I've missed you, darlin'! Please come on in. How about a cup of hot cocoa?"

Gaynelle nodded, then blurted, "That round part of your house looks like the turret of a castle!"

"That's because it is. My husband always called this my castle," Anne said solemnly. She waved them into her parlor. "I'll be right back with that cocoa. Water's already on. Have a seat."

Flames crackled behind an iron grate in the fireplace. Brushing off her coat, Gaynelle perched on the edge of a paisley, silk-cushioned sofa with delicately-carved legs. She gazed up at the chandelier that hung from the ceiling. Even unlit, its profusion of crystals sent light dancing across the striped wallpaper.

"Such wonderful timing. I received a new book for you just yesterday." Anne entered the room, beverages steaming on a silver tray. As she placed it on the coffee table, she slipped out the volume she'd been carrying beneath it.

Eyes wide, Gaynelle accepted the blue-bound storybook. *The Wonderful Wizard of Oz* was imprinted in gilded letters on the cover. "Oh, thank you," she breathed.

"And we brought *you* a little somethin'." Clayton fished out the tin of marshmallows from his coat, smiling as he handed them to her.

Gaynelle's eyes danced as she settled back into her seat. He'd bought those for Mama, but they wouldn't have helped much there, anyhow.

"How perfect for the cocoa!" Anne exclaimed. "I declare, it's like Christmas." She took one and set the tin on the coffee table. "Please share with me, you two. Just plop them in your cocoa. Oh, here. Let me refill your cup." Placing a marshmallow in Gaynelle's cocoa, she poured more from the silver pitcher.

The white puff swelled irregularly, increasingly cloud-like. Gaynelle took a long sip of the sweet, rich cocoa then sank into the sofa cushions, resisting the urge to pull her feet up. When she grew up, she would have a couch just like this. She'd wear thick socks and curl up with a book, right in front of the fireplace, with a big silver pitcher of cocoa and fancy teacups. Exactly like this, except without shoes.

Placing her book carefully in her lap, Gaynelle started reading. After just two pages, however, she realized that she had to pee. She found her way out the back door but returned shortly, baffled. As she waited for a break in the grown-ups' conversation, she shifted from foot to foot until at last they looked up at her. "I didn't see the outhouse."

"Right down the hall," Anne said automatically. Then she added, "It's inside the house."

Gaynelle nodded, feeling foolish. She'd entirely forgotten there were indoor bathrooms. On her way back from the fancy restroom, she lingered in the hallway to look at an elaborate tapestry, all-too-perfect for Queen Anne's castle. It depicted a young woman in a high tower. Impossibly-long, honey-colored hair flowed out the tower window to the ground, where a raven-haired young man in royal garb stood. He was surrounded on all sides by thick, shadowed forest.

On her next trip to the restroom, Gaynelle paused to scrutinize the scene again. This time she noticed a stooped, sinister figure on the forest edge. She traced the crooked shape with her fingertip.

Anne spoke softly from behind her, startling her. "My husband ordered this tapestry from Brussels years before this Great War started, when it was easier to get such things. He said I needed one for my castle—because all castles used to have tapestries, you know—and Rapunzel was a favorite story of mine."

"Rapunzel?" Gaynelle repeated curiously.

Anne smiled at her. "Don't you know the fairy tale?"

She shook her head. "Will you tell it to me?"

"I can do better than that."

Before Gaynelle and Clayton took their leave, Anne had located a book of Grimm's fairytales. Her heart sang at the sight of Gaynelle clutching not one, but *two* books upon her departure. It reminded her of how Caroline had once pressed her beloved dime-novels to her chest. Anne's own chest tightened, however, on recalling that Caroline had been dressed far better than Gaynelle now was. Pressing her lips together, Anne sighed. *Out of sight, out of mind—and completely out of style.* Chiding herself for her lapse, she resolved to make Gaynelle something soon. Practical, everyday wear would be best. *Those threadbare garments need to be thrown out. I'll bring some things for her to wear to school, too, and a suitable dress for church, of course.* Her lips thinned even more tightly. *Jessie will just have to let me.*

Vivian, though, should be quite a bit easier, bein' under Stephen's roof for now. Anxious once more to see Caroline's daughters clothed properly, Anne sucked in a deep breath and resolved to pay a certain local visit as soon as possible. She hadn't spoken with Dr. Stephen Connor in many years, but it seemed that the time had arrived to break her avoidance of him.

10 • Veneer of Sanity

JESSIE STOOD BY THE DOOR, plucking at her apron as the wagon pulled up to the farmhouse. She rubbed her face briskly and took a deep breath. The past twenty-four hours had been the most agonizing she'd experienced in her entire married life. Even during the blighted days surrounding her heartrending miscarriages, Clayton had at least remained by her side.

When Clayton had first left with the girls the night before, she'd been livid—and Clayton's favorite young rooster, Ivanhoe, had borne the brunt of it. That preening fowl had been nothing but another mouth to feed and trouble to boot. She and Clayton had long argued about keeping the second Dominicker cock, but she'd grudgingly allowed the creature to live. Until now. Before Clayton and the girls were half-way to Kingstree, the creature hung upside-down and headless, his blood draining into the soil of Jessie's dormant flower garden.

As she washed hands bloodied from wringing the bird's neck, Jessie began to croon to herself. She sank to the cold wooden floor. Crossing her arms, she wailed and rocked, increasingly possessed by grief. Her wails eventually subsided to moans, however, and she fell asleep from sheer exhaustion.

Hours later, she awoke to an eerily quiet, dark house. Stiff with cold, she lay still. Her heartbeats were palpable, interminable and solitary. Clayton had left her here like this. Just left her here alone. Shivering, she pulled herself up from the floor. After getting the oven going, she resumed preparing the bird—cleaning out the innards and plucking his corpse. Once the chicken was stewing in a big cast-iron pot, she began scrubbing once more. She washed the butchering knife, the floor, her clothes, and finally herself. The previous evening's dishes were ignored, still piled high on the table and counter. Her normal household routine had been neglected; even the old mule was unattended in the stable, and the chickens never had been put away.

As she shivered and scrubbed, she fought down hysterical screams that threatened to break through her thinly-controlled veneer of sanity. Her thoughts tumbled over themselves. *They're all against me. Yet I do everything for them. I scrub their clothes, cook their food, clean their dishes. I keep them safe and groom them, but I'm just a maidservant to them. They left me here, disrespectin' my good judgment. As if I've ever let anythin' bad happen to a one of them.* The memory of Clayton's callous words cut like a knife. *No matter how much I do for them, he'll never consider me one of them. Not really. I'm a secondary wife, an afterthought. A nursemaid and a housekeeper. He never loved me. Only ever had eyes for that whore. Even when she's gone, he still sees her in his daughter. It's her fault that I can't make Clay love me. She's ruint everything. She's always ruint everything.*

Jessie's tendency to conflate Gaynelle with Caroline had only been validated by Vivian's confusion the night before. Now the two jumbled together in Jessie's whirlpool of a mind more than ever. Bundling up, she began to attend the usual chores. Her thoughts continued churning as she collected the previous day's eggs—just a paltry, wintertime few. Instead of returning to the house, however, she turned down the lane, towards the main road. The moonlight seemed to guide her. She was barely aware of where she was headed, so muddled was she by overpowering emotions.

Soon she found herself within the bowels of the nearby New Market Cemetery. Though she almost never came here, her feet knew where Caroline's grave lay. Unlike most of the burial plots, no overgrown weeds covered Caroline's marker. No, this grave had never known neglect—that much was obvious even in the scant light of the moon. Someone, and she could fathom *whom* with excruciating certainty, had been regularly tending this hallowed grave, and he probably had been for the entire past decade.

Loathing and resentment festered deep within her bosom until a primal, ferocious scream burst forth. When it began to subside, she hurled an egg at the grave marker. The dull thunk elicited a shard of elemental satisfaction. Slimy contents coated her dead rival's name. Jessie's pain found a splintered release in angry sobs.

"I hate you! I hate you! I hate you!" Another egg was cast at the headstone each time she uttered the phrase. The eggs were spent all too soon, and so she picked up loose gravel, flinging it at the stony target until her hands were scraped and dirty and her voice raw and hoarse. Ceasing the fruitless onslaught, she gazed in frustration at the marred but implacable headstone. Her rage was depleted. After what seemed endless moments, Jessie slowly trailed her way back to the farmhouse, dejected. Her life would be perpetually thwarted by a mere memory.

Once at home, Jessie sat motionless at the kitchen table. When the quiet emptiness began to seep into her mind, a lonely ache prompted her to pick up her darning to busy herself, but she couldn't blot out the fear of loss that went even deeper than her attachment to Vivian—not even when she stabbed her finger with the needle. Jessie's world revolved around Clayton, and it always had.

As her blood stained his sock, she reflected how she'd grown used to being his wife, had taken for granted that her position was permanent. But men sometimes divorced their wives. *Especially barren wives*, Jessie thought with a pang. It could happen. And since he didn't really love her, a confrontation like that of the previous night could spell ruination. Anxiety and fear began to course through her spine, and Jessie painstakingly reconsidered her choices.

She could do little about her opposition of the night before, but she could still deal with the remains of the rooster. The mess was already cleaned up, but the aroma of stewed chicken still wafted through the house. Springing to her feet, Jessie scooped Ivanhoe's remains from the pot. With a sudden, vicious hunger, she scarfed down two tough, stringy drumsticks—Ivanhoe's swaggering legs—for her breakfast. Then, squeezing out the juices from his cooked carcass, she wrapped the remainder of the rooster in paper and placed the meat in a satchel.

Taking the time to first clean the dishes, she threw the bag over her shoulder, strode to the stable, and saddled Button, the remaining mule. As she climbed astride the old beast, she thought worriedly, *I don't know when they'll be back.* Directing Button onto the main road, Jessie set her jaw and attempted to ground herself, combatting the swell of anxiety and anger. *Control yourself. Don't lose sight of what's important.*

Within a quarter hour, they arrived at an immense green house. Large square columns supported an overhanging Turbeville porch. Paint peeled from the plank siding, and loud voices poured forth from inside. Steeling herself, Jessie knocked on the double front door.

"Come on in, Mrs. Bell!" An older, bearded man answered, gesturing for her to enter the house. His breath reeked of alcohol.

Jessie forced a pleasant smile but didn't budge. "Hey, Mr. Barfield. Just wonderin' if your grandson Henry was home."

"Him and his bride are over at her mama's, but they been by here already. Guess you lookin' for your horse, huh?" He winked knowingly.

Jessie nodded. "And I wanted to apologize. None o' this had anythin' to do with me or Clay. Our daughter was sick and not in her right mind when she lent that horse. She sure didn't have our permission. I'm so sorry."

"No need to apologize! We're pleased as punch. Henry and Rosa are a right fine couple, jus' like Zingle and Rennie. We's celebratin' now. Come on in."

She blinked. "I can't stay. I brought some stewed chicken for y'all, though. Maybe you can add it to your celebratory feast." Handing him the wrapped packet out of her satchel, she tried not to cringe at his effusive, malodorous thanks.

"Oh," Mr. Barfield added congenially, "and thanks for the use of yore horse, too, even if you didn't know nothin' bout it. He's tied back at the barn. I told them chillun he'd had enough ridin' and to give him a break, but I s'pose you can take him home now, since you're here."

By late afternoon, Julep was back in his stall—watered, fed, and groomed. Jessie loathed the tasks, reflecting that it was good for Julep that he hadn't been there the night before. She completed the chores as quickly as possible, scowling all the while at that infernal perch Clayton had installed for Gaynelle to waste her time on. Jessie itched more than ever to tear it down, but she vowed not to touch it, telling herself that it at least kept that useless novel-reading out of the house. Truth be told, Jessie was pleased with how she was recovering the situation.

She was figuring it all out. When Clayton got home, she'd admit to being so upset that she hadn't locked up the chickens the night before. Young Ivanhoe's disappearance would be blamed on one of those ever-lurking raccoons.

Filling a bucket with water, she resolutely marched back towards the desecrated grave marker. She wanted nothing to upset Clayton. *After all, it's just a stone, and Carrie's only a distant memory*, she told herself. *Gotta keep my priorities in line and my position in mind.*

By the evening, Jessie had herself a bit more pulled together, the house and her thoughts both in better order. She kept cleaning, rearranging the shelves as she failed to push away newly-emerging worries about Vivian's condition and why Clayton was taking so long. *He has to come home sometime… but he was so mad. Hope they weren't in an accident. He better not have taken a notion to haul her all the way to Charleston, to one o' them fancy, expensive doctors. We'd end up sellin' our farm to pay for it. That kinda thing is bound to happen when he won't listen to me. I hate when he won't hear reason. Who knows when they'll get back. Or if they'll get back.* She frowned, imagining him making funeral arrangements or consulting with a lawyer about getting a divorce. Whatever it was, their delay couldn't be good. As the minutes ticked past, she found it more and more difficult to continue cleaning, and by the time she heard the wagon, she'd been huddled by the stove, motionless, for a while. Relief flooded through her, and she hurried onto the porch, nervously plucking at her apron, exhausted by the events and emotions of the past day and fearful of what she had yet to face.

Having been braced for Jessie's wrath, Clayton was stunned to find her fairly calm and amenable upon their arrival. He carried a sleeping Gaynelle to bed before returning to face his wife at last. She accepted his explanation about Vivian without protest, to his astonishment. She looked so miserable, however, that his heart swelled with sympathy.

"I'm so blessed sorry for what I said last night, Jessie. You've been a wonderful mother to these girls, and I was wretched for rubbin' salt in your wounds like I did." He cast regretful eyes at her.

"Alright Clay, it's been a long day." Jessie sighed, but a glimmer of resentment flickered across her face. "I'll just ask that you respect my role as mother to the girls in the future. I don't see how we can be a real family if you don't."

"We are a family," Clayton insisted. "I'll do my best to act like it from now on."

Biting the inside of her cheek, Jessie fought the urge to demand that he fetch Vivian back. It was hard enough having him leave once, and she didn't want to send him off again. Besides, he hadn't actually apologized for leaving their daughter there—just for upsetting her.

A penitent husband and a somewhat-comforted wife made their way to bed that night in the small farmhouse, where a bright young girl with a dimpled chin already lay contentedly asleep, blissfully unaware that their patchwork existence was just beginning to unravel.

11 • A Necessary Reconciliation

ANNE SANDERS DIDN'T KNOW WHY she'd avoided Dr. Stephen Connor for so long. There really was no good reason. They'd each lost the same wonderful individual—such an important person to them both.

As Caroline's best friend, Anne had witnessed their engagement, their break-up, and their subsequent pregnancy. She'd also been there when he'd lost Caroline a second time. By no means had he been perfect, but his pain had been palpable—yet she'd left him to it, figuring he didn't deserve her sympathy.

Since then, she'd only occasionally caught glimpses of the doctor bustling around town, and she'd formed the impression that his life was dedicated to his medical practice. Her heart ached for his losses more charitably now. She, too, still grieved the loss of Caroline, and she'd likewise lost her life's love when she became a widow.

I wanted to show my allegiance to Carrie's girls and Clay, Anne admitted. *Stephen was the last of my concerns. But apparently Clay's decided it's time to include Stephen in the fold again, after all these years.*

Smoothing the skirt of her blue afternoon dress and straightening her velvet-trimmed collar, she rang Stephen's doorbell. She'd lost no time in arranging a visit with him and Vivian. Now, on the appointed day, she found herself surprisingly nervous—or maybe it wasn't so surprising. After all, it had been a mutual extended silence.

He answered the door looking as handsome as ever, if not as impeccably groomed as he used to be. He sported a five-o'clock shadow, and his dark, silver-streaked hair was rumpled. His outfit included his typical white linen shirt and black slacks, topped this day with a gray tweed coat, but they could stand to be pressed. Stephen's smile didn't quite reach his eyes. "Please come in, Anna."

Anne followed him up into the apartment and promptly embraced Vivian. The girl was pale and thin, but she'd at least stood to greet her. Anne hadn't been sure what to expect.

"I'm so happy you're here." Vivian tugged at Anne's hand, pulling her down on the sofa next to her. The enthusiasm in her gaunt face was heartwarming. As Stephen poured tea, Vivian murmured admiringly, "I could eat that hat."

Anne's slender fingers reached up to the sloping brim of her pale-pink straw hat. It was set off with a dark-blue velvet ribbon matching her collar trim. Vivian's compliment and trusting touch warmed her heart, reminding her again of how sweet Caroline was.

With a contented sigh, the teenager leaned against her as if she'd simply been waiting for her stylish Georgette shoulder.

Maternal instincts rising, Anne glanced around the small space and sipped her tea. Then she promptly informed her host, "Goodness, these accommodations simply won't do at all for raisin' a young lady."

Laughing as he sank into the chair across from her, Stephen assured her, "There's not a better spot for her in all Kingstree. My medical supplies are on hand downstairs."

"And you think they'll be necessary?" Anne's eyebrows shot up.

"Vivian seems to be recovering rapidly, but long-term sequelae are possible—and I prefer to be close to my office in case an issue arises. Let's just pray there's no internal organ damage. Time will tell."

"So you think it's for the best to stay where you are." Anne sighed.

"For now, though I appreciate your concern." Stephen had wondered what to expect at this meeting, so he wasn't particularly surprised at the slight sting in her voice. Beyond a few civil words of greeting, he couldn't remember them speaking at all since his return from the Philippine-American War—an experience so hellish he'd not once considered volunteering for the Great War—but he hoped any grudge she held had faded by now.

They sipped their tea through the deafening silence that blanketed the room. Finally, Anne asked, "What about school? Will she be returnin', do you think?"

"You can see for yourself that she's not yet in any condition for school. I'll send her when the time is right."

"Of course." Anne's eyes narrowed. "And are you sure you're up to watchin' her, Stephen?"

"Dr. Davis has taken over some of my patient load."

"And what about your business at the horse races?"

Stephen regarded her for a long moment, then answered evenly, "I haven't been there for ages. Those days have long since passed."

Anne set down her teacup, queasy at her own rudeness. Taking a deep breath, she patted Vivian's hand where it rested on her arm. *Stephen is perfectly capable of figurin' out their living arrangements. He is, after all, a skilled professional at taking care of people. My tactlessness, especially regardin' his past indiscretions, is inappropriate. What has possessed me?*

Maybe I can't forgive him for hurtin' Carrie—and my concerns for Vivian are not unwarranted. What man can truly understand a young lady's needs? It's my duty to ensure she is properly tended. I should really be taking care of her myself. In fact, I should invite her to move in with me… except that I have a ridiculous itinerary, and she's not up to all that travel. Besides, I know nothing about her medical needs. With respect to that, she's surely in more competent hands with Dr. Connor.

Anne sniffed and tossed her head, still feeling stubbornly antagonistic. "Well, at least let me get the girl fitted for some new clothes before my spring tour begins."

"Oh, yes please!" Vivian breathed.

Nodding, Anne added, "Now that she's a town girl, we want her fit to meet society, which will come callin', regardless of her health."

"I'm happy to leave that to you." Stephen stood to refill her teacup as memories of their entwined past engulfed him. Once, Anne had painstakingly crafted Caroline's wedding gown. Back then, she'd wholeheartedly supported his relationship with Caroline—before his unexpected departure, that is. They'd been planning for Caroline to work with Anne even after their marriage. Those plans had been undone all too soon by the surprise pregnancy, a pregnancy entirely his fault. Feeling conciliatory, Stephen added, "We'd be quite pleased for Vivian to benefit from your assistance with her wardrobe."

"Can I help pick it out?" Vivian chimed, her voice high with excitement.

"Of course you may." Anne patted her hand again.

"It might be wise to keep it fairly modest for now," Stephen warned, but he smiled indulgently. "Her size could shift as we get her to a healthier state—but no doubt you can take that into account. I'm grateful for your help in this matter, as I couldn't hope to know what a young woman requires."

Flushing with pleasure—such words were unexpectedly considerate after her barbs—Anne replied, "Don't worry about a thing, Stephen. We'll put together a complete, if basic, wardrobe for now. It will be simple, I promise." She squeezed Vivian's hand to let her know it wouldn't be too plain.

"I definitely need a hat," Vivian said with conviction.

"We'll get that right off," Anne promised.

"I appreciate it." Stephen looked around thoughtfully. "And you know—you're right that this space is rather small. No smaller than many families have, but I could do better, I suppose. If she isn't soon ready to spread her wings and fly off to school, I would like to give Vivian her own room." He heaved a sigh. "The thought of moving is hard to contemplate after all this time."

"I'm sure there's no rush," Anne answered, still abashed at her rudeness. Deeming her visit successfully concluded and not wanting to further impose on Stephen's time and patience, Anne finished her cup of tea in one long sip, kissed Vivian's crown, and rose to take her leave.

Accompanying her down to the street, Stephen paused before opening the outside door. "You know, I never did get to pay my respects after your husband passed."

Anne shrugged sadly. "I hardly remember who was there. It was all a blur. Such a difficult time for me."

"A number of my patients have perished from this influenza. It's been a rough couple of years, and I am often reminded of your loss. Mr. Sanders was a remarkable man."

Anne's eyes misted. "Thank you, Stephen. I owe him everything, and I miss him dearly, but we keep a little bit of those we love in our hearts, I believe. Don't you?"

"Of course." Stephen nodded politely as he opened the door to the street. When he closed it after her, he leaned against the cool wood, allowing the pain to mar his face. Time had tempered his grief, but Caroline remained omnipresent in his life—in his heart, his daily thoughts, and his dreams.

"Dr. Connor?" A melodic young voice filtered down the stairs, pulling Stephen from his sad reverie.

"Yes, it's just me," he called, a smile breaking through his melancholic countenance. Thinking of his daughter and their afternoon plans, which included a selection of phonograph cylinders and a certain backgammon board, he bounded up the stairs.

12 • The Neighbors

FOR THE NEXT SEVERAL DAYS AFTER RETURNING to Greeleyville, Gaynelle walked with ginger steps around Mama, like a mouse wary of being pounced upon. She was half-certain a beating was coming to her after her defiance on the night that they went to Kingstree. Gradually, however, she relaxed. Mama was actually nicer than usual—quieter, more to herself, maybe. A couple more weeks passed before Gaynelle realized that their dynamic had subtly shifted—Mama now simply ignored her unless she was giving instructions.

Meanwhile, Gaynelle attended school as if engulfed in a solitary bubble. She sat alone at the table where Rosa used to be. A new student with skinny brown braids had long since filled her old seat next to the girls nearer to her own age. Trailing after them like a lost puppy, she re-joined the girls at recess only to find that their conversations and games were no longer of much interest to her.

Worse yet, the condition seemed to be a mutual one. The other girls didn't shun her so much as forget her presence altogether.

On her rides home from school, Gaynelle always picked a spot so that she was on the same side of the wagon as the yellow shack. She'd twist in her seat, clutching the wagon slat, often bumping into the child next to her. Her eyes stayed peeled for Shirley and Barney, even though she knew they tended to be out working in the fields at that time of day. Sometimes they saw her and returned her waves.

She came home only to do her chores and then slip into her bed alone at night, a solitary figure in a room as quiet as a deserted island. The ache had grown so great that she dared to bring her novels inside the house at night, reading by the soft glow of lamplight until she caught herself nodding off. On the now-rare occasion that Mama bothered to check in on her, Gaynelle would slip a textbook on top of her novel. So far she'd garnered no more than a scowl and a few trite words about wasting time on learning she wouldn't use and didn't need.

On her way home one day, Gaynelle saw Shirley and Barney in their front yard once more, this time lounging in newly-rigged hammocks. Upon disembarking from the school wagon at her lane, she started directly towards them.

She wasn't halfway there when they slid out of the hammocks and put their foreheads together. Their brief glances in her direction confirmed that they were talking about her.

Panicked that they might decide to leave, Gaynelle began to run in their direction even before the school wagon was out of sight. Breathlessly, she called out, "Hey, remember me? I'm Gaynelle!"

"I remember ya, li'l miss Gaynelle," Shirley called back, wriggling her shoulders and hips as though to suggest Gaynelle put on airs.

Gaynelle didn't care. Their faces were now turned towards her, and this time Barney met her eyes more directly. He was even taller than Shirley. Gaynelle slowed, trying to hide her excitement at catching them out in their yard at last. "What y'all doin'?" she asked, looking around.

"Shootin' da breeze."

"Can I join in?" she asked hopefully, setting her pile of schoolbooks on the ground.

"What's a li'l white girl like you doin' over here wid us?" laughed Shirley.

"Ain't nothin' to do at home but chores! I hate Vivian bein' gone."

"Dat your sister?"

Gaynelle nodded. "Can I try out your hammock?"

"Don't see why not. Here, you can share dis one wid me. You sit on dat side, and I'll sit on dis side."

The hammock swayed precariously as Gaynelle climbed into it, and a moment later she was holding onto the sides like a rowboat as Shirley climbed in. Soon Gaynelle was nestling happily, Shirley's long legs right up next to her. Sighing contentedly, Gaynelle stared upwards. Until that moment, she hadn't at all appreciated the spring weather that had so recently burst forth—and there weren't even any mosquitoes yet. A clear blue sky framed the red oak leaves that rustled overhead. Her heart felt suddenly full. "Pretty day out," she murmured dreamily. "Hear them leaves whisperin' up there? Whatcha think they're sayin'?"

Shirley laughed. "You somethin' else. How old are you, anyway?"

"I'll be thirteen real soon," Gaynelle hedged.

"Twelve, den. Jus' a baby."

Barney laughed. "Like you so much older."

"How old are y'all?" Gaynelle turned in the hammock, pressing down on the side of it to peer out at Barney.

"Fifteen," Shirley said. "Dat's an awful lot older dan you."

"And you?" Gaynelle asked Barney.

"We're twins," he replied.

"Twins," Gaynelle repeated. "I ain't never met twins before. Y'all ain't never been apart?"

"Not fer long."

"Sounds nice. Y'all got the day off?"

"Naw. Ma and Pa had to go into town 'til tomorrow. We're s'posed to be workin' in da field like usual. But dey know we're not," Shirley laughed. Her laughs were so rich and deep that they made the whole hammock vibrate.

"I don't blame you." Gaynelle leaned back again, putting her hands on her stomach, enjoying the last vibrations. "I could stay here forever."

They swung in the hammocks, a companionable silence falling between them. Eventually a wagon rolled by, closer than Gaynelle was used to, but she just smiled to herself, content that nobody could see who was actually inside the hammocks. They rocked beneath the swaying branches of the supporting oak trees. A nuthatch flitted about in its upside-down way on one of the trunks. After a while, Gaynelle broke the spell with eager questions, wanting to know all about their lives. The twins answered good-naturedly. Soon she learned that they hadn't attended school at all for the past three years. They spent most of their days helping their parents on the farm, expecting its very first harvest within the next month. Their older siblings had moved out a long time ago, most of them married.

"You don't get to see them at all?"

"Dey all back in Manning," Barney said. "Fella what owned dis land offered ta let us live here real cheap, almost free. Said he ain't got no other use fer it right now."

"Who dat?" Shirley lurched up in the hammock.

Despite Shirley's wide eyes staring out, it took a moment for Gaynelle to realize she wasn't asking about the land owner.

"Dat woman goin' up your lane," Shirley clarified, nodding in that direction.

Even then, Gaynelle stayed where she was, preferring not to be seen. She figured it must be her mama.

"You sure it's okay fer you to be up here?"

Gaynelle sighed then rolled again, this time peering backwards out of the hammock. It was Mama, of course. She'd apparently gone all the way to the road and was now returning to their house, her back to them. Though she'd already guessed who it must be, the sight of Jessie sent a jolt of alarm through Gaynelle, and she rolled right out of the hammock onto the crabgrass beneath them. From her sprawled position on the ground, she glanced once more towards Jessie but was relieved to see that she was still continuing on her way back.

"You alright?" Barney was out of his hammock in an instant, helping her to her feet.

She nodded and began to brush herself off, afraid to answer aloud.

"Maybe you betta get home." Shirley spoke in a sober tone.

Gaynelle shook her head, finally answering in a whisper, "Nah. Let's go inside your house so nobody sees me up here."

"You sure?" Barney looked down the lane uncertainly.

Gaynelle nodded.

"Girl, you crazy. You betta get back up there," Shirley repeated, hands now on hips.

"But..." Gaynelle looked between the twins, blinking away sudden tears. "I've been wantin' to see y'all for so long, and you finally have the day off."

"Yo mama's lookin' fer ya," Barney said in a cajoling tone. "Betta go let her know you're home. Den if you can, you can come back up here."

Nodding, Gaynelle took a big breath. As she started to leave, she glanced once more at the hammocks. "Don't take 'em down yet."

"You jus' go on," Shirley said with a wave of her hand. "Get on outta here."

Surprised at being shooed away, Gaynelle picked up her schoolbooks and began to trot towards her house. For a moment she wondered if she should be offended, but then decided she didn't care. She'd be back up to see the twins the first opportunity she got.

Gaynelle stole back to their place that very evening. She hadn't asked for permission to visit the twins, guessing it would only restrict her further. Besides, she was busy until then with chores, including cleaning up after dinner. It was dark when she slipped into her room to gather the prettily-wrapped soap off her windowsill. As she headed back down the lane, she prayed Mama wouldn't look in on her. She didn't most nights anymore.

The hammocks were gone. At Gaynelle's knock, Barney opened the door of their shack and knit his brows.

"I brought Shirley a present." Gaynelle presented the soap.

"What's dat?" Shirley appeared behind her brother's shoulder. She laughed aloud when she saw the cake of soap. "Somethin' else, fer sure. Come on in here."

Eyes bright, Gaynelle stepped inside the one-room shack. She was surprised to see just one bed. It was covered with a patchwork quilt. The hammocks were strung up on either side of it, rather like the bed had wings. A long, low trunk lay beneath each hammock. "You sleep in them at night?" Gaynelle asked in awe.

"Better dan da floor," Barney said.

A kerosene lantern perched on a shelf, casting light over a little table spread with gamecards. The cards looked worn, with bent edges, and they were lying all around two wooden bowls that contained what looked in the lamplight like sweet potatoes.

"Jus' playin' some gin rummy," Barney explained.

"You know how ta play?" asked Shirley.

Gaynelle shook her head. "Will you show me?"

"Have a seat."

The twins commenced playing cards with her, seeming as delighted with Gaynelle as she was with them, laughing at how excited she was at the novelty of being in their shack, of playing with their cards, of everything there that was new to her. She forgot entirely about the trouble she'd be in if her folks discovered she wasn't home. After a while, Barney picked up a poker, and she watched for him to stir the ashes of their small fireplace. Instead, he cleared off the lid of a cast iron pot then retrieved a sweet potato as carefully as if it were a hot coal.

"Here ya go." He dropped it into another bowl and handed it to Gaynelle, looking pleased with himself. "Can't have company goin' hungry."

"Oh." She looked towards the fireplace, wondering if they had more sweet potatoes for themselves. "I don't want to eat your supper."

He waved a hand at their bowls, now jutting precariously from the shelf next to the lantern. "We already ate."

Shirley nodded.

Reluctantly, Gaynelle brushed off a few ashes that had fallen onto the sweet potato, but after the first soft, sweet bite, she ate it with relish. Smiling, Barney fetched her a canning jar full of water to wash it down with.

They continued playing cards into the wee hours of the morning, but eventually Shirley stowed the card deck in her trunk and flopped onto the bed. "I been lookin' forward to dis! So soft. Wanna try it out?" She patted the area next to her.

Gaynelle glanced shyly at Shirley's corner of the room. "Actually, can I swing in your hammock again?"

"Go right ahead." Shirley stretched out her limbs to take up the entire bed.

Gaynelle picked her way over Shirley to climb inside her hammock from atop the bed.

Soon Barney had dimmed the lantern further and was climbing into his own hammock, saying, "Remind me to turn off dat lantern when Gaynelle leaves."

After they were all settled, the twins began asking Gaynelle about her own life. Before long she'd told them all about Vivian's recent drama, glad to have something to share, and they were soon arguing about whether or not the doctor was Vivian's birth father—Shirley was of the decided opinion that he was, while Barney held out that it was a stretch. After that, however, Gaynelle spent most of the time telling them about Aunt Anna and her almost-castle with its indoor bathroom and treasure horde of books. She'd begun summarizing each of her favorite novels and was in the midst of telling them about *The Little Princess* when she realized they'd grown very quiet—quiet but not silent. Not the silence that made her ears and heart ache when she was alone in her own bedroom. No, their deep, rhythmic breathing was comforting. She liked having Shirley next to her, right there on the bed, so close she could reach out and touch her. She liked Barney hanging in a twin hammock at the same level as hers, just across from her. Only now, as she pushed her foot against the wall in unison with their breathing to rock herself back and forth, did Gaynelle realize that the hammock she was in was pungent with Shirley's scent. She really didn't mind at all—it made her visit with them all the more real. She liked being there with friends. She'd stay for just a while longer. Gaynelle closed her eyes, daring to rest them for a bit, just to enjoy the company for a few moments longer.

Some time later, Gaynelle's eyes flew open. An owl was hooting just outside the shack as though to warn her. Alarmed, unsure whether it was even still nighttime, she fumbled her way out of the hammock. She tried not to step on Shirley, who muttered something to herself and turned over. The lamp had apparently long since gone out.

Slipping out of the yellow shack, she made her way home, heart in throat. All was silent within the white clapboard house, to her relief, and it was still dark inside. Just to be sure they weren't out looking for her, she peeked briefly into the stable, but the mules and Julep were all there. She sighed to herself with relief, certain that everyone must still be sleeping. On tiptoe, Gaynelle let herself back into the house and crept back to her room. As she settled at last into her own bed, wearing her nightgown as usual, her eyes finally closed again, and only then did a sense of elation wash over her. She hadn't been caught. She'd made it. It had totally been worth it.

Gaynelle had not been wrong that she'd gotten away with her night out. She hadn't been wrong, but that didn't matter. The very next day, instead of dropping Gaynelle off at the side of the road as usual, the school-wagon driver turned down their lane, driving right up to the Bells' house. The old bonnetted busybody told the children to remain in the wagon while she spoke with Gaynelle's parents.

Disregarding her instructions, Gaynelle followed her swishing skirts into the house. Soon the old woman was seated at the table, telling Jessie all about how Gaynelle had run over to see their colored neighbors the day before. She'd driven back by to double-check a little while later and had spied Gaynelle in one of the hammocks, where she wasn't alone. Bare, dark skin was all pressed up against her light skin—it'd been a tangle of black and white limbs.

"I couldn't believe my eyes." The driver leveled a dire glance at Jessie. "I don't know why I didn't drag her straight outta there. I should've hauled her up here and told you about it right then and there." She paused and waited for Jessie to speak, but Jessie just nodded, her eyebrows pinching.

"Maybe it was cuz I still had to drop off the other children and needed to get home." The old woman shook her head at her own poor excuses. "I fretted about it all night. Jus' never woulda expected it o' *Gaynelle*."

Jessie maintained a fairly cool demeanor, occasionally nodding. When the diatribe seemed at an end, Jessie waved a hand dismissively. To Gaynelle's utter amazement, she lied outright to the school-wagon driver. "We sure do appreciate your concern, but there ain't a thing to worry 'bout. We've known them folks since she was a baby," Jessie shrugged. "Their family used to work for Clay's family a long time ago. That's why they moved up there. Harmless as cooin' doves."

"Sure they ain't lovebirds?" The woman pursed her lips.

Jessie shook her head as though this were a reasonable question. "More like… family. They been watchin' her since she was tiny. You know how them chillun pile up like puppies when they have sleepovers. Done it ever since they were knee-high." Jessie held her hand towards the floor to indicate how small they'd been. Her smile was an afterthought, but as bright as if she thought it all perfectly adorable.

"These are not *children*," the woman insisted, eyes flashing. "She's far too big to be climbin' into hammocks with the likes of—"

"Oh, I'm sure you're right," Jessie cut her off and stood to her feet, making it clear that their visit was over. She took a step towards the door. "I forget how big she's gettin', and I guess they do, too. Old habits, you know. My own fault for not puttin' a stop to it sooner. I'll have a talk with her. Sure do appreciate you keepin' an eye out for these chillun."

"See that you do speak with her," huffed the driver, her bonnet brim trembling about her face as she marched past Jessie. She turned to Gaynelle on her way out. "I never woulda imagined it of you. The other children look up to you."

When the wagon driver left, Gaynelle could barely move, she was so stricken. A lead weight sat in the pit of her stomach. She couldn't think at all of how to answer Jessie's strident questions and accusations. When Jessie spanked her with Clayton's leather belt, Gaynelle did cry out, but the cries were only partly from pain—for she'd finally recognized what those cool nods, that seeming nonchalance reminded her of: it was the same expression she'd had when Gaynelle had told her about Vivian loaning out Julep. Things had gone horribly awry then. Gaynelle had lost her sister altogether. She dreaded what was to come of this.

Gaynelle was so consumed with worry that she didn't even react to her mama calling her a little whore as she spanked her. It only came back to her later that evening, when Jessie ranted about the incident to Clayton.

"Don't call her that, Jessie," he said warningly.

"Have you seen that boy up there?" she insisted, her face flushing. "Your daughter was rollin' around in the hammock with him like the worst sort of tramp. What do you call that?"

"I was not," Gaynelle interjected, heat flooding her own face. "I was in the hammock with Shirley!"

Clayton looked unhappily between them. "Prob'ly best if you don't do that anymore, Gaynelle." Then he cast Jessie a glance that said, *Watch your tongue.*

"Alright." Jessie's eyes were blazing. "If you wind up with a li'l colored grandbaby, don't say I didn't warn you."

Just to be safe, Gaynelle waited before trying to visit the twins again. She couldn't go at night, as their parents would be there. And she couldn't go straight after getting off the school wagon, as the busybody had taken to driving her all the way down the lane, even waiting for her to go inside her house. It was humiliating, but it was at least a small comfort that the other children didn't seem to be aware of why she was doing it. One little girl even complained that she didn't take the rest of them all the way to *their* houses.

Gaynelle shrugged. "I'm older than you."

Despite knowing she wouldn't be able to spend time with the twins directly after school, Gaynelle still kept her eyes peeled for them each time the school wagon passed by their yellow shack. She spotted them in the field a couple of times that first week after the incident, but then she didn't see them at all for more than a week. At last she dared to steal down to their shack, only to find it empty.

She raced back home, her heart thudding in her chest. She didn't dare ask Mama, but she found her daddy repairing a section of fence on the edge of a field. He was just sinking post-hole diggers into the earth when she ran up to him.

"Do you know where the neighbors went?" she panted breathlessly. "They're not there anymore."

He looked up at her mournfully then tried to paste on a smile. "Nothin' to fret about. They're jus' fine."

"Where are they?"

"Moved back to Manning, actually." He returned his attention to the hole.

"Did not," Gaynelle spat furiously. "They were plannin' on bringin' in their first harvest in jus' a couple more weeks."

He didn't answer, merely scooping another mound of earth onto a small pile.

"They weren't plannin' on movin' nowhere," she insisted. "I know that for sure. What happened to them?"

"Don't get so worked up." He sighed and turned back to look at her, propping himself up with the post-hole diggers. "You know how we save up to buy a little more land each year, right?" He cast her a thin smile once more. "Well, jus' worked out that the land they were on was a 'specially good deal."

"No." Gaynelle took a step backwards, staring at him horror-stricken. "We didn't take that land from under them."

"They didn't own it."

"They lived there. They were nice!"

"It's alright," he assured her. "I made sure they got set up in another house. A real nice one there in Manning. Took 'em down there myself. Seemed glad to be back near their other children. I even paid them some for the work they already done here. Not only that, but I promised to take 'em some of their harvest when it comes in."

"You're… you're a bully," Gaynelle fumed, unable to even see straight. The ground seemed to swim under her.

"I didn't hafta do all that for them. Ain't nobody bullied no one. Didn't take much persuadin' at all."

"Persuadin'," Gaynelle snorted.

"It's all for the best."

"It's not fair! They didn't do nothin' wrong!" Tears flooded her eyes.

"Your mama thought it was better this way."

She'd immediately suspected as much. Her nod was almost a spasm. "I hate her!" Gaynelle sobbed. "She's not my mama!"

"Enough! We did it for your sake. Behave yourself."

Trembling, Gaynelle fled from her father, running towards the stable to find comfort with Julep. Apparently he was the only friend she was allowed to have.

13• New Farm Help

Two years later
April 1920, Greeleyville, SC

"I'LL BE RIGHT THERE, DADDY. I jus' hafta wash these here dishes," Gaynelle hollered from the porch. She rushed inside to finish that particular household chore. It would be twice as hard to clean the dishes if the grits dried on them.

Spring had arrived and life on the farm was a whirlwind of activity. This was always the busiest time of year, and she found herself staying home from school time and again to help her daddy in the fields. Since he cleared a new field each winter, the work of planting and weeding and tending the crops had long since become too much for him alone.

Clayton burst into the house with a scowl. "Jessie, do you mind if I go ahead and take the girl out to work the rows now? I'm afraid it's gonna start rainin' soon. Can you finish up them dishes without her, please?"

Bowls in hand, Gaynelle paused, looking wide-eyed from Mama to Daddy. It never paid to displease Mama.

"Of course, Clay." Jessie pursed her lips. Her husband's dependence on his daughter had only increased in the years since Vivian's absence. Resentment curdled in Jessie's stomach as Gaynelle tugged on work boots and a straw hat over still-untidy hair, then raced to catch up with Clayton. The girl had grown in the two years since Vivian had moved away. Her childish figure had developed subtle curves overnight, unnecessarily enhanced by the fitted cut of a new everyday dress, courtesy of that high-and-mighty Anne Sanders.

After finishing the dishes and tending to the rest of the morning chores, Jessie strolled down to the fields to watch her husband work for a while. She often did so—especially since that September before the Great War ended, when they'd expanded the draft age and she'd had to make sure Clayton didn't go off and register. During that terrifying period, Jessie had found it difficult to get her own work done for following Clayton around everywhere, heart in throat. Checking in and knowing that things were in order—or, as the case had been then, out of order—unfailingly comforted her, especially when her mood was out of sorts.

Despite the heavy cloud cover, it hadn't started pouring yet, though she didn't mind if it did. She enjoyed a good rainstorm. As she walked down the still-dusty road, she spotted them working in the field. Clayton's massive figure loomed large beside his petite daughter's form. His bare skin gleamed with perspiration. Jessie halted, catching her breath. Clayton had stripped off his shirt, and his muscles rippled. Her husband was a specimen of a man, even in his mid-forties, and she moistened her lips as she watched him.

Clayton made some unintelligible remark to Gaynelle, and the girl's tinkling laughter followed. She shot back a reply. As he guffawed and grinned, Jessie pressed her lips together in irritation. *Thinks she's clever—just like her mother.*

Gaynelle tossed her curly head, her hat apparently discarded, and Clayton redoubled his efforts with his hoe.

Look at the impudent hussy, flirtin' with her own father, tossin' that hair she's so proud of. Jessie's bloodlust rose until she could taste bitter bile on her tongue. Her well-developed husband's naked torso was gleaming and bulging for Gaynelle's iniquitous enjoyment. Abruptly, Jessie turned and headed home as the first drops of rain began to fall.

I'll put a stop to this foulness, she swore.

"Dry off that dripping mop." Jessie shoved a towel at Gaynelle as they came in from the field, but other than that, Jessie betrayed none of her anger. When they finally settled down to the table, however, with large helpings of perlou and collards filling their plates, Jessie broached the subject as soon as their mouths were full. "Clay, I think you should hire a boy or two to help you out in the field."

He blinked in surprise and swallowed. "You said we couldn't afford it, that we needed to save for buyin' that neighborin' field. And I thought you didn't want no more people round here cuz o' that influenza."

She nodded. "I know I said that, but I been rethinkin'. If it ain't one thing threatenin', it's another. Ain't never gonna end." She paused, recalling how their fool neighbor had brought the Spanish flu back with him from Charleston, killing his mother with it. Over the past three years, countless folks had fallen victim to the epidemic, but at least it wasn't as bad here as in the cities. "I s'pose the good Lord decides who he wants to carry home, after all. Besides, if Vivian ain't caught it all this time down in Charleston, maybe we're okay here."

"Jus' what I been sayin'," he agreed, nodding effusively.

The metallic taste of blood filled her mouth as she bit down on her tongue. For so long, she'd been begging him to bring Vivian home from Charleston, but even after the flu killed their neighbor, it had made no difference to him. Blinking to clear her vision, Jessie struggled to keep her voice even. "I'm just thinkin' maybe you're right. You could earn more here on the farm, in the end, with some extra help."

"I guess tomorrow I'll go ask Ms. Moultrie if she knows anyone who might be interested," Clayton mused.

Jessie shook her head. "I'd rather not have everybody around here knowin' our business. Maybe you could hire boys from Manning or Kingstree."

"They could stay in the little yellow house," Gaynelle suggested, eyes bright.

Jessie's scowl quickly morphed into a motherly nod, and she settled a hand on the shoulder of their damp-haired girl. "Just what I was thinkin'. Besides, Gaynelle's been missin' too much school. She's a young woman now, and it ain't right for her to spend all her days laborin' in the fields. I know how important her schoolin' is to you, and I could use her help more back here at the house."

"Hallelujah!" Clayton whooped. "I been thinkin' I couldn't take this much longer with just Gaynelle to help me out there. Thank you, darlin'."

On the very day that the new help arrived, Gaynelle returned to school. She'd been absent for nearly a fortnight. A teetering pile of textbooks threatened to avalanche as she stepped down from the school wagon that afternoon. She was shuffling down the lane when a smooth voice asked, "Need some help with those, sweetheart?"

"Oh, yes," breathed Gaynelle, casting a relieved smile at what must be the new help. She could get used to extra hands in no time flat, she decided. Just as she was about to relinquish the pile to him, however, she drew back, staring at his 'extra' hands. They were caked with dirt.

"I been in the field." He brushed them carelessly on his trousers. A one-sided smile crossed his lean face, and his gaze wandered down her figure.

She flushed. By the time his sparkling blue eyes came back up to meet hers, her heart was racing. She let him have the books.

"I'm Tommy Salters, your pa's new help. Come on, then." Adjusting his flat tweed cap, the boy shouldered the stack.

As he strode forward, Gaynelle scanned him thoroughly in turn. His hair was sleek and black under the pageboy cap, his body lithe and muscular. He sauntered with the confidence of a young man who owned the world.

After depositing her textbooks on the kitchen table, Tommy nodded at Jessie then left to rejoin Clayton in the field. Gaynelle bit her lip, her gaze lingering on the empty doorframe after he'd gone. The next moment, her braid was abruptly snatched backwards, her backside deposited into a chair.

"Hussy!" Jessie stared down at her, eyes narrowed. "You stay away from the farmhands, y'hear? That is all we need."

Gaynelle gasped. "I didn't do nothin', Mama."

"It's in your blood, you little tramp. You so much as speak to those boys again, and I'll make your Daddy fire them. Then he'll not have any help, and it'll be entirely your fault. Understand?"

Tears spilling down her cheeks, Gaynelle nodded.

"Alright, then. Get them god-blasted books off the table. I shoulda known they'd send you home with a mess o' homework. Set the table and help get this dinner ready."

Stricken, Gaynelle hastened to complete her chores. At suppertime, she avoided meeting the eyes of either of the new farmhands, only daring to nod in reply to their greetings. She could hardly believe the youths would be taking meals with them. How she could make it through entire meals without speaking with them was hard to fathom, even if Mama did divert the conversation away from her. The unfairness of it all blistered her heart. She so rarely saw new faces. She burned with curiosity but dared not do more than glance at them while Mama was around.

Gaynelle took her studies into the room she used to share with Vivian. By the time she dimmed the kerosene lamp, even her wraith of a stepmother had long since gone to bed. With a lonely ache—despite having spent the day around more people than she almost ever saw—Gaynelle hugged her pillow and drifted off to sleep. She dreamt of her sister, of vainly clutching for her as Vivian rolled out of bed and then out the door, into the obscurity of the night.

14 • Can't Hurt Nothin' to Say Hello

GAYNELLE FROZE BENEATH THE RIVETING GAZE of Tommy Salters. She'd heard the stable door creak open and had slipped from her morning perch to greet her daddy—but she'd unlatched Julep's stall to find herself face-to-face with the farmhand instead.

"Well, hey there, Gaynelle." Tommy set down the bucket he was carrying.

She retreated, closing the stall door between them.

"What's the matter?"

Hesitating, Gaynelle admitted, "I'm not allowed to talk to you. Mama says I can't."

His skewed smile returned as he looked around with exaggerated care. "Hmm, well, I don't see no one but us, so it can't hurt nothin' to say hello, now, can it?"

"I s'pose not. Hello." Gaynelle laughed with a touch of relief, but it was short-lived. His blue eyes were so fixed on her that her heart skipped a beat. Her hand drifted self-consciously to still-unbraided hair.

"Whatcha doin' in here so early in the mornin'?"

The silence fell thick until Gaynelle stammered, "I... I like to come out here early in the mornin' to read my stories... and spend time with Julep." When she realized she was staring into his eyes, her gaze shifted upwards. Then she tilted her head quizzically. "What happened to your other hat?"

His hand shot up to the brim of the straw hat now perched on his head. He pulled it off with a scowl. "Your pa said this would be better than my regular cap while I'm workin' in the field." He waved the straw hat at Julep. "Lucky beasts don't have to wear stupid straw hats. He gets to be just as fine-lookin' out there as anywhere. Come to mention it, that one's handsome enough to bring a mighty decent price at the auctions."

His words yanked Gaynelle straight back down to earth. She glared at him. "No, he wouldn't. We ain't gonna sell Julep—never."

"Alright. Don't shoot. I was just tryin' to say that he's a fine horse."

She heaved a sigh. "Sorry... Guess I'm kinda protective. He belonged to my mother."

"But he don't now?" His brow creased.

"Oh, Mama's not my real mother, though she done raised me ever since I was a baby. There's not much to remember my birth mother by, 'cept Julep. Daddy says she loved him like *he* was her firstborn instead o' my sister."

"Bet your Ma was a pretty woman. I was wonderin' where you come from. You're the prettiest thing I ever did see." Tommy extended an arm over the stall door and traced her cheek with one finger.

Heat flooded her face, and she stared downwards.

"Hey, it's alright. You ain't got nothin' to worry 'bout." He withdrew his hand, glancing back at the stable entrance. "You gonna be here tomorrow?"

Nodding silently, she looked back up at him with wide eyes.

"Alright, then." Stepping back from the stall door, he settled his hat back on his head. "I gotta grab these mules and get out to the field before your pa gets mad at me."

"Daddy's not comin' this mornin'?"

Tommy was already in Button's stall, fitting the harness. "Nah, he's already out there. Me or Willie will be comin' to get the mules ready from now on."

With dismay, Gaynelle climbed back up to her perch. Clasping *1001 Arabian Nights* tightly in both hands, she stared at the open pages as she listened to him leave. If only she could leap straight into them, like a genie disappearing into a lamp. Her reality was quite the opposite, though. As long as Tommy could show up at any moment, it would be a remarkable feat for her to ever lose herself in her morning-time novels again.

The next day, she waited for Tommy to appear. When the stable door opened, she slipped from her perch, heart thumping. She peered through the slats, but to her disappointment—or relief, she wasn't quite sure which—the other farmhand was the one retrieving the mules, oblivious to her presence. This scene repeated over the next several mornings until at last Gaynelle stopped expecting Tommy, and once more she was able to delve into her readings.

Tommy didn't let her forget about him, though. At supper, he didn't try to speak with her beyond simple pleasantries, but she was acutely aware of his hand brushing hers. It happened so often that Gaynelle was sure he was doing it on purpose. When passing behind her, he'd sometimes trail his finger across her shoulder or down her arm. Shivering at his touch, Gaynelle prayed her parents wouldn't notice.

Several weeks later, Gaynelle entered the stable before dawn on a June morning. She was startled to find Tommy there—already there—leaning easily against Julep's stall door.

"Mornin', sweetheart." He cast his audacious, lopsided grin at her.

Instantly dizzy, she leaned on the wall for support. "What are you doin' here?"

"Heard tell it was your birthday." He shrugged. "You're fifteen now, ain't that right? I brought ya a present."

Gaynelle blinked as he handed her a package wrapped in brown paper. Daddy sometimes gave her a whole dollar to spend on herself, but otherwise, no one ever made a to-do on her birthday. She tore at the wrapping.

The stoppered-glass bottle inside was glazed, fluted, and painted with pale flowers. Gaynelle gasped reverently. "It's beautiful!"

Taking the bottle from her, he unplugged the stopper and waved it under her nose. "It's perfume, silly. Here, put some on."

Uncertainly, she held out her hand. He turned her palm upwards and rubbed the stopper against her wrist. "There now, see how you like it."

Sniffing at her wrist, she coughed.

"Oh yeah, don't whiff too hard. It's kinda powerful at first."

Shyly, she said, "Me and Mama made yellow-jessamine water once, but it weren't near this strong."

Taking her hand, he lifted it towards his own face. Inhaling the fragrance, he murmured, "This one's rose. Yeah, that's nice."

Gaynelle sniffed once again, a bit more tentatively, and nodded her agreement. Gazing rapturously at the ornate perfume bottle, she said abruptly, "Mama'll never let me have it, and I can't tell her you gave it to me, neither."

"Don't you have somewhere you can keep it?"

Her cubbyhole was only yards away. "Maybe I do, actually." Striding over to Julep's stall, she called, "Thanks for the perfume. I'll see you at dinnertime."

"Hey, hold on a minute." His hand descended on her shoulder.

She turned back to face him, her thoughts on the scent of the floral perfume. "Hmm?"

"Just this." Tommy leaned forward, quickly kissing her. He chuckled at her surprised gasp. Dashing out of the stable, he called, "Happy Birthday! See ya at supper."

When Willie came in a while later to retrieve the mules, he was none the wiser as to the presence of a barely-fifteen-year-old girl perched in Julep's stall, smelling her wrist and touching her lips in wonderment.

15 • Scissors

To Gaynelle's surprise, Tommy was once more waiting for her in the stables the next morning.

"You again?" She looked around nervously to make sure they were alone.

He responded without hesitation, looking more serious than the day before. "Here to see you, sweetheart."

"Ain't my birthday," she croaked, heart catapulting in her chest.

"Nope, but I like talkin' with ya, and I done figured out that this is the only time I'll get to." Tommy's no-nonsense expression suggested that he found this logic irrefutable—he was there because he must be there.

"I'm not allowed to talk to you," Gaynelle whispered, feeling lightheaded as he drew closer.

"Alright, well, your Ma ain't said nothin' bout kissin' me, did she?" His hands slipped around her waist.

The words that had been perched on the tip of her tongue drifted away as his soft lips brushed hers, not waiting for a response. His hands slid to her hair, and he tilted her head back as he continued to kiss her.

Her trembling hands rose, clinging to his sinewy shoulders. A spark of heat ran through her.

"You're so pretty," he murmured repeatedly, breathing between kisses. His hands were trailing over her figure, grazing her hips, her back, her breasts.

Gaynelle felt herself responding to his caresses, returning his kisses. As his hands began to search more insistently, however, she pulled away.

"Stop that, Tommy," she managed to utter, her voice uncertain.

"Alright," he agreed, but he stepped forward to kiss her again.

She responded with increasing abandon until his hands began to explore her form again.

"Stop," she insisted more certainly, drawing back.

"Aw, come on, Gaynelle." His voice was urgent. "You feel so nice. I ain't never wanted to touch no one so bad."

Realizing she better draw the line while she could, Gaynelle demanded, "What if Willie walks in here? I'm gonna be in trouble, and you'll get fired."

"Alright," he agreed, "just one more kiss…"

Several minutes later, Gaynelle finally extracted herself from Tommy's embrace. Somehow, she managed to complete her chores and get ready for school, just as if nothing had happened, as if all were as usual in the world.

At suppertime, Tommy kept his leg pressed against hers, brushing her hand with daring frequency. He flashed intermittent smiles at the potatoes, to her discomfiture—and exhilaration. To her amazement, no one seemed to notice anything out of the ordinary.

He continued to meet Gaynelle in the early morning hours, even bringing a blanket for them to lie down on. She began to anticipate their rendezvous—and dreamt of him all other hours, both day and night. Everything else in her life soon paled, dreary next to his smooth kisses and caresses, now a welcome tonic. Never before had anyone plied her with so much attention, and though he continually pressed for more, he'd eventually stop at her insistence. She wasn't quite sure what exactly she was stopping, but she knew beyond a doubt that her parents would most certainly not approve even of the kissing.

Still, she thought of Tommy through chores and during long, bumpy rides to school. In her bed at night, she drifted off to sleep anticipating their embraces. Dreams of the thrilling young farmhand gradually, steadily replaced her nightmares about Vivian.

Pouring a dollop of gravy over her rice, Gaynelle tried to look natural. Her other hand was prying away the fingers that had slipped onto her thigh under the table.

"What you thinkin' 'bout, Gaynelle?" Clayton asked.

She started at the question, jerking up as if he'd shot at her. Relinquishing her struggle with Tommy's wayward hand, she scrambled for an excuse. "Um, well, I have to write a paper on Socrates for school. Did you know he was poisoned?"

"They know that for sure?" Clayton frowned.

"Yes, sir. Everyone knew it." She exhaled, certain he was thinking of the words she'd overheard Dr. Connor murmur to him so long ago. They were, after all, why she'd picked the story. "He was poisoned to death as a punishment for criticizin' all sorts of bad stuff his countrymen were doin'. They made him drink hemlock. He coulda escaped, but he said he wasn't afraid to die, since he was a philosopher and all."

Clayton stared at her, seeming to mull this over.

"Why on earth are we sendin' the child to that school?" Jessie interjected. "What nonsense they're fillin' her head with. Why, she plum forgets to do half her chores these days, and her head's all in the clouds. What use is there to her learnin' 'bout philosophers? She needs to be learnin' how to tend a home."

"I like hearin' 'bout what she's studyin' at school," piped up Willie. He virtually never spoke at the dinner table, but his steady gaze regarded her as it sometimes did. His eyes were medium brown, as medium as everything else about him. Gaynelle would hardly even remember he existed if it weren't for the fact that she was reminded of him every time she got off the school wagon—he stayed in the yellow shack with Tommy, so she didn't dare try to visit Tommy there.

"Waste o' her time," muttered Jessie.

Clayton shook his head. "Nah. It's only fittin' for her to learn history, too. She still has to do all her regular cipherin' and such, right?" He threw a questioning glance at Gaynelle.

"Yes, sir." She blushed self-consciously, admitting, "This is kinda extra, actually. My teacher wants me to enter a paper for a district contest. Only a couple other students are writin' essays—and I'm the only girl. We got to choose any ancient philosopher, but I picked Socrates cuz the poisonin' was so interestin'."

"Ain't it, though." He shook his head.

"It's ridiculous, that's what it is." Jessie stood abruptly and started clearing supper dishes from the table.

"Well now," he mused, "Dr. Connor thinks it's a lot more common than we know. He said it sometimes happens by accident."

"Hogwash," she spat.

"Nah, it ain't. In fact, he seemed to think maybe Vivian had gotten into somethin' like that." His voice dropped to a low rumble.

Jessie stared. "He said that?"

"Not 'zakly, but he went on like Gaynelle there, 'cept he was talkin' 'bout some composer fella. Guess he mighta been onto somethin', cuz Vivian sure is better now."

"'Cept she still might be done in by that Spanish flu, stayin' in the city like she does. And if that don't get her, she's still gettin' ruint with all sorts o' high-fallutin' notions," Jessie seethed.

"Can't believe she's goin' to college this fall," Gaynelle said, eyes shining. "Wonder what she's gonna do after that? Maybe run for Congress like that lady from Montana she was talkin' about."

"Republican nonsense," Jessie interjected.

"Sky's the limit." Laughing, Clayton settled back in his seat. "I think them's the words she used. Sure am proud o' my smart girls. Musta got it from Carrie, cuz it sure weren't from me."

Gaynelle's eyes grew round as small globes. "Oh, Daddy, I knew she was pretty, but was she real smart, too?"

Dishes clattered into the sink. Venom shot from Jessie's eyes. In a barely-contained voice, she said, "Time for y'all to go on and clear out." Her calloused hand waved their dismissal. "I gotta straighten this here kitchen, and y'all in my way."

"Guess you're right," Clayton sighed. "Dinner was real good. Come on, fellas."

Once they'd left, Gaynelle began to help Jessie with the dishes, humming to herself as she digested this newest morsel of information about her birth mother. Just as she hung a ceramic cup in the cupboard, her head was yanked backwards.

She gasped as Jessie unceremoniously thrust her into a chair. "We need to take a gander at your scalp, Gaynelle. Thought I saw lice creepin' round in there earlier."

"Lice?" Gaynelle clutched at her braid and looked up in horror.

"Hold still." Jessie pulled off the girl's hair tie and shook the braid loose, leaning close to inspect as she roughly parted the curly tresses in various ways. "Mmm-hmm. Yep. Li'l vermin will be all over this house if they ain't already." Lifting a long ringlet, she took up the scissors and snipped close to Gaynelle's scalp.

Gaynelle cried out but didn't dare move. The metal blades rang together, right by her ears, again and again. Within moments, her fair curls were shorn.

Stepping back to view the nearly-bald head with satisfaction, Jessie wondered why she hadn't done it sooner.

"How can I go to school like this?" Gaynelle sobbed, tears coursing down her cheeks.

Jessie sniffed. "What a vain creature you are. Wear a scarf over your head. You'll learn just as much, if that's even why a li'l hussy like you is there. Maybe you'll actually learn more now." Nodding at her wide, stricken eyes, Jessie hissed, "Yes, ma'am. I know you better than you think. And since you really wanna know about that tramp that gave birth to you, I'll tell ya. You *are* just like Carrie. She did everythin' for attention, and your daddy weren't the only man she went with. But all the while she was puttin' on airs, like you with your Socrates. A self-absorbed, spoiled brat, too. You're her spittin' image, cryin' over here about not gettin' the chance to give the rest of us your vermin. I ain't gonna cater to none of that foolishness, so if you expect me to feel sorry for you, you got another thing comin'."

Shame and humiliation racked the girl's body. It was true, she realized—she did care too much about everyone's opinion of her, and she hadn't worried for a moment about spreading lice to the rest of them. No, she was too wrapped up in her vanity. When the boys cast glances at her, her chest fairly swelled with elation. She reveled for minutes on end when anyone flattered her about her hair. Mama was so right. Even her good grades were an effort to win approval.

"Mama," Gaynelle pleaded for comfort, barely able to speak through the sobs shaking her body.

Jessie rolled her eyes. "Go on now, git. You ain't no use to me in your state."

Blinded by tears, Gaynelle ran towards the door and fumbled for a scarf. She pulled it over her head, then ran out of the house to safe haven in the stables.

Curled on her perch in Julep's stall, she wept bitterly. After a while, a gentle hand touched her knee, and she stopped mid-sob. She hadn't heard Tommy enter the stall, but she knew it was him.

"What's goin' on?" he asked.

Moaning in humiliation, Gaynelle hunkered further, pressing her head into her knees and pulling the scarf more tightly around her head.

He waited for a while, allowing her to cry. Finally, he tugged her hand, "Come on down here, Gaynelle. Let me hold you."

She sniffled, "I can't."

"Why not?"

"I'm hideous."

Her tone left no room for doubt, but he laughed. "What?"

"I'm ugly and repulsive," she insisted.

"Nah, you're the prettiest girl I know. What's the matter?" His tug became more robust. "Get down here."

Allowing herself to be pulled off the perch, Gaynelle crumpled against him.

He held her in his arms, trying to soothe her as she burst into a fresh round of sobs.

"What's the matter?" he murmured. Pulling back, he held her at arm's length, searching for the source of her pain.

When he began to push her scarf back, she squeezed her eyes shut, murmuring by way of explanation, "Mama cut off my hair."

Several agonizing moments of silence passed. Gaynelle was envisioning his look of disgust when she felt lips pressing against hers. In surprise, she opened her eyes. He drew away slightly, stroking her head with his free hand.

"You're still the prettiest girl I know." Flashing his lopsided grin, he gave her another light kiss before she could even speak.

She burst into tears again, and Tommy brought her securely into his embrace. Her misery gradually relented under Tommy's tender ministrations, and she pressed herself into his sweaty shirt, wishing to remain in his arms forever.

"I love you," she mouthed, holding on to Tommy, her life preserver in a tumultuous emotional sea.

16 • Tommy's Reassurances

Razor-sharp talons slashed at Gaynelle, jolting her awake from a vivid nightmare. She was in a cold sweat. Though it was earlier than usual, she climbed out of bed, shaking with fright and longing for Tommy's comforting embrace. *Maybe he'll know to be there for me this morning,* she hoped, but her footsteps faltered as she remembered her hair. *Will he even bother? I'm so awfully bald.*

When she saw his statuesque form silhouetted against the tangerine-lit back wall of the stable, she braced herself for rejection. As she drew closer, however, she could tell that he was smiling warmly—with not a hint of reserve about him.

Emotion caught at her throat, and she could only admire him. Jet black hair was combed to the side, sleek as an otter's. His golden skin was inexplicably radiant in the gloom of the stable. Blue eyes pierced her as though she were in the presence of a god.

Wordlessly, he pulled her onto the blanket and began to kiss her deeply. Discarded were the lighter, playful kisses that they often spent their mornings sharing. She generally pulled away from him when he tried to further their lovemaking, but this morning she felt depthless gratitude for his touch. When his hands began to explore her body, Gaynelle allowed them to go where they would, responding with pleasured moans. Soon, Tommy had disrobed them both. Their bare skin came together, warm and supple as he kissed her once more. Within moments, he was pressing into her.

When he entered her fully, she gasped. He repeated the movement again and again, but after the first sharp pain subsided, it didn't hurt so much. She was still trying to figure out whether or not to push him away when he paused deep within her and held quite still. Then he groaned with ecstasy and shuddered. A moment later he gave a small laugh, murmuring in her ear, "That's over now. It'll feel nice from now on."

He collapsed to her side, spent and breathless. After a moment, he leaned over to kiss her cheek. "You're amazin', know that?"

Gaynelle could only manage a faint smile. The air brushing against her bare skin felt all the more peculiar with even her scalp vulnerable and exposed. Wetness spread between her legs, and she looked to Tommy with uncertainty.

"Don't worry," he laughed again, apparently in a wonderful mood. "I'll help you get all situated."

After that fateful morning, Gaynelle and the lithe young man began making love frequently in the early workday hours. Her qualms and inexperience gave way to passionate eagerness as Tommy's guidance brought her into the delights of womanhood all too early. Gaynelle blossomed as she reveled in his touch and felt comforted by his love.

17• Saying Goodbye

"**Y**OUR PA JUST DON'T NEED ME RIGHT NOW. Leastways, not for a couple o' months. But he will in the spring. We'll figure it out," Tommy placated the distraught girl as they stood together near the road. Winter had arrived, and they were making their final good-byes.

"I love you, Tommy," she cried, her wavy, short mop spilling across his shoulder.

"I love you, too." Tommy extricated himself from her grasp. "We've had a lot of fun, you and me, haven't we?"

"Yeah, I suppose so." Gaynelle wiped at her eyes.

"I'm gonna be workin' over at a store in Manning for a while, but maybe I'll be able to come back here real soon." His tone was hopeful.

She released a wavering breath, gazing at him ardently. "I'll miss you so much."

"I'll miss you, too." Tommy picked up his few items, including the blanket they'd shared, and cast his skewed grin at her. "See you soon, sweetheart."

Gaynelle blinked away tears as he turned and sauntered down the lane. His lean body strode with confidence, and she didn't know whether to laugh or cry when she heard him humming a jaunty tune.

She stood there until he was gone, doing both. When she finally made her way back towards the farmhouse, she paused at the water pump to wash away the evidence of her loss before her parents saw her.

18 • Jessie's Birthday Surprise

THE COLDEST PART OF WINTER DIDN'T BOTHER GAYNELLE as much as it usually did. Vivian's warmth had been sorely missed on chilly nights, but now Gaynelle found herself grateful for room to toss and turn. Her icy appendages used to be routinely bundled during winter with socks and sometimes mittens, but now her hands and feet stuck out from her quilt as if mocking the Frost King's weakened powers so far from his glacial palace at the North Pole.

The girl had never been told about the mechanics of pregnancy, nor had she spent time around expectant women. Months passed with her none the wiser about her quietly-growing child. She'd never experienced monthly cycles, assuming her first bleed to be trauma from too much clandestine activity with Tommy. She'd begged him off, and after a few days everything had seemed right again. Never had she had another issue with bleeding.

Then it seemed perfectly normal to feel unwell after Tommy's departure. She ached with longing for him, crying well into the nights, and her morning nausea seemed only a natural consequence. Even on those rare mornings that she hadn't cried the night before, it wasn't a whit surprising that she'd feel sick to her stomach at missing their special morning time together, at not knowing when she would see him again.

Disconsolately, she settled for the pleasure of food. She thought about it all of the time—if she wasn't pining for Tommy, she was thinking about eating. Even though she could hardly eat in the mornings, she'd never craved meals so much, and she found herself eating seconds and sneaking snacks. Even though she was gaining weight, she felt compelled to seek food out, despite the teasing that was starting up at school. Two of the boys had taken to slyly calling her 'Gainer' during class, looking at her belly and laughing. They'd say, 'Excuse me, Gainer,' and 'Good job, Gainer,' right in front of the teacher and other students. The whole class snickered.

Gaynelle's cheeks would flush, but those boys were nothing compared to Tommy. Awash with contrary spirit, she'd stare at her slate and wonder what Mama was cooking for dinner.

"My word, that catfish stew was wonderful. You have outdone yourself, Jessie." Clayton leaned back and surveyed the supper table with satisfaction.

"Nothin' is better than your mama's recipe." Jessie agreed, trying to hide her smile of pride. They'd all eaten their fill, Gaynelle once again scarfing down as much as her massive, labor-weary father. *My, how that girl can eat when she has a notion.* "Mr. Barfield dropped off that fresh fish earlier today, and you grew everythin' else, 'cept for the rice. I just put it all together." Trying to suppress a grin, she added, "I made a little somethin' for dessert, too… Get the sweet potato pone, Gaynelle."

Generous slices were doled out, and Gaynelle closed her eyes with pleasure at her first bite. "Mama, this is even better than them marshmallows I tried in town."

Clayton murmured, "That's for sure. They were somethin' else, though."

"When was that?" Jessie blinked with annoyance.

His fingers drummed the table for a moment. "Ah, Gaynelle was with me when Vivian was so sick and we took her to Kingstree. We tried 'em at the grocery store there."

"But they were even better in cocoa," Gaynelle added eagerly.

"Where'd you have cocoa?" Jessie asked.

Gaynelle shook her head, looking away. "Some… somewhere in town."

"Don't lie to me." Jessie pursed her lips, turning to Clayton. "Where'd y'all go for cocoa?"

"Well… we stopped by the Sanders' place." He fiddled with his fork, regarding Gaynelle reproachfully.

"Anne Sanders?" The name was an accusation.

"Yeah." Clayton wiped his mouth and rose from his chair. "I gotta go finish up outside. Dessert was delicious."

Jessie narrowed her eyes as the screen door banged shut after him. Her gut was busy clenching into a knot as Gaynelle followed his lead.

She was aghast, wondering why it had taken her this long to suspect that her husband was dallying with that snooty woman. Just his type and rich as sin to boot. He'd never stoop to low-class whores and cheap women, but Anne was exactly his cup of tea. No doubt she reminded him of that ever-sacred tramp Caroline. After all, they'd been such friends. Now he was using Anne being a widow as an excuse to cozy up with her, to share sweets—sweets Jessie, his own *wife*, had never even tasted. He knew perfectly well she didn't want him associating with Anne, but apparently her feelings on the matter made no difference to him, so long as he thought she wouldn't find out. A blinding rage surged over her, and her hands shook. *At heart, all men are dogs.*

Two mornings later, Clayton opened the stable door and quietly entered. Walking softly towards Julep's stall, he paused to admire his daughter on her perch. He recognized her latest novel, *The Secret Garden*, in her hands. She was nibbling on a biscuit, oblivious to his presence. His heart warmed at the sight. "Gaynelle…"

Startled, she dropped her book ribbon. Then she laughed, rubbing at her eyes as he bent down to pick it up for her. "Thanks. I didn't hear you."

With a furrowed brow, he rubbed his palms together. "Honey, I'm in a heap o' trouble 'bout those marshmallows with Aunt Anna."

"I'm sorry, Daddy. I didn't mean to say nothin' wrong."

"I seen Jessie mad before, but never so mad at *me*. Sure does make my skin crawl."

Gaynelle nodded sympathetically. "It's horrible. I'm sorry."

"I was thinkin' maybe you could help me put together a birthday dinner for your mama. Maybe that would help."

"Sure, if you think it would." At once an ecstatic hope began to swell in her chest. Trying to control the excitement in her voice, she suggested, "We can invite Granny and Uncle Simms—and maybe Tommy and Willie."

He nodded. "Yeah, that sounds good. Let's make it this Saturday. I'm takin' some eggs and stuff over to my mama's in a while. I'll make the invites while I'm out there."

"Get Mama a present, too. Not marshmallows."

He grimaced. "Figured I'd take her to the shops here in town Saturday mornin' and buy somethin' nice for her to wear. You can cook the birthday dinner while we're out. Think you can handle that?"

Her bright, cheerful nod contrasted with Jessie's recent scowls so much that he sighed, resting his forehead against the reading perch. "Dang it, can't stand her givin' me those hateful looks. Hope this helps."

Gaynelle slid down from her perch, hugging him. "It's a sweet idea, Daddy. Mama loves you so much—she can't stay mad forever."

His troubled eyes lifted heavenward. "Sure hope you're right."

On the appointed morning, Clayton lured his still-sullen wife out of the house for a rare shopping venture.

Though she preferred not to fritter away her time and money, she felt compelled to go along with it. *I'd best let him*, she decided, *before he takes a notion to shop for Anne.*

Perusing the racks of new apparel, she frowned at striped, loose jersey tops that reminded her of sailor outfits for children. "Why I'd wanna look like a child, I don't know."

Clayton didn't reply. Looking up, she saw that he was yards away, chatting with the sales clerk, Ms. Moultrie—and the pair seemed to have an inexplicable familiarity.

"Why certainly, Mr. Bell. Right back there," the middle-aged, dark-skinned woman was saying. With a gesture towards the rear of the store, she gave him a brilliant smile before returning to the jewelry counter.

Jessie was still catching her breath when he returned to her side, holding a silky shawl embroidered with colorful flowers.

He fingered the macramé fringe as if it were strings of jewels. "Looka here, how d'ya like this?"

"What on earth would I do with a piano shawl?" Jessie raked it with a scathing glance.

He was too busy tracing the print flowers with his fingertips to notice.

She sighed. *Maybe if I wear it he'll look at me like that.* "But it *is* beautiful, Clay. I would… I would love it."

He draped the rayon shawl around her shoulders.

She pulled it close, pretending to admire it. The smooth cloth slid over her skin, and the bright flowers caught the light so that for a moment, she forgot she was faking. "Oh, roses and lilies, like my flower garden."

For a fraction of a moment, her smile was genuine. As angry as she still was with him, there was no question that her heart would always be devoted to Clayton—and she felt comforted at the notion that he was currently more solicitous of her than at any point in their past. Like a snake closed up in a piano cabinet, her venomous anger quelled.

Clayton blew out a breath. His shoulders relaxed. "Come on, let's get you a ready-made dress, too."

Stifling a sigh, Jessie was soon trying on a pale green afternoon dress with a loose, overly-long bodice and a pleated skirt. As she emerged from the dressing room, she said, "I think this upper part is too long. It at least needs a belt."

"No ma'am," Ms. Moultrie said. "That's the new dropped-waist style."

"That's right." Clayton's eyes tracked the swish of her skirt as Jessie distrustfully turned in front of the mirror, adding the piano shawl to the ensemble.

Reminding herself once again that she had to let him waste their money on her so he wouldn't find some other woman to indulge, she asked grudgingly, "You wanna buy it?"

"It looks good."

"Alright then. I guess it's decent."

Clayton's eyes brightened. "Maybe after you get used to wearin' a dress like that, you'll be more comfortable makin' 'em that way fer Gaynelle, too. Lots o' girls are wearin' 'em low like that now."

"There's an idea." She managed to feign a smile, but the piano-cabinet lid had burst open at his suggestion; the snake slithered out, hissing from the depths of her soul. Jessie clenched the shawl tightly, twisting the smooth cloth until it wound into a tight wad in her sweaty hands. *What a scheme this was, just to make me sew these ridiculous fashions for Carrie's daughter. Like Anna would do. He's dreamin' of that fashion designer. That's all there is to it.*

She took a deep breath, trying not to seethe. *But I guess this ain't really so different from those hair ribbons I once wore for him.* Forcing her smile to be even brighter, she said, "I'd love a new dress, and I'm sure I can get used to this one. Let me go change so we can pay out."

Clayton beamed. "Shucks, no need for that. You go ahead and wear that dress today, Jessie. It's your birthday."

"No call for me to wear my fine new dress today. I ain't got *that* many clothes," Jessie laughed, looking at him like he had lost his senses.

"You have to. It's your birthday dress." He took her elbow, leading her to the counter, where he picked up a parcel wrapped with brown paper. "I done paid out with Ms. Moultrie. Let's go home."

The supper was cooked and the cake baking in the oven. Pleased with herself, Gaynelle checked her hair in the mirror. Wavy locks had grown out to frame her face quite nicely, curling in towards her cheeks in a way that her longer hair never had.

Smoothing her eyebrows with a wet fingertip, she puckered her lips, admiring their exaggerated fullness.

"You look beautiful." The quiet words broke the stillness.

Startled, Gaynelle jumped back from the mirror. Heart hammering, she turned towards the porch screen door—and then her heart sank. "Oh. Hey, Willie. How ya doin'?"

"Pretty good. I been workin' down at the lumbermill." The quiet, plain boy came in, glancing around. "Am I that early? Where's everybody else?"

"Daddy took Mama to buy some new clothes. This dinner is a surprise for her. I gotta hurry up with it, though."

"Can I help?"

Gaynelle soon had him whipping the icing. She smiled, charmed at how good-natured he was being about putting his hand to women's work. "I can get distracted by anything," she chatted amiably. "If I don't have a book, I just daydream, and if I don't have a daydream, I apparently make faces at the mirror."

"I'd stare at it, too, if I saw your face when I looked in the mirror." Willie's voice was even, as even as the icing he was now smoothing onto the cake.

Gaynelle laughed with surprise. Willie had never said more than a handful of words to her, and they had all been along the lines of 'Pass the butter, please.'

When he finished, Gaynelle picked up the frosted cake and carried it to the table. He followed right behind her, and as she set the cake down on the table, he slipped his hands onto her hips, pressing his length against her.

Clumsily, Gaynelle stepped away from the table and gaped at him. "What do you think you're doin'?"

"Oh, Gaynelle." Willie sounded not at all contrite. "Whippin' that icing got me all whipped up, too."

"Don't go losin' your head." Rounding the table, Gaynelle swallowed a lump in her throat. It hadn't occurred to her to worry about being alone in the house with Willie, of all people. She tried to redirect him. "Would you pour that jar of pears in a serving bowl and put them on the table, please?"

As he busied himself with the pears, she tried to insert tapered candles into silver candlestick holders. They hardly ever used them, and the candles kept slipping out, but at least they could serve as small clubs if he tried anything. Hands unsteady, Gaynelle finally gave up. Shakily, she slid into a chair at the table and watched him apprehensively.

After setting the pears in place, he came around the table to sit next to her. She stiffened as he slid one arm around her shoulders and put his other hand on her thigh.

"What's the matter, Gaynelle? You liked it when Tommy did this sort of thing. Must be awful lonely without him." He was almost crooning.

Heat rushed to her face. She stood abruptly, but he tugged her back towards him.

Just then the front door opened, and Willie released hold of her. Granny and Uncle Simms shuffled into the farmhouse. She'd never been happier to see them.

Only moments behind them, Clayton and Jessie trailed in. Jessie's new clothes provided a welcome distraction. Everyone started exclaiming over them like she'd just flown in from Paris, no one so much as remarking upon the blood rushing to Gaynelle's face.

As they seated themselves at the dinner table, Gaynelle sandwiched herself between her granny and her father, even though she knew she might regret it if Tommy showed up. Her nerves were so rattled that she hardly gave further thought to his absence.

The birthday dinner was soon polished off. She nodded at their compliments, glad that Jessie didn't seem to mind her receiving credit this once. But after all, she'd done it in Mama's honor, and nobody seemed to forget that. They kept admiring the new outfit and repeating, "Happy birthday!"

"Well, as happy as you can expect," cackled Amarintha as Gaynelle began to clear the dishes.

"What do you mean?" asked Jessie, licking a bit of icing from her fork.

"You must be right sore 'bout yore smart girl gettin' knocked up." Amarintha pointed a knobby finger at Gaynelle, who was at that moment cornered in the kitchen by Willie. He'd followed her with a handful of plates. She was trying to slide past him, but he was making it impossible. Redirecting her words, Amarintha clucked, "Get away from dat boy. Dat's what got you into dis trouble to begin wid."

"What trouble?" Gaynelle glanced at her, face flushed once more.

"You ain't old enough to be spittin' out babies, missy."

Clayton sputtered, "What are you talkin' 'bout, Mama?" and then, "Come here, Gaynelle."

At last Willie made way for Gaynelle, and the flustered girl stepped towards the table. The room went silent for several moments.

Uncle Simms spoke first. "Must be dis boy's baby. He was messin' wid da chile when we came in here."

Willie began retreating towards the farmhouse door. "No sir, ain't mine. Musta been Tom—"

Before the words were out of his mouth, Clayton launched forward, slugging the boy in the face. Blood spewed from Willie's nose as he continued to stumble back towards the door.

"No sir, no sir. It wasn't me!" he protested, his voice rising as the farmer lunged again. Willie took to his heels, and a moment later the screen door clattered closed behind him.

Clayton stood wild-eyed, at a loss until Jessie grasped his shoulders, pulling him back into his seat. "Calm yourself, Clay. Slow your breathin'."

Turning to Gaynelle, she hissed, "Go to your room. We'll deal with you in a little while."

Once there, Gaynelle touched her swollen stomach in wonderment. A flutter of movement brushed against her fingertips, the same flutter she'd begun to feel every so often. She'd presumed it was digestive unrest from eating too much, from gaining so much weight, so quickly. The notion of a baby had never occurred to her; she'd thought only married women could have babies.

As she leaned back onto her bed, she concluded that she did *feel* married. She loved Tommy, and he loved her. *Maybe we are truly supposed to be a family*, she thought. *Like Rosa and Henry. They got married when Rosa was my age, and now they have little Jack.*

The idea soothed, frightened, and excited her, all at once. She could imagine living with Tommy, preparing his meals and tending to their home and children. Hadn't Daddy said that he hoped she'd one day marry a man who could help him with the farm? Surely Daddy would help Tommy build them their own little house right here.

On the other hand, Daddy had thought Willie was the father, and he'd hit him. Maybe it wasn't safe to tell them about Tommy yet.

19 • The Curse

Gaynelle had never seen her daddy like this. He was pacing back and forth, scowling and muttering to himself like Uncle Simms did when he was drunk. She watched from the couch, her heart in her throat, while Jessie sat in a rocking chair, waiting placidly.

Halting, he stared at his daughter with large, raving eyes. "I won't let it happen."

"You can hardly make it disappear," returned Jessie, a matter-of-fact, almost satisfied expression on her face.

As his anguished gaze bore into Gaynelle, it seemed to her the hands of time had caught up with him at last. Her daddy was forty-eight, but he had almost transcendentally maintained a youthful air and bearing. Sun and hard labor seemed to fall upon ageless shoulders, but now, as if divine privilege were abruptly rescinded, lines crossed his forehead and crow's feet adorned his eyes; his blonde hair had turned white, seemingly instantaneously. Broad shoulders bent in abject grief.

A pang of sorrow struck Gaynelle, then a surge of guilt. "Is it truly so awful, Daddy?"

"Of course it is," snapped Jessie.

Clayton crossed the room and sat next to Gaynelle. He braced his head in his hands, too overcome for speech.

Gaynelle waited, bewildered. She was stricken with the intensity of his pain, a pain that seemed to prey on his mortality—but she was the one pregnant, not him. Despite her own fears, she was still excited by the thought of an infant. She'd always hoped that Mama would have a baby, and everyone would have been thrilled had Jessie been the one pregnant. *Is it really true? Is this a child in me? How can I be a mother?*

"Here's what's gonna happen." Jessie leaned forward with her hands clasped in a business-like manner. "You'll hafta stay here at home until the baby arrives. You can't attend school or go to church anymore. Once the child is born, you'll need to nurse the babe until it begins solid food. Six months should do just fine. Then we'll send you to Kingstree to live with your blood mother's relations; your life will go on there, apart from us, as your sister's has. We'll adopt the child and let the community know that the youngun is ours. Until then, no one must know of your condition. Granny and Uncle Simms can help us in the meantime. You understand?"

A moan escaped Clayton, and he began to rock in his seat.

Gaynelle was so overcome with her father's state that Jessie's words passed through her only half-processed. The transformation in his constant, stalwart presence was disconcerting and frightening. "Must we?" she asked in confusion. "Can't I stay with you? Perhaps I could get married?"

Clayton sat up in sudden anger. "No!"

Gaynelle gasped then threw herself against his unreceptive, hostile form, clinging to him. "Please, Daddy! Please don't hate me. I'm sorry. I'm so sorry. Don't send me away."

Rising, Jessie pried the girl away from her father. "We're done here. You need to go to your room. I think you've upset your father enough, don't you?"

She led away their pleading daughter as her husband's wretched eyes followed them.

Hours later, the door to Gaynelle's room opened, and her father entered. He now appeared calm and grave.

She sat up as he gestured for her to follow him. Shrugging into her boots and grabbing a woolen shawl, Gaynelle hurried after his mute form. They were headed towards the fields when she caught up with him.

He seemed to be appraising the farm, gazing right and left as he walked. Hardly seeming to notice her, he said, "Maybe it's a curse, I dunno."

She remained silent, striding beside him.

"I want you to understand, Gaynelle, that I love you more than life itself. What we're doin' is for your own good." He met her eyes briefly. "No one did it for my mama, and look how things turned out. Her parents helped her with me, but it ruint her reputation to have a kid. She never did marry. She'd been born out o' wedlock, too, and her mama did marry, but she married down, jus' grateful to find someone willin' to have her an' the baby."

Reflecting on this, Gaynelle kept by his side and quietly waited to hear more.

"I have a confession to make, darlin'. You can't never tell no one what I'm about to tell you, but it's important that you understand why we hafta do this." Clayton turned tormented eyes upon her. "What happened to my mama's mama is what happened to your own mother, too. I mean Carrie."

Gaynelle inhaled sharply.

"She was already expectin' your sister when I married her. Coulda done a lot better than me. So beautiful and smart, readin' them books all the time." Pausing, he glanced at Gaynelle. "You got a lotta her in you, but I can't even begin to describe how special she was. Not just to me… everyone saw it.

"I ain't sayin' I shouldn't have married her. She didn't have a lotta options, an' so she married this poor farm boy."

Stopping in her tracks, Gaynelle protested, "But Daddy, you're wonderful!"

He smiled ruefully. "I did my best for her. I thank the Lord for my years with her and for you and Vivian… but I'm not gonna condemn you to that kinda fate. I love you too much, and I ain't convinced that a farmhand can take care o' you and appreciate you like you deserve. At least I was a grown man." Clayton shook his head sadly.

"But she loved you, right? That makes everythin' okay, doesn't it?"

"Nah, it don't make everythin' alright," he insisted. "She deserved better. She deserved nice clothes and a fine home. She shoulda had a lot more." He turned fervently to Gaynelle. "I swear that you're gonna have your future. You're gonna keep goin' to school. I'm not gonna let this hold you back. I was selfish 'bout Carrie, cuz I didn't wanna live without her and didn't see how it could go no better for her, but I ain't gonna be selfish with you. We'll take care o' that baby. Don't you worry 'bout that. You still need your chance in life."

Stupefied, Gaynelle tried to consider his words, but she was still reeling from finding out about her pregnancy. The sheer magnitude of his disclosure and their plan overwhelmed her. Weakly, she pleaded, "I don't wanna leave you, Daddy."

Clayton clutched her shoulder. "Looka here, Gaynelle. I ain't gonna do less for you than I did for Vivian. It tore my heart out to leave her there with Dr. Connor, but I knew it would be the best thing for her, an' look at her now. She's a real fine lady, and I am *so* proud." Clayton touched his chest. "I know, in here, that this is what I need to do for you, too. You ain't goin' nowhere but downhill if you stay here, whether or not you marry a pitiful farmhand."

"It ain't the same." Gaynelle protested. "Is Vivian even really your daughter?"

With a ferocious gleam in his eye, Clayton stated evenly, enunciating every word, "Yes ma'am, she is my daughter. I don't wanna hear you say nothin' like that ever again. I didn't throw her away—I did what I needed to do for her future. I'm gonna do the same for you, no matter how you choose to look at it."

Swallowing the lump in her throat, Gaynelle realized he had made up his mind. It didn't matter that she loved Tommy. He didn't care that she might want her own child, that her heart would break yet again over missing him and even Mama. She'd already ached over Tommy's absence these past couple of months, and the prospect of even more loss was unbearable. Daddy wanted to take away every shred of everything and everyone she'd ever loved, for her own prospective good—and there was no convincing him otherwise.

20 • A Letter and a Shift

J ESSIE HUMMED AS SHE FOLDED THE LAUNDRY. It was a new beginning. Everyone pitied her because of her barrenness, but now she was going to have her own child—one who not only called her 'Mama' but actually believed she was 'Mama.' This time they'd do it right, and how often did one get a fresh start?

Thus content, her rare sympathy was elicited by Gaynelle's swollen, distended figure and unhappy face. The child was bearing all the tribulations of pregnancy, so Jessie was doing her part. These days, she asked less and less of Gaynelle—after all, she'd best get used to not having her help—and she even indulged the girl's whims as she never had before. In fact, she'd made one of Gaynelle's favorite everyday dishes, a potful of tender butterbeans, just the night before, and

Gaynelle had inhaled most of it right along with a healthy portion of peppered rice.

Despite Jessie's unprecedented kindness, Gaynelle spent endless days brooding in her room—fearing the birth, dreading her banishment, and most of all pining for Tommy. Neither fieldhand had been asked back.

One afternoon, Clayton brought a large wooden crate into the house. A thick tarp had been carefully wrapped around it.

Jessie eyed it sharply. "Why you bringin' that in here?"

"For Gaynelle. I know you don't care for books, but the chile ain't got a blessed thing to think about 'sides all this mess. Just let her have 'em. I'm tired o' seein' her mope."

Without waiting for a response, he entered Gaynelle's room—she was just lying on the bed—and presented her with the crate. He carefully untied the rope that held the tarp on it. "These books belonged to Carrie. She read 'em a lot when she was pregnant. Her sister sent 'em to her from Georgetown."

Gaynelle sat up, her lackluster expression shifting to one of mild interest. She picked up the novel lying on the very top and gasped.

A grin broke out on Clayton's face as he read the title—it was his first grin in weeks. Scratching his head, he laughed. "Yeah, well… I told you she liked to read, didn't I?"

Lifting weary eyes to her father, Gaynelle managed a small smile. She would read *Willful Gaynell* first, of course.

***

172 Rutledge Ave.
Charleston, S. Car.
March 3, 1921

Dearest Gaynelle,

I cannot begin to convey the depth of my sorrow at hearing your news. Were you not wearing pigtails and skipping rope when last I saw you? I have difficulty conceiving of your current state, though it seems I must. Daddy has related the very private nature of the situation and has forbidden me from alluding to your condition to our mutual friends and relatives, excepting, I presume, between ourselves.

I have been given to understand that you are not a fast adherent of the course that our parents have now outlined for you, but I want to extend my support of the plan. I hope that my words may comfort you in this heavy hour, and that my own perspective—after, we must admit, a somewhat analogous experience—may soothe you, especially in your months of prolonged anticipation of your mysterious new life. Such foreknowledge of the impending separation I would not have wished upon you. I suspect it is more agonizing than the reality will be.

Firstly, I wish to express that I understand your desires to stay with our parents, to raise your child, and perhaps even to marry the child's father, if the opportunity presents itself. Those feelings are completely natural and to be expected in any girl worthy of claiming her family.

Additionally, you have been confined to quaint, small-town perspectives on life, isolated from what's really happening in the world. I'm sure you hardly realize the revolution that has occurred for our gender since the war ended. Ideas are changing about family, about the role of women.

Women are no longer simply vessels for furthering the human population. We are not merely handservants of our families. Are you aware that we are now deemed full, legal citizens by our federal government? Our worth has finally been acknowledged with the passage of the 19th amendment to our nation's constitution; once we come of age, we will finally, for the first time in our country's history, have the power to vote. Can you believe it? I can't wait to register.

That said, while I understand your very natural desire to remain home with family and raise this child, I support our parents' sagacious decision to look out for your future as a well-rounded woman, as a fully-educated citizen of our great nation. I have no doubt that you will one day appreciate the sacrifice required of both you and them in this dark time.

Aside from political gains, young women are discovering a new, independent existence. We may have led absurdly sheltered lives under Miss McBee's watchful eye at Ashley Hall, but I've now joined the first wave of female students at the College of Charleston, and it's even better than I thought it would be. We move about the city unchaperoned, in shortened skirts and with bobbed hair. Many of my friends even smoke cigarettes, like the men! Old-fashioned conventions are falling away, beloved sister, in ways that you must see to believe, and we are the beneficiaries of decades of effort on our behalf. Therefore, I beg of you to allow our parents to give you this opportunity to join the modern world, to become the woman that you can be.

Little comfort though it may be, I will be sojourning only a few more weeks here in Charleston. I expect that I will be back in Kingstree before you arrive. Even if I am not, I eagerly anticipate our reunion. Once you've seen the modern world, Gaynelle, there will be no going back to your simple, rustic life. You, my dear, are in for a treat.

Your Loving Sister,
Vivian

P.S. I've enclosed a novel by a new British author, Virginia Woolf. What can I say? The title seemed appropriate: <u>The Voyage Out</u>. *Anyhow, I skimmed through, and I expect yours will be closer to the protagonist's than what you may be anticipating—the sinking of the Titanic, perhaps? May Woolf inspire you to look forward to your own voyage into life in a new, refreshing light, as marriage certainly isn't our only option. An unimaginably brilliant future awaits you, darling.*

Bemused, Gaynelle folded the letter to her chest. Such big words from someone who had clearly not loved as she had. Her sister was full of hope, confidence, and worldly knowledge, but the truths underlying love were eternal. The bond between her and Tommy was sacred, and the idea of relinquishing their child, the manifestation of their love, was reprehensible. Well-intentioned encouragement would not make her forget what was important to her.

Despite her swollen, unattractive state, Gaynelle maintained a steadfast faith in Tommy's love for her, bolstered by her memory of his unwavering devotion to her when she was shorn nearly bald. She comforted herself with reassurances of their future. Once he became aware of her condition, she had no doubt that he would staunchly fulfill his family obligations and marry her. *Daddy will just have to relent when he sees how sincere Tommy's love for me is.*

"Somethin' troublin' you, girl? You feelin' alright?" Jessie's forehead creased with concern as she handed Gaynelle another dirty sock. She'd experienced the devastation of miscarriage too many times, and she was nervous about losing this baby, too.

As Gaynelle scrubbed the garment, she felt the words swelling up inside. The baby would be here any day now, and Tommy still had no idea of her condition. She glanced at the fragrant red roses gracing the

80 111 CB

flower garden's fence and considered their hidden thorns. *But what could it hurt to tell Mama?*

Biting her lip with trepidation, Gaynelle glanced at Jessie's concerned countenance and then averted her eyes again. *Mama's never treated me so well. Maybe when I'm doin' fine, she just figures I don't need her care as much. Maybe she really will help if I need it.*

Finally breaching her reservations, she said in a rush, "Mama, I shoulda told you before, but Willie isn't the baby's father. I ain't never had nothin' to do with Willie."

Jessie blinked, her hands tightening on the cotton slip she was holding. "Who's the father, then?" Her tone was suddenly harsh, the muscles in her neck protruding.

Taken aback, Gaynelle already regretted her impulse to confide. With Jessie glaring at her like that, however, it was too late to change her mind. She stared down at the washtub and whispered, "Tommy Salters."

Jessie's taut body melted like wax. A deep, gnawing fear—one she'd managed fairly well to repress—was at last dispelled. She mulled the admission, rather more pleased than not to find out that the father was Tommy instead of Willie. The youngster was more likely to be attractive, and Tommy's dark, smooth hair was closer to Vivian's and her own. He had a better personality, too, even if he seemed perhaps more shiftless. But overall, Tommy had some fine traits for a birth-father.

As Jessie visibly slackened, Gaynelle took hope. "I love Tommy. I wanna tell him about the baby."

On guard once more, Jessie surveyed her warily. The girl's eyes shone with hope, even now. Jessie's shoulders set with resolve. *I can't let her see him.* Her voice dripping with concern, Jessie lamented, "Oh Gaynelle, I had no idea the father was Tommy. He didn't force himself on you?"

Gaynelle shook her head, her cheeks turning pink.

"Well, I'll be. I have to tell you I'm at a loss for words. I never thought to ask you about what happened. After what Uncle Simms saw, with you tryin' to get away from Willie, we just assumed Willie had gotten that child on you. You shoulda told us about Tommy a long time ago."

"The baby's not born yet. We can still tell him, right?" Gaynelle bit her lip, dropping a shirt in the washtub.

Jessie shook her head regretfully, her mind scrambling for an excuse. "I'm sorry, honey, but your daddy found Tommy in Manning back in March to tell him about the lack of work this year. So Tommy told *him* that he was gonna head off to work at one of them car factories then, maybe up north. Must be long gone by now."

"He's gone?" Gaynelle echoed.

"We sure didn't know what a state he put you in, but never mind that. Ain't neither one o' you chillun ready to be gettin' married."

Gaynelle slumped. She felt too tired to cry—both physically and emotionally. As they silently finished the laundry, she thought dejectedly about her mother's romantic novels. She'd been reading them voraciously—and had indeed learned something from them. In those books, the love interest didn't just nonchalantly walk away. Never did he just whimsically leave, without a word to his beloved.

Indignantly, Gaynelle twisted the water out of a pair of overalls. *Tommy should've found a way to see me by now, no matter whether or not I'm pregnant. I'm tired of waitin' for him. Maybe Mama, Daddy, and Vivian are right.*

After supper that evening, Gaynelle settled down with a different book—the book that Vivian had sent to her. If her fate was unavoidable, perhaps the time had arrived to embrace her destiny at last.

21 • Gaynelle's Egress

T HE INFANT WAS SWADDLED NEATLY in a soft blue receiving
blanket. Drops of milk still clung to her lips, lips that made tiny
nursing motions as she slept. Gaynelle stroked one of the cheeks that
seemed almost too plump for her face. Her skin was fragile, delicate as
gossamer. Soft, wispy blond curls lay atop her head. *She's just like me,
down to her blue eyes and that dimpled little chin*, thought Gaynelle.

As Jessie retrieved baby Ginny, Gaynelle sucked in a fortifying
breath and looked away. Walling her heart from the child wasn't
actually so hard. Her time with Ginny was limited, as Mama generally
kept the baby with her.

Gaynelle had relegated herself to the dictates of her parents. It
was a relief to be done with the pregnancy, even if it had been
immediately followed by the unpleasant experience of dealing with
sanitary belts and towels; she'd been appalled to find out that those
would be monthly fixtures of her routine, but just as she tried not to

think about losing her daughter, she would try not to think about having to endure monthlies.

Instead, she distracted herself with more pleasant thoughts. What a delight to be thin again—to lie on her stomach in bed while reading, to tie her own boots, to skip down the stairs. Such taken-for-granted, simple things were only fully appreciated after losing them for a spell.

She could once more climb up onto her perch in Julep's stall, and she was soon riding her beloved stallion again, inhaling his soothing horse scent. She'd neglected Julep shamelessly—and needlessly—but now that she knew she could stand being away from him, she was less afraid to revel in her remaining time with him. On difficult days, Julep unfailingly nuzzled her with his velvet nose, seeming to intuit her pain. When she cried, he tenderly ministered to her, and when she felt better, he helped her to outrun her troubles. He was still a fast horse, despite his age. He seemed to take pleasure in galloping until his smooth chestnut coat was speckled with lather. Julep was a safe, comfortable focal point for her attentions and love, an essential distraction from the beautiful baby that threatened to break her heart.

The months had slipped by, and the time for her departure was eminent. Coddling a vague hope that had formed regarding her cherished mount, she stopped her father in the stable one morning. "Daddy, I wanna talk with you."

"What is it?" Concern registered on his face in thick brow wrinkles so deep now that they reminded her of a washboard. After the baby's delivery—it had gone well, thanks to her granny's skills— he'd seemed to take over from Jessie in continually asking if she was alright.

"I'm fine right now," Gaynelle began, "but I don't know how I'm gonna make it away from home without any of you."

His expression flattened. "We done been through this. I don't wanna hear another word about it."

"No, wait." Gaynelle said as he brusquely turned to leave. She took a deep breath, noting how impatiently he lingered, fingers tapping on the stable door. "I jus' wanted to ask if I could take Julep with me to Kingstree." There it was, her request in a nutshell. It seemed senseless to plead, but she had to ask. Julep had always been there for her, through everything, and his company would make her move more bearable. "It's only fair, if you won't even let me keep my baby."

Stroking his dimpled chin, Clayton murmured, "Well now, I don't know."

"Really? Oh, Daddy, it would be so wonderful."

"I haven't agreed yet."

Gaynelle threw herself into his arms and hugged him tightly.

It was a hug they had not shared for well over a year. Clayton's eyes began to brim at the thought that he might never again receive such a hug from her.

Her face shone with such excitement at the thought of taking Julep with her that Clayton knew he couldn't deny her. It would be like turning back the hands of time and refusing her mother's request that he take care of Julep. In fact, he had the peculiar notion that Caroline's spirit shone through her child, conveying the message that he'd done his part, that she was ready to take back her horse. As Caroline had entered his life on the farm, so would her daughter leave it—astride Julep, her beloved and constant ally.

Jessie had been disappointed at the baby's arrival. *Maybe somethin' is wrong with Carrie's entire family. All they seem to birth is girls.* Despite this failing and the blight of blond, curly hair that refused to go away, she'd followed through on becoming the baby's mother. Yet how was she supposed to embrace the child, to love her as her own, with Caroline's irrepressible curls adorning her? Why couldn't the child have been more like Tommy?

She should have known Gaynelle would yet again disappoint, but Jessie would simply adjust to the situation. At least this baby would truly regard her as its mother. The curls could, thanks to the current fashion trends Jessie had never much bothered with before, be cut and maintained at a short length, as unlike Caroline's as possible. The chin dimple? Well, Jessie didn't mind that, as it reminded her of Clayton, and her child should, of course, look a bit like Clayton.

With a sigh of surrender, Jessie resolved to patiently tend the baby's needs. She'd tolerate Gaynelle's presence as a wetnurse, counting the days until her departure.

Before Jessie had even had the chance to tell them what she'd planned to name the child, Gaynelle had started calling her Virginia, after some author. It had been just moments after she gave birth, and

Jessie had bitten her tongue, seeing no need to argue about it. She figured the girl would be gone soon enough, though Clayton had already delayed her departure too long. Despite their plan, he'd refused to put her out just before the holidays. And all the while Clayton had continued to affectionately refer to the now nearly 8-month-old baby as Ginny, too.

Perplexed as she was, Jessie continued biding her time. When Gaynelle left, she would simply insist upon the name Anne instead—a clean start for after Gaynelle was out of their lives. The idea that Gaynelle wouldn't even know the child's name elated her, and so Jessie had been sure to use the name Anne only behind closed doors, when she was alone with the child. Clayton would soon adapt. He couldn't really mind, given his long-term friendship with Anne Sanders. No doubt that would persuade him faster than the fact that it was his wife's own middle name. Regardless, after all she was doing for him and his troublesome daughter, surely he wouldn't balk at this perfectly reasonable request. She'd always secretly wished to be called by her middle name, and Anne Sanders' privileged use of it had chafed. Jessie didn't have to let her have it all to herself. By renaming her own daughter Anne, Jessie could at last take ownership of the name.

The anticipated day arrived, and Clayton and Gaynelle left in the early morning hours with the young woman's few worldly possessions, including Julep and the crate of books. Jessie had been pleasantly surprised to see her take the thoroughbred. It cost an arm and a leg to feed—and she was relieved that her own baby would not develop an attachment to the creature. No, she wanted things done right this time, and if the horse could mollify Gaynelle, that was fine by her. She was ready to clear out such an enduring, unsettling memory.

Jessie shook her head. She didn't often dwell on Sam Swann's death anymore, though it once held a rather morbid fascination for her. Now and then, she still dreamt of watching and caressing his handsome, lifeless face—like a marble statue, it never changed for her. The day that Mr. Swann had met his fate had been the day that Jessie's profound power to affect human destiny had been realized.

Though she had not planned for the accident to occur—she had not meant to startle Julep and thus end Sam's life—it had jolted her into the awareness that she could consciously take possession of her power. As others, in their infinite feebleness and short-sightedness, abjured their potential, she recognized and exerted her own control in a timely manner. When she did so, very little stood in her way.

People were, overall, a quite malleable lot. They were fearful, impatient, insecure, and weak-willed. Small, insignificant details confounded them. Even before Mr. Swann's accident, Jessie had never been plagued with such uncertainties. Setting her sights on her goals, she was undistracted by the daily nonsense that consumed most people. Others did occasionally trip up her plans with their unpredictable, unstructured responses to life events, but by remaining clear and purposeful about what she wanted, her persistence had inevitably granted her goals, with few exceptions.

It wasn't that Jessie was heartless; she was far from heartless. She merely had carefully chosen which feelings were important enough to commit to—like loving Clayton. She had focused on obtaining him, and now she had him. Feelings of guilt were unproductive. When they threatened to surface, Jessie identified them as the pathetic instruments of human downfall that they were. Leaders and winners in life were the most successful at discarding these ineffective, treacherous emotions, she had long ago realized.

So, when she identified her own occasional weak, human impulses for grief or even affection for Gaynelle, she stomped them like roaches, crushing them from her thoughts without further qualms. Instead, she focused on her modest goals. She didn't ask for more than her fair allotment—only for the man she loved and for a child of her own. One could hardly begrudge her those.

Jessie had already settled the baby down to sleep when Clayton returned home. The percentage-method formula of powdered milk, canned cream, and sugar she had so successfully used with Gaynelle had been well received by the baby. Jessie turned to her husband, pressing her hands together. "How did it go? Is she all settled in with Mrs. Sanders?"

He nodded wearily as he took off his coat. "Anna is a saint for taking her in like this. It's a shame her Aunt Mary and Uncle John couldn't make room for her, though. I'd ruther her have a family to live with."

"Well, you can hardly blame them for wantin' to keep such influences away from their grandchildren. She'll do just fine with Mrs. Sanders." Jessie forced a smile. After all, she'd helped to coordinate all this for Gaynelle, knowing well that Clayton would never leave her in a less-than-savory situation. Resenting that the child had landed in such fine straits despite her sins was counter to her own goals.

Casting Jessie a stony look, Clayton sank into a chair before his prepared place setting at the table. "How's our Ginny doin'?"

"Sleepin' right now." Jessie took a cast-iron skillet from the oven and began scraping leftovers onto a plate. "But I've been meanin' to talk with you about her name."

"How do you mean?"

"Well, I was thinkin' we might call her Anne instead, now that Gaynelle's not here anymore. Don't that have a ring to it? Annie Bell?" Jessie set his plate in front of him, glad to share the baby's real name with Clayton at last. She might scream if she heard the name 'Ginny' one more time.

"Too late for that. Them adoption papers done list her name as Virginia Mae Bell. That's what Gaynelle told 'em, and that's what they put."

Dumbfounded, she stared as he began to shovel in succotash. "But that's just what *she* wanted to call the baby—bet it's after that author lady and… and some bawdy actress. Shouldn't we name our daughter what *we* wanna call her?"

"We signed them papers, too. And Ginny is a fine name. Just fine. Virginia's a real common name. Ain't no call to be complicatin' everythin'." Clayton's mulish look left no room for discussion. He took one last bite and then stood up. Striding towards the door, he muttered, "I got chores to tend."

Her lips tightened into a thin line. Her motherly rights were already being impeded. So this was how it was going to be? Supposedly her baby, but she couldn't name her own child? He reckoned she'd just pretend to be the mother of a child she hadn't named nor birthed, blithely calling her 'Ginny' while brushing those accursed blond curls? Disappointment engulfed Jessie as she realized her dreams had been thwarted yet again by the cruel hands of fate. She was still, despite everything, just a nursemaid to Caroline's offspring.

22 • Illness

"YOUR ROOM IS JUST DOWN HERE. I hope you like it." Anne Sanders strolled down the hall, past the tapestry, and gestured towards an open doorway.

Casting a longing glance at the restroom, Gaynelle followed her into the bedroom despite her aching chest. Warm milk was leaking straight through the tight wrappings, saturating her rayon slip.

She gasped with delight, momentarily forgetting her discomfort. The bedroom was larger than their old farmhouse's living area and kitchen combined. Oak bookcases with elaborately-carved scroll designs rose to the ceiling along the southern wall, and gold-trimmed, patterned wallpaper lent a majestic air to the room. Large, westward-facing windows overlooked the manicured lawn; cream-colored satin curtains were drawn back with braided rope, just like the matching canopy on the bed. A vanity dressing table with a plush, velvet-cushioned chair held a silver brush and comb set. Next to them sat a tray with a curious array of implements and jars that drew Gaynelle to them.

Fascinated, she picked up a rod by its wired handle. "What's this?"

"That, my dear, is an electric curling iron. You simply plug it into the light socket."

Raising an eyebrow, Gaynelle tugged a curl outward.

"It's not just to make your hair curly. You don't need that, obviously. But in only five minutes, your hair can have the most perfect, sophisticated Marcel waves."

"Ah. And are these hair combs?" Gaynelle lifted three rather plain combs, confused by the extra teeth on the bottom.

"Water wave combs. You can use those on nights when your hair is wet to create your waves. I'll show you how." Anne patted her shoulder. "You'll need wave lotion and a hairnet, but it's a cinch."

Gaynelle turned around, admiring the four-poster, canopied bed. It looked like something she always imagined a princess might sleep in. Approaching it, she fingered the lace-trimmed cotton nightgown laid out for her. "Aunt Anna, it's all so beautiful…"

"I thought you might like it. I'm hopin' you'll feel comfortable here." Anne touched the wallpaper pattern of green-and-blue shrubs with yellow berries. "I thought of you when I saw this print, what with all our fairy tales." She smiled conspiratorially. "The paper's old-fashioned, but I thought you'd appreciate it. It's s'posed to be a rowan tree to protect against evil spirits. Magicians of old used it for their wands."

Gaynelle laughed. "I'm not a little girl anymore!"

"Magic stories aren't just for children." Anne shook her head. "You need all the protection you can get right now. I want you to feel secure here."

"Thank you, but I'd feel a lot better if I could use the bathroom," Gaynelle admitted with a sheepish smile.

"By all means, go refresh yourself." Anne stepped closer to hug her, oblivious to the pain she was causing. "Eddie will bring up your things."

When Gaynelle finally climbed into the luxuriously warm bathwater, she tried to express her milk. Only the initial, easily expelled, more watery milk came forth, however. With the most urgent pressure relieved, she gave up, re-wrapping her breasts before donning the new nightgown.

Despite her throbbing chest, she perused the ornate bookshelves before going to bed, nodding at *Heidi*, *Black Beauty*, *Little Women*, and countless others as if to old friends. She moved a framed photograph in order to stroke the spine of the book of fairytales perched at the very end of a shelf. Anne had placed all of the books she'd provided over the years here, with enough room to spare for Caroline's dime novels as well. A welling of gratitude and wonderment overcame Gaynelle. She thought nothing could have made her feel more welcome, but when her attention was caught by the framed photograph, she gasped aloud. Anne was unmistakable in what looked to be a chic wedding gown, her hands resting on the shoulders of a brunette girl in white. The two blond ladies in matching gowns on either side of Anne riveted her attention, however—especially the older one, nearer to Anne's age and more likely to be *her*, to be Caroline. Surely it was. A tingling sensation ran over Gaynelle as she drank in her mother's features. Caroline looked bright-eyed and happy, as joyful as the bride. The smiling visage was so like her own, though Caroline had no dimples and Gaynelle's face was rounder in every way. Still, it was familiar—and yet it wasn't. Not really. After all, she wouldn't have begun to recognize her if she'd passed her by on the street.

Gaynelle's hand trembled as she considered how in similar fashion, Ginny would forget her, too. Her breasts throbbed emphatically, and the photograph swam in front of her. Carefully, she set it back on the bookshelf and made her way to bed. That delightful discovery was impossible to appreciate fully when it reminded her so keenly of being separated from her own child.

Not that she could forget for long. Her aching chest incessantly reminded her of her need to be with Ginny. The rich hind-milk that Ginny usually extracted had sat there far too long. Pining for her daughter, Gaynelle climbed into the bed, soaking the pillows of the large four-poster with a sorrowful sea of tears that flowed far more easily than her milk.

During the night, Gaynelle woke to the insistent throbbing of her swollen breasts. They'd become quite hard. Turning on the electric lights, she found with horror that they were streaked with red. At the bathroom sink, she determinedly squeezed out now-coagulated milk of a cream cheese consistency, white and yellow. Despite the excruciating pain, it seemed imperative to clear the old milk, so she continued to press on her swollen, tender breasts.

In the morning, Anne Sanders found her charge delirious and consumed with fever. Placing a cool cloth on the teenager's burning forehead, she left to ring for Dr. Stephen Connor. When Vivian answered, she left a message with her instead.

Soon he was there, taking Gaynelle's temperature and pulse, listening to the girl's recent history with an implacable expression. Anne shivered as the doctor gently unwound the wrappings. Angry red streaks ran outward from her nipples like sunrays.

Re-covering her with the blanket, Stephen said, "Mastitis can be severe like this, but it's generally not life-threatenin'. Her body's fightin' the infection with this fever."

Anne pushed wet tendrils of hair away from Gaynelle's flushed face. "But stagnant milk keeps contaminatin' her bloodstream?"

"It does." He sighed. "She'll just have to get through this. Vivian could come over to sit with her. She was anxious to join me when you called with news of Gaynelle's illness, but I wanted to check with the both of you first."

His lucid voice cut through Gaynelle's delirium, yet she had trouble formulating a reply. Vivid faces—startling manifestations of her imagination—loomed so closely to her own. Mama, Amarintha, and Simms scolded relentlessly, while Ginny's incessant bawling came from somewhere behind them. Her wails drowned and garbled their words. Illusory cries ebbed and flowed, faces mingling before her in a blur, making it difficult to focus on Dr. Connor—but at last a coherent answer penetrated the confusion. Clutching the bedspread, she uttered, "Vivian! Yes, please!"

Gasping, she let go of the covers, flattening her hands on the mattress for stability. Her own arm had bumped her breast excruciatingly. The room spun. Her body ached. Her breasts throbbed. The mildest brush was sheer agony. Her mind wandered through the delirious taunts and spinning landscape, never allowing her to see her wailing child. She'd never felt more ill.

"Three minutes of hot, thirty seconds of cold," Anne recited as she walked Stephen to her door.

"Then repeat three times."

"Three times per session. Three sessions per day," Anne clarified. She sighed, envisioning the mountain of towels this so-called hydrotherapy would entail.

"It'll promote circulation to the area," Stephen reiterated. "I'll send Vivian over to help out."

Anne nodded.

"I'll get her to bring over a pokeroot tincture that some of my patients have had success with. I've come to believe it helps clean the lymph, but don't be overzealous with it. More is not better. Too much pokeroot can sicken the stomach—and worse. It can be deadly."

"If anythin' happens, I'll just call you again," Anne promised. Closing the door behind him, she pressed her back against it and covered her face. A shaky laugh escaped through her fingers. It quickly turned into a moan. Once she'd thought Stephen a poor choice as guardian for Vivian, but here she hadn't managed a single day with Gaynelle as her ward without him.

Gaynelle woke to a gentle prodding on her cheek.

"Drink this." Vivian's anxious face hovered over her.

Gaynelle rose to take a sip of water, then dutifully swallowed a spoonful of dark-red tincture.

"It's about time." Vivian capped the tincture bottle, then ran fingers through her short, sleek bob. "I've been having trouble gettin' that into you. You're wearin' half of it."

Gaynelle rubbed her throbbing brow. "I have a terrible headache."

Bringing the water glass back to her sister's lips, Vivian said, "Probably dehydrated."

As she lifted her head, Gaynelle winced.

"We'll get you right as rain in no time." Hardly had Gaynelle settled back onto the bed than Vivian flipped back the covers, exposing her sister's breasts.

"Oh my God!" Gaynelle yanked the covers back up over her.

"We have to apply this heated cloth while it's still *heated*." Vivian waved a steaming towel and sighed with exasperation. "You're worse than patients I don't even know. Now let me put it on before it gets cold." A moment later, she was efficiently tucking the warm cloth over Gaynelle's chest, layering an extra wool blanket before adding back the covers. "I've been doing this for you for the past couple of days, dingbat. Aunt Anna is letting me stay here while you recuperate. In fact, she's at her shop right now, making a new frock with her assistant Fletcher. Honestly, I don't think takin' care of sick people is her cup o' tea."

Gaynelle managed a wan smile.

"Thank God you're finally awake. I'm goin' stir-crazy here, just lookin' at sick little ole you."

As Vivian chattered over the next couple of minutes, Gaynelle took in the changes in her sister—the new hairstyle, and her clothes were different. When Vivian removed the lukewarm towels in a sopping heap, Gaynelle tried not to think about being exposed. Instead, she admired her sister's straight-line, mid-calf-length dress, similar to styles she had seen in magazines. "You weren't kiddin' about the new fashions. You look like a movie star in—" Gaynelle gasped as Vivian laid an icy towel on her chest.

"You should see when I get all dolled up with lipstick and one o' my sleeveless numbers," Vivian said cheerily. About the time Gaynelle had knocked the chill from the cold towel, Vivian leaned close to swap the cold towel for another warm one. In a conspiratorial whisper as though they weren't the only ones in the room, she said, "Maybe you'll recover faster if I let you in on a little surprise Aunt Anna has planned for you. There's an absolutely gorgeous evening dress just waitin' for you to try it on, when you're all better.

"Of course," Vivian straightened with a smirk, "the neckline on mine plunges more than yours." Then her face fell. "But never mind that. Your bust is twice the size of mine."

Despite her achiness, Gaynelle erupted in weak laughter. "Trade with you."

"Humph!" Vivian tossed her dark, smooth bob. "Do you like my hair? I got it done again at a beauty parlor here last month, and I think she did alright."

"It's real glamorous." Gaynelle's voice was full of awe.

"Shall we get yours done, too? It's all the rage."

"Oh no," Gaynelle said quickly. "I've had enough of short hair to last a lifetime."

Vivian sighed. "Dr. Connor would agree with you. He likes it better long." She pouted for a moment.

"Prob'ly most o' the old folks do," Gaynelle said charitably.

Vivian grinned. Then she asked thoughtfully, "Have you thought about what you're gonna do with yourself now that you're here in Kingstree?"

"Daddy wants me to go back to school. He says the school is better here in Kingstree," Gaynelle said reluctantly. She hadn't yet warmed to the idea of meeting hordes of new people.

"He's right. But maybe you should wait to start back until the fall. Adjust to your new life here first." Vivian blinked at Gaynelle hopefully. "I could use the company. Dr. Connor's patients are mostly old and rickety, and half o' them can't even hear me." She wrinkled her nose, making Gaynelle laugh.

"Are you goin' back to the College of Charleston?"

"Prob'ly. I liked it there, but I knew you'd be here, and Dr. Connor was payin' gobs o' money for me to be able to go there. I figured I'd pay off some o' my debt to him by helpin' out at his clinic for a while."

Gaynelle nodded more seriously.

"I wish we could send you to Ashley Hall," Vivian went on. "You'd learn heaps, even if they do lock you up like a prisoner. We never got to go anywhere without chaperones, but we sure saw how much fun we were missin' out on. I was itchin' to check it all out. That's why Aunt Anna suggested that I apply to College of Charleston. Since they were finally acceptin' female students, y'know."

"Oh, I thought maybe you wanted a professional career." Gaynelle's face squinched.

Laughing, Vivian admitted, "Yeah, maybe, but all I could think was that they better not ship me back home before I got to experience the big city. I still had a curfew at the college, but it was way better."

Smiling ruefully, Gaynelle said, "Kingstree seems pretty big to me."

Vivian rolled her eyes.

Sighing, Gaynelle tugged a loose, chin-length curl. "S'pose you're sorry now that you decided to spend your time here with me instead of stayin' in Charleston."

"Oh, I'll go back later." Vivian tossed her head breezily. She was glowing, her energy palpable and contagious. "First things first. My real responsibility—my obligation, mind you—is to help you enter this modern world at last. You're my sister. It's the least I can do."

"I've missed you." Gaynelle's voice wavered. She cared nothing for her sister's progressive agenda, but it was a relief to have her back at last, even if she was now a new and very different Vivian.

"Oh, I've missed you, too."

They sat together in silence for a long moment before Gaynelle suggested, "Maybe you can help me find Tommy. Mama said he's—"

"Not gonna do you a lick o' good to dwell on him, baby sis," Vivian said sharply. Leaning close, she stroked Gaynelle's brow more sympathetically before proceeding to swap the warm towel for a cold one. "You've been through a lot and probably wanna talk about it, but maybe you should just try to forget all that for now. Gettin' worked up won't help a thing."

Gaynelle shivered. The urge to confide in Vivian had indeed been surging forth, but at her sister's impatience, she clamped her lips shut. Turning her head away, she closed her eyes, reminding herself that Vivian didn't understand what it was like to love someone so much. This time, Gaynelle didn't even look at Vivian as the final heated towel was applied. Settling into the warmth, she drifted back to sleep.

When Gaynelle next awoke, Anne was sitting by her side, studying a magazine. The sun shone through the window, its brilliant rays piercing between the thick drapes.

"Where's Vivian?" Gaynelle blinked in confusion.

Anne smiled, replying with mock reproof, "Good afternoon to you, too. Glad to see you're awake. How you feelin'?"

"Oh, sorry, Aunt Anna." Gaynelle grimaced. "I still have a headache, but my body doesn't hurt so much."

"Glad to hear it." Anne looked visibly relieved. "Vivian is movin' her things over here as we speak. Dr. Connor's apartment has always been too crowded, and she wants to be near you. She's been runnin' back and forth like a woman possessed."

A titter came from the doorway. Vivian marched in holding out a narrow box, her eyes sparkling with excitement. "Speakin' of possessed, look what I found on my closet shelf here."

"Oh my!" Anne laughed, holding her hand to her mouth.

"Oh, yes!" Vivian patted the box in confirmation.

Gaynelle sat up with curiosity. "What is it?"

Setting down the box, Vivian pulled a wooden board from it and brought it closer for Gaynelle's inspection. It was covered in letters. "A spirit talking board. At Ashley Hall, Cecilia had one that we snuck out at night to commune with all the ghosts. There are a lotta them in Charleston."

With an amused tone, Anne recalled, "My husband used to pull this game out when company came over and there was nothin' else to do. It always generated conversation."

"How does it work?" asked Gaynelle.

"You simply ask a spirit a question," Vivian answered authoritatively. "Your fingers go on this little pointy thing—"

"The planchette," Anne interjected.

"—and it moves to spell a message. Or it can just point to the little sun or moon up here in the corners for yes or no. It's the bee's knees!"

"Oh, let's do it," Gaynelle cried, despite her headache and chestache and less-than-suitable garb.

"Maybe when you're feelin' better," Anne said mildly.

"I think she's well enough." Vivian smiled conspiratorially at Gaynelle.

"I think I am, too." Gaynelle sat up straighter.

Succumbing to their exuberance, Anne said, "Alright, tell you what. If you're able to get up and eat supper with us, then why don't we play with it tonight?" She had to wait for their clamor to die down before she could add, "*After* supper. Agreed?"

After taking her tincture again and complying with another hydrotherapy treatment, Gaynelle gingerly made her way to the tub. There she marveled at how the warm, running water seemed to wash away the last vestiges of her illness. Refreshed and cleansed by both the heat of fever and the bath, she looked forward to an evening of spooky fun with her newly-reconstituted family.

23 • The Spirit Talking Board

WHEN AT LAST THEIR SUPPER CONCLUDED, Vivian solemnly rose, grasping the still-burning tapered dinner candles. Wordlessly, she headed towards the parlor.

Gaynelle and Anne followed her, their anticipation growing. Settling onto the chaise lounge, they observed Vivian's preparations with silent interest.

Once the candles were arranged, Vivian left the parlor, returning momentarily with a crystal bowl of water.

"You see," Vivian uttered mysteriously, "spirits are drawn to water."

"And to candle flames?" asked Gaynelle.

"Hmm, I'm not sure, but the light helps us to see the board." Vivian laughed, disrupting the ambience for a moment. She pulled a chair opposite Gaynelle and set the board between them, perched on their knees. "Aunt Anna will read what the spirit spells for us, okay? We just need to let the spirit guide us. We can even close our eyes."

The young women allowed silence to settle on the room once again. Their fingertips rested lightly on the planchette, guiding it in slow, gentle circles. Once the eerie mood had satisfactorily returned, Vivian inquired ceremoniously, "With whom are we speaking?"

The planchette began to move almost before the words were out of her mouth, and Anne transcribed the letters G-E-O-R-G.

"George?" Vivian breathed. Neither she nor Gaynelle had closed their eyes.

The planchette glided up to the sun. The women nodded 'yes' together, echoing the confirmation.

"Did you live in Kingstree, George?" asked Vivian.

The planchette glided to the moon.

"No," they repeated in unison.

"Where did you live?"

B-L-A-K-R-I-V-R. The planchette stopped.

"The Black River," Vivian confirmed.

"What happened to you, George?" asked Gaynelle.

F-I-R-E.

"A fire," echoed Vivian. "Did you die in the fire?"

The planchette moved to the moon, and then, without further questioning, it traveled to the letters H-O-W-S.

"Why did your house burn?" queried Vivian immediately.

W-A-R.

The girls looked at each other, and Vivian asked, "Are you our ancestor, George Bell?"

Their eyes grew wide when the planchette moved to the sun.

Gaynelle shuddered. Her skin felt like it was crawling all over with invisible insects when the door to the parlor burst open. She jumped to her feet, shrieking, and the board tumbled to the floor.

Anne rose, a slight blush tinging her cheeks. "Why hello, Stephen! We were just playin' a little game."

Vivian laughed as she picked up the board.

His arms full, Stephen said, "I brought over that phonograph, like Vivian asked me to. Where do you want it?"

"In here is fine. How about on the sideboard?" Anne gestured towards the mahogany surface, trying to disguise her discomfiture.

"What are y'all playin'?" Once he'd set down the phonograph, Stephen turned to survey the scene before him.

Vivian was in no way abashed. "We have a spirit talking board. Wanna join in?"

"Do you think it's… safe?" Stephen gazed at them with surprised concern.

"Such a bluenose," Vivian chided, rolling her eyes.

Laughing, Anne coaxed, "Oh, it's all fun and games. Take a turn with me."

With a smile, Stephen sank into an armchair. "Your merry faces are irresistible. What do we do?"

Vivian led Anne to the seat opposite him. "Okay, slide a bit closer and balance the board between your knees."

As their knees bumped, Anne cast her eyes downward like an awkward schoolgirl. Her face grew warm again, and she was glad that they were only using candlelight. As their fingertips rested on the planchette, she tried to ignore his finger touching hers. Hurriedly asking the first question, she was surprised to see the planchette spell out E-L-E-A-N-O-R. Gooseflesh arose as she asked, "Is this my husband's first wife?"

The planchette pointed to the sun.

Her voice caught as she asked, "Is he with you?"

Again the pointer went to the sun.

"Are you both happy?" she asked tremulously.

The planchette spelled out F-I-N-A-L-L-Y-A-T-P-E-A-C-E and then pointed to the small circle at the bottom center of the board, saying 'goodbye'.

The company was subdued for a moment, then Vivian slipped the board from their lap. "Wow, fantastic. Are you alright with us takin' another turn?"

This time, Gaynelle and Vivian conversed with a chatty, recently deceased patient of Stephen's whose love of sweets was well-known. The whole party laughed when the spirit answered the question, 'Do you miss anyone?' with the phrase, I-M-I-S-F-R-U-T-C-A-K.

"I'll have another whirl at it," Stephen volunteered.

"I'll pass." Anne pressed a hand to her waist, still overwhelmed by her previous message. She was not inclined to risk the heartache of speaking directly with her husband, and the message from Eleanor, whether it was truly Eleanor or only her own psyche's machinations, had unsettled her.

"I'm in," Vivian announced. "Bring on the spooks."

"Sit here," Gaynelle told the doctor, standing up so that they could balance the board between them. The planchette slid in slow circles around the board as Vivian inquired, this time in melodramatic, sepulchral tones, "With whom are we speaking now?"

C-A-R-O-L-I-N-E was slowly spelled out.

"My mother?" she whispered, her tone at once vulnerable.

The sun was indicated.

"What is it you wish to say?" she asked softly, eyes glued to the planchette.

B-E-C-A-R-E-F-U-L was indicated by the planchette.

"Of what?" Vivian's forehead creased.

D-O-N-T-F-O-R-G-E-T.

"Forget what?"

F-I-R-E.

Vivian probed urgently, "Will there be another fire?"

After a pause, there was a slow indication of the moon.

"Are you speaking of the fire in which you died?"

The sun.

"Was it an accident?"

The moon.

At this, Stephen interjected, "Who caused it?"

The planchette only moved around the board in slow figure eights.

In anguished tones, Stephen insisted, "Carrie, we need to know who caused the fire."

Fearfully, Vivian cried, "Was it me, Mama?"

The planchette flung to the moon.

As the planchette began to whirl again, relief flooded Vivian. Afraid they were about to lose Caroline, however, she blurted another question that had been bothering her for quite a long time. "Is Dr. Connor my father?"

The planchette came to an abrupt halt as Stephen's hand fell off of it.

"Come back!" Vivian cried.

No longer paying attention to the board, Stephen was staring at Vivian, eyes wide with incredulity. "You know?"

"So it's true?" She looked up at him, her face crumpling. Tears were now flowing, a sudden torrent down her thin face.

"I'm so sorry." Stephen gazed at her with concern.

Sobbing, Vivian flung herself into his arms.

He stroked her back, waiting for her tears to subside.

When they finally did, she pulled away from him, dashing at her eyes and straightening her blouse. Then she glared at him. "How could you?"

"I loved her, Vivian. We were engaged. I can explain everything," pleaded Stephen.

Her fury mounted. "That's not what I meant. What I meant was, how could you not tell me? Why do you think your uptight secret negated my right to know who my own father is? I'm sick—so very sick—of the outdated Victorian values that you arrogant prudes apply to yourselves and to everyone else around you. I've been calling you 'Dr. Connor' for all these years like every single stranger that walks through your office door. How could you keep me in the dark? I had a right to know!"

Stricken, Stephen stood wordlessly.

Gently, Anne said, "There's more to it than you know. Stephen was halfway around the world when you were born, when Clay became your daddy. We didn't think it our place to bring it up, even though we both wanted to."

"Not his place? Not my father's place?"

"When you were tiny, Carrie kept it all as quiet as possible. I don't know when she planned to tell you, if ever. Clay tried to be as good a father to you as he could."

As if in a cloud, Gaynelle watched the scene unfolding before her. She'd pondered Daddy's admission many times but was still dumbfounded to hear it once more confirmed. Somehow, it had always felt like a mysterious fantasy, not truly reality.

Frowning, she remembered how Daddy had insisted Vivian was his daughter. In sudden sincere perplexity, she asked, "Well then, who is *my* father?"

After a surprised silence, the others burst into laughter.

Vivian wiped her cheeks and answered with sudden gaiety, "Gaynelle, you slay me! Nobody with eyeballs to see you with has ever wondered that. You were branded with Daddy's dimple from Day One."

24 • Water Combs & a Pile of Mush

WHILE RECUPERATING OVER THE NEXT COUPLE OF WEEKS, Gaynelle was inundated with information on the current trends in fashion, hairstyling, and cosmetics.

Anne demonstrated how to style her unruly hair with the water combs. "I like to wear my own hair in a low chignon at the nape of my neck, but we'd best trim your curls into a bob—perhaps without any bangs. It'll look wonderful."

Despite having told Vivian that she didn't want a short cut, Gaynelle did allow Anne to trim her hair—and was relieved to see that it soon did 'look wonderful'.

Taking charge of Gaynelle's cosmetics instruction, Vivian began with the fundamentals. "These are meant to stay on," she warned.

"They can stain your skin worse than grass stains dungarees. If you don't put them on right, you'll be scrubbin' at your face for days."

Alarmed at Vivian's warning, Gaynelle gained an almost instantaneous, expert skill with rouge, powder, and lipstick. The eyelash curler proved more confounding, but she eventually obtained proficiency with that, too, after only a few troubling and painful mishaps.

The time passed quickly, and soon Gaynelle was familiar with all manner of fashion implements and powders, perfumes, and hair lotions. She often gazed with satisfaction at the array of bottles, amongst which sat, with seeming innocence, her fluted bottle of perfume from Tommy.

Neither Anne nor Vivian showed any willingness to hear about Ginny's father, so Gaynelle had learned not to mention him. She couldn't stop herself from thinking about him, though, even if logic bade her not to cling to such memories. When her longing for him welled greatest, she would dab just a miniscule amount of rose perfume on her wrist. Sometimes she fell asleep with the lingering fragrance pressed to her nostrils, recollecting sweet mornings of long ago—mornings that had produced a beautiful baby girl named Ginny.

By the end of their first month together, Anne brought up Gaynelle's education but readily agreed that she could wait until the next fall term. "Too many questions if you enter mid-term. Besides," she admitted, "I need to leave for a fashion show in New York City. Then Philadelphia is next month, and I'd love for both of you to join me. Two of my regular assistants usually accompany me, but they need to attend a workshop in Atlanta, and those dates overlap those of my trip."

"Yes! Yes! Yes!" Vivian bounced with delight and clasped Gaynelle's hand. "We've never even been out of the state, auntie. It sounds smashing."

"Ah, that reminds me." With a slightly perplexed air, Anne clasped her hands together in front of her. "I have certain reservations about this, but I am going to ask you girls for a favor."

Settling, they waited attentively.

"As y'all no doubt understand, I do have a fashion reputation to look out for," she began. With utmost gravity, Anne hesitated, meeting the gaze of each young woman in turn. "You're aware, I'm certain, that youth and independence are highly overrated in my line of work, particularly for women. So from now on, I have to ask you to call me Anne, not auntie and not Aunt Anna, *especially* when we're traveling or addressing anyone associated with my work."

The sisters regarded her with surprise.

Gaynelle started to protest, "But we've always—"

"Keep in mind that I am not technically your aunt, nor am I even a blood relative. Once y'all are used to it, the occasional private endearment is fine, but I will look like the old dowager that I am if two such fairly-grown women traipse around after me callin' me 'aunt' at my work events."

"But you were married to Mr. Sanders, and he wasn't young," managed a thoroughly dismayed Gaynelle.

"Pshaw, that doesn't matter. In our business, beautiful young women marry older, successful men all the time. That doesn't have the least effect on me, except to link me with the very best in the industry." Anne smiled, falling into a contented reverie.

Vivian grinned at her with impish delight. "It's a brilliant idea, Anna. Can we still call you Anna?"

"Anna is fine. And to be clear—you're not traveling as my wards but as my assistants." Anne struggled to keep a straight face as they gaped at her. In point of fact, Anne felt just the vaguest bit of shame at her request—but business was business.

Gaynelle gaped at Anne. "Assistants? Is this why you've been teachin' me so much about fashion since I've been here?"

"My word, no." Anne rolled her eyes. "Darling, I taught you that because you desperately needed it. Any woman fit for society needs to know just about everything I've shown you so far." She shrugged with amusement. "But you know, you're right that it's time for you to learn if y'all are gonna be my assistants. You seem up to it now, Gaynelle. Let's get started at my shop tomorrow, bright and early."

At this, the young women bade her goodnight, each heading to her own room. Gaynelle was turning her doorknob, wondering about the mysterious new curriculum of the morrow, when Vivian dangled into the hallway from her own room's doorframe and called out, "Anna underestimates how much she's already taught us. It'll be a cinch."

"You think so?"

"I'm certain." Vivian winked in blissful ignorance.

Stephen lost little time in coordinating an afternoon to spend alone with Vivian. It would be their first meeting by themselves since he had confirmed his paternity to her, and he felt relieved yet awkward at dispensing with the charade of acting solely as a family friend. It had been both a shield and an insurmountable wall. When Vivian answered the door, however, he could only halt and blink.

She beamed at him. She'd taken extra care in dressing for the occasion. A gypsy girdle and flounced skirt accented a jaunty yellow crepe jacket and dress in what she'd only just learned to term 'analogous colors'. Makeup had been carefully applied, more attention than usual paid to covering the shadows under her eyes with powder; she'd stayed up late yet again practicing another new stitch Fletcher had taught her. Vivian touched the brim of her matching cloche hat to salute him. "Hello, Dr. Connor."

Grateful for this reprieve from her intensive new studies, Vivian seemed not to notice his silence, but only that he smelled like castile soap when she grasped his arm. Soon she'd escorted him off of the porch and towards the nearby town park, where the trees still retained an array of autumn colors—'complementary colors', she now deemed them to be. They'd agreed to walk and talk there until suppertime if the weather remained fine, and the sky seemed to promise a clear, crisp January day.

"I've decided to skip callin' you 'Father' or anything of the sort," Vivian informed him at once. "I think it best to keep things as simple as possible."

Stephen blinked once more in surprise, "But I thought—"

"How about Stephen? Shall I call you Stephen?" The sheer modernity of the idea called to her. Vivian turned to him with big, excited eyes made more dramatic by the application of kohl eyeliner; dark eyeshadow near her nosebridge served to deepen them.

"Hold on, hold on. Give me a moment." Stephen paused to consider then shook his head. "Where did you get this notion?"

Sighing, Vivian told him about Anne's request.

"Ah, I see. And in our case, you've never called me 'Father' to begin with, so to start at this point would be awkward," he admitted.

"Right-o! It's a new world, Stephen—a world where we are all considered equals."

"Alright, I hear what you're sayin'. We are equally important as individuals."

"Check!"

"I agree with that wholeheartedly, and since Stephen is my given name, it's logical you might call me that," he ceded.

"Just so!" Delighted, Vivian danced the next several steps.

"However, as Anna made her request because of her business, I must do the same. You do, after all, assist me there as well. She prefers Anna, or Anne, I'm assuming, right?"

"Mmm-hmm." Vivian's thinly-plucked eyebrows drew together, her enthusiasm fading.

"Well, in my line of work, it's best for me to be called 'Dr. Connor'. I need to be seen as an authority in order for my instructions to be taken seriously."

"So, you want me to continue calling you Dr. Connor?" Vivian frowned with disappointment. "But that's no different than I've been doing."

Stephen stopped walking and turned to face her. "Precisely. Nothing has changed. I have always loved you as my daughter, no matter the distance, no matter what you've called me. Getting you back, even without acknowledgin' our familial bond, has been the best thing that ever happened to me. When you came to stay with me, you called me 'Dr. Connor'. Hearin' you call for me those first few times warmed my heart as nothin' else has, not since I lost your mother. What you called me then was 'Dr. Connor', and that memory is indelible. We can't undo that, and I don't want to."

Vivian's lips were trembling as she whispered, "But why don't I call you Daddy? What happened?"

At this, Stephen took a deep breath and plunged into the speech he'd prepared. "Well, Vivian, the truth of it is that I made a lot of mistakes. The biggest one was in leavin'. I didn't know that Carrie was pregnant with you. She was alone and scared, so she married Clay. I happen to know that he loved you and raised you as his own, just as proud as any papa could be. I had no right to disrupt your life or his, but I thank God that Clay saw fit to bring you to me."

"So... Caroline wasn't in love with Daddy?"

Stephen laughed uncomfortably. "Well, I hate to admit it, but I think she loved him, too. But I was the one she'd agreed to marry, until I messed it up."

"So you were left with nothing?" Pity brimmed in Vivian's eyes.

"Well, I've spent a lot of time thinkin' about that, and the fact is that I wasn't left with nothing. I've had my medical practice and a whole community of people who think about me and depend on me. I'm invited to all the neighborhood events and many private family celebrations, and, you know, there are even a handful of Stephens and Connors here in town, named in my honor. As for your mother? Well, I still cherish memories of our time together—and I keep a little angel pendant she used to wear."

At his mention of the pendant, Vivian started. "I've seen that on your bedside table. I thought it was a religious memento."

"Yes, that's it," Stephen affirmed. "She was an angel to me then, and she's an angel to me now, so it's not so different, is it?"

Vivian blinked away tears at the avalanche of profound feelings overwhelming her. She sniffed and wiped at her eyes, exclaiming with a shaky laugh, "For cryin' out loud, I can't stand this, Dr. Connor. I'm gonna melt here into a pile o' mush if we keep talkin' this way."

Stephen smiled back at her affectionately. "I know it's a lot for you to take in, and I'm glad to have told you. I've been thinkin' about that pendant and plannin' to explain it to you, so I bought you a necklace of your own to commemorate this occasion."

As he spoke, he presented a jeweler's gift box and raised the lid, revealing a small golden heart. Lifting it from the box, he clasped it around her neck, vowing solemnly, "You're my daughter, and I love you. I will try my utmost to treat you fairly and, like you say, as an equal. This is a reminder that I don't expect you to be perfect, that I will always love you no matter what."

"Here I go!" Vivian blubbered as the watershed of tears opened. In acceptance and gratitude, she hugged him, mopping her eyes on his shoulder all the while.

25 • An Origin of Troubles

A couple of months later
March 1922, Greeleyville, SC

VIBRANT YOUNG TENDRILS OF EARLY PEAS boasted the soil's fertility, and Clayton was pleased that it was time to hire help again. He'd been particularly lonely on the farm since Gaynelle's move. With only the baby and Jessie, Clayton hadn't had anyone with whom to banter for a long while. Jessie treated him well enough and tended the baby, but she was not one to throw around light-hearted conversations, and Clayton was anxious to bring on a farmhand for both the company and the help.

As he finished plowing the last row of the field, Clayton mused, *I won't hire that blasted Willie again, but Tommy's a pretty decent hand, if a bit slow to show up in the mornings. He's right good company, to be sure, always eager to oblige.*

While putting away his plow and mule, Clayton strategized on Willie's replacement. *Maybe I don't need to go all the way to Manning to find help. I know that's what Jessie wants—to keep everyone 'round here outta our business—but it jus' ain't worth the hassle, 'specially as I don't need 'em year round. Surely that shopkeeper here can help me find someone. She knows everyone—and chews on gossip more than Ginny chews on her blanket.*

As Clayton pondered in the field, Jessie washed dishes with Ginny still strapped into her raised seat at the table, eating grits. As Jessie rinsed the last dish, she heard a clank.

"Naughty!" Jessie scolded, picking up the spoon to wash it.

The bowl clattered down then, scattering a puddle of grits across the floor. Impenitent eyes stared expectantly at Jessie.

Lowering herself to look in the child's face, Jessie hissed, "Try that one more time and see what you get, you little nothin'."

Ginny screamed, striking Jessie in the nose with her small fist.

Jessie's nose gushed a crimson creek. Horrified, she mopped at it, wondering if she could get by with throwing the child down the well. *No faster way to lose Clay,* she decided. *But when she's old enough, she's gonna earn her keep around here,* Jessie swore. *Just a pauper brat from rotten seed. Even worse than the other two I raised. More stubborn than a rusty gear. No amount of scoldin' or shakin' or smackin' is ever gonna straighten that little hellion out, but I'll just have to do better, make up for the way Clay spoils her.*

Ginny was a deceitful thing. She nearly always acted as though she were sweet when Clayton was present. She would smile and beam and call "Dada!" joyfully when he came inside. If Clayton were inside the house, Ginny would crawl to him and settle on his lap or by his feet, pretending like she was always so docile while, in fact, the child did nothing but throw fits all day. When Clayton left to go out to the fields, she would prostrate herself on the floor and scream for a half-hour or more. If Jessie spanked her, she'd just holler louder, and if Jessie tried to pick her up, she'd sometimes bite her.

Eventually Ginny would quiet down and crawl outside by herself. Independence should be encouraged from an early age, Jessie told herself. The best part of her day was when she could push the door closed—mostly closed—and pretend the child didn't exist. It was a normal reaction to the demands of motherhood—or servitude, in this case—but one day the tables would turn, assuming the child didn't fall

off the porch or get bitten by a snake out there, of course. If she did…
well, it would be God's doing, hardly Jessie's fault. No, she deserved
the designation of sainthood for raising a third child not her own, with
so little appreciation for her sacrifices.

In fact, if Clayton arrived at the house to find Ginny alone in the
yard or on the porch, he would level a poignant glare at Jessie, a glare
which she resented in the worst way. This go-round he didn't display
the gratitude he'd shown when Vivian and Gaynelle were young.
Now he judged instead, always interfering, fussing about warm
clothes and dry diapers like it was his business. He didn't have to
change the pest. He most certainly did not have to wash and hang the
diapers out to dry. Jessie did all those things, but Clayton's
unhappiness with her had grown steadily worse until finally, in sheer
frustration, she started changing Ginny's diaper and bringing her into
the house before he came in from the field at mealtimes, as if she had
time for that. She'd been doing a perfectly good job with the brat
already.

At dinner the following afternoon, the couple ate in blessed
silence while Ginny took a nap. After his last bite, Clayton finally
broke the quiet. "You know, I wonder if we never had kids cuz we're
related. Ms. Moultrie told me up at the store yesterday that they been
passin' a bunch o' laws bannin' cousins getting married, sayin' it don't
make for healthy younguns."

"Ain't a lick o' sense to that, and you know it. Why, half the
people I know are married to cousins—an' uppity folks is always
marryin' their cousins, too. Now, why would they do that if it weren't
good for their babies? Besides, aren't there lots o' cousin marriages in
the Bible? Like Mary and Joseph?"

"Yeah, s'pose so. Guess it jus' set me to wonderin' again 'bout
why we ain't had none. I wouldn't have minded havin' a little fella to
follow me around here an' learn the farm." Sighing wistfully, he rolled
his sore shoulders and rubbed his neck. "I sure ain't young like I once
was. Don't know how I made it through last year with no help at all.
Like to have killed myself out there." Back aching, he reluctantly rose
to head out to the fields.

Jessie followed him to the door, reminding him, "Your help starts
tomorrow."

"Yeah, guess that'll have to do, hmm?" He cast her a rueful smile
before heading back out to the field.

Ms. Moultrie can burn in hell, thought Jessie. *Sounds like he's taken to visitin' her somethin' regular. Just knew it when she was makin' eyes at him on my birthday. Tryin' to steal him for herself, plain as day, fillin' his head up with nonsense like that.*

Jessie brooded as she washed the dinner dishes. Despite herself, a thread of doubt coursed through her mind. Perhaps her pregnancy difficulties did stem from their shared bloodline. Jessie set her lips, reluctantly identifying what may have been the invisible barrier to her ultimate goal of being the wife Clayton wanted. In her experience, few obstacles were insurmountable so long as she demonstrated due patience and persistence.

Maybe I am perfectly capable of givin' him his wish. Maybe there's nothin' wrong with me, after all. What if it's only our lineage that stands in the way of me givin' him a son? A son… somethin' even Carrie couldn't give him. If she could only bear a son, Jessie would triumph at last over those pitiful, distant memories that were now Caroline.

26 • The Sophisticated Life

GOLD-SATIN, BUTTONED-STRAP SPANISH HEELS CLICKED boldly onto the catwalk. Gaynelle's painted vermillion lips smiled slightly, and her shoulders were thrown back to better display vertical rows of iridescent sequins. Sashaying carefully in step to the jazz music being played, she followed the slender, towering woman just ahead of her, mimicking the sway of her walk. As she pivoted and returned, countless fashion buyers were following the blue net gown she wore. It was exhilarating.

Wordlessly, she arrived backstage. Vivian unzipped the back of the dress to help her slip it off. The next number, a sleeveless pink-satin evening dress with asymmetrical draping and a boat neckline, was already pulled free of its muslin packing, laid out next to T-strap beige military heels. With clockwork precision, Gaynelle began to yank it all on.

Dabbing her forehead, Vivian left her sister to manage buckling the shoes by herself. She reapplied powder while admiring the ankle-length black velvet gown that accentuated her slender silhouette. The sisters had worn three model gowns apiece, and they still had two more each. As they rejoined the mannequin line-up for the catwalk, Vivian reminded her, "No smiling."

Vivian was the better of the two about remembering to appear haughty and disdainful, which she managed by pretending to be Coco Chanel herself. Even though the young women were significantly shorter than the six-foot mannequins some designers brought to the shows, both Bell girls showed an aptitude for displaying Anne's haute couture model gowns. Gaynelle wore the dresses that required curves, while Vivian sported the sleeker, garçon fashions.

"I've been considering hiring my own mannequins," Anne had confided to the girls during their training, "but I'm fortunate my assistants continue to double so nicely for the task. The assistants used to always display the dresses, but designers are using mannequins more and more so they can hire better seamstresses, focusing on their talents rather than their looks." She sighed at the ever more complicated expectations of her industry. "That never used to be the case… except, well, I suppose I'm taking Fletcher for granted. She's never traveled with me, but I don't know what I'd do without her at home. I'd give up my right arm before I let go of her, so I guess maybe there is something to all the specialization."

The day after the Philadelphia show, while on the train to New York, Anne narrowed her eyes thoughtfully at the girls. "You both make better mannequins than Bernice and Gloria. They are talented, of course, and have always paraded my model gowns adequately, but you two have panache. Maybe we can make this a regular gig. Would you like being my dedicated mannequins?"

Vivian and Gaynelle nodded a sleepy agreement, rubbing their temples from the previous night's riotous gaiety. They weren't used to the constant, demanding schedule of the fashion world, a world that required not only a normal workday but expected after-hours socializing as well. Aside from the scheduled parades, random private showings of the model gowns could be required at any time.

Anne was singularly oblivious to the hung-over state of the girls, having always eschewed excessive consumption of alcohol herself. She nursed a solitary drink throughout each night as she dutifully made her rounds, greeting other prominent designers who imbibed to varying degrees, none of which was any of her business. She bore the parties as an obligation of her profession, mentally ticking off the minutes, sparing not a thought for the dissipation surrounding her.

Because she'd been guided through the social world of the couturiers by the experienced hand of her now-deceased husband,

Anne had never been drawn into the risqué side of the parties, which had grown increasingly wild over time. The most extravagant and flamboyant were drawn to the world of fashion, but Anne remained sheltered through ingrained habit, retracing the steps that she had followed for so many years with her husband.

Gaynelle and Vivian, however, had been sniffed out as fresh fodder for the jaded, uncurbed participants. By the end of a single night in Philadelphia, Gaynelle had smoked her first cigarette and they were both tipsy on spirits. To their surprise, liquor had flowed far more easily at this party than sweet tea, despite prohibition.

"Alcohol's not banned here?" Gaynelle had asked, hesitating when the willowy, titian-haired mannequin with a husky New York accent proffered her first drink. The tall woman had invited her to join their circle, presenting the teenager to the group as if she were a prize.

A bored-looking designer, recently returned from Paris, said drily, "*Merde.* How naïve she is."

Gaynelle had been trying to decide if the designer's complexion was naturally swarthy or if he was sporting a trendy tan, but at his words such thoughts flew straight out of her head. She bit her lip self-consciously.

The red-haired woman laughingly reassured her, "No, baby—they got plenty of this stuff put away for us—or maybe it's from their own barrel house." She snickered. "It's only illegal to buy booze, but there's no trouble with drinking it. Our treat for all the hard work we do."

The debauched group eagerly watched as Gaynelle choked down her first drink and the posh designer plied her with another. Thanking him uncertainly, she dutifully started to sip it as well.

Meanwhile, Vivian danced to live jazz music with a group of design assistants. By the time she located Gaynelle, her sister was already a bit unsteady on her feet. "You flapper! Look at you. You've already got an edge."

"My, you can get a wiggle on." The willowy model gazed with interest at Vivian, sizing her up as the bored designer handed the older sister a cocktail.

Vivian laughed, accepting the drink as if she were behind in the game.

"Anyone got a fag?" another mannequin asked. She was a dead-ringer for Lillian Gish, the silent-screen star whose face was everywhere—including here, apparently. Vivian peeked curiously at her as cigarettes were being passed around, wondering if she might indeed be related to the actress. Vivian was just about to ask her when Gaynelle started gagging and gripping at her arm.

"I need to get outta here," Gaynelle coughed.

She was tugging Vivian away from the others, waving a hand altogether too obviously at the smoke-laced air.

Exasperated at her sister—and the sniggers of the group—Vivian deposited her empty glass on a passing waiter's tray as Gaynelle led her out of the building. She stood by patiently, however, while the younger girl closed her eyes and breathed in the fresh air.

When Gaynelle opened her eyes, she found Vivian still puffing on the cigarette she'd been given indoors. "You like smoking?"

"Why not?" Vivian answered coolly. "Did it all the time in Charleston. Give it a whirl."

Uncertainly, Gaynelle took a drag from the cigarette and began to cough again. "I'm gonna be sick."

Vivian watched as Gaynelle ran to a nearby shrub, where she heaved fruitlessly. After waiting what seemed an interminable time, Vivian's patience wore thin. Grasping Gaynelle's elbow, she said, "Come on, let's go."

The pair reentered the party, where they found Anne and persuaded her to say her goodbyes.

Despite the early end to their evening, Vivian felt gratified as she dozed off that night. She'd paraded model gowns to a crowd, danced at a ritzy party, held her liquor, and tasted her first cigarette in ages. She'd been complimented and admired and felt like a truly liberated woman—a real flapper. Vivian had never felt so content in her life. She fell asleep with a smile, repeating the word 'flapper' and giggling to herself.

Nearby, Gaynelle lay on the other bed. She'd barely managed to stumble there without hurting herself, she was so nauseated. The alcohol had tasted vile and the cigarettes worse. They made her clothes reek, too—adding to her nausea. Then there was that fashion buyer who had squeezed her bottom as he passed by. She missed Julep, who was all alone and probably pining for her back in Kingstree. She missed her daddy and her mama and Ginny… and even, or maybe especially, Tommy, despite everything. Gaynelle had seldom felt quite so desolate in her life.

27• An Extra Farm Duty

TOMMY STEPPED OVER GINNY, pulling open the creaky screen door of the farmhouse. Inside, Jessie was folding laundry. He'd been hoping to catch her alone. His attempts to ask about Gaynelle at dinnertime had met with Clayton's answering glare. It had shut him right up, but now that the farmer was in the field, Tommy wanted to try to speak with Jessie. He was sorely disappointed at not seeing Gaynelle.

Taking off his straw work hat, he nodded. "Mornin', Mrs. Bell."

Jessie placed a folded sheet on a stack. "What is it, boy?"

"Well, ma'am, jus' wanted to chat. You know, 'bout stuff, like what you're doin' and what Gaynelle's up to. I jus' don't ever get to talk with you, really." He smiled his most persuasive, lopsided grin.

Jessie observed him with cool regard. He was, as she remembered, a handsome boy. "How old are you now, Tommy?"

"Eighteen next Thursday, ma'am."

Jessie favored the youth with a rare smile and made an abrupt decision. His sudden appearance had simplified things. She was unconcerned with the boy's own agenda, of course. It probably had to do with Gaynelle, and Jessie was reticent to discuss the young woman with him. Time was of the essence, and she didn't want to detract from his primary farm duties by wasting it. "So young," she murmured. Then she smirked, her voice growing more assertive. "But as I recall, you're already pretty experienced in gratifyin' the ladies."

Tommy's face registered shock. "I—I don't know what you mean, ma'am."

"Come now, Tommy. I understand you. You aren't a boy to forego what you take a fancy to." Jessie stared at him intently. "I know about you and Gaynelle."

"No, ma'am. I didn't do nothin'," stammered the farmhand.

"Oh, but you did, Tommy. You did the most amazin' things with Gaynelle, and I have to say that I'm curious to know what it's like." The young man's fearful reaction was oddly scintillating. She took a step closer to him.

"No, ma'am. I ain't sure what you're talkin' 'bout, but I gotta get back to work. Mr. Clay's waitin' for me." Tommy began backing towards the screen door.

As it jangled open, Jessie called after his retreating form, "Alright, since you don't have time now, perhaps I'll come out there and we can continue our discussion with Clay. That work better for you, Tommy?"

Stopping in his tracks, he turned back to face her. "No, ma'am, please. He'd shoot me dead. I know he would. He done said he was gonna shoot Willie if he ever showed his face 'round here again. He wouldn't say why, but he meant it."

"Well, then, settle down and chat with me for a moment." Jessie patted the space next to her on the loveseat, shaking her head as if amused.

"Yes, ma'am." Tommy nervously made his way to the edge of the seat.

"What's Clay up to, right now?" she asked, as if they had only been discussing the weather.

"He's in the middle o' the field with Marion. We're gonna be out there 'til dark, an' he don't wanna take a break. I'm jus' s'posed to be fetchin' water."

As he began to stand, Jessie reached out to stop him. Rising to her feet, she faced him, reveling somehow in his skittishness. Reaching behind her head, she pulled out the pins holding back her hair. Slowly, she leaned towards him, shaking out the dark tresses. "I'm not so awful, now, am I?"

He gazed up at the loose black hair tumbling down her shoulders. Her large brown eyes stared down at him purposefully. Swallowing hard, he managed to ask, "Ma'am, what is it you want from me?"

"I've just taken my own little fancy to you. What do you say?" Jessie smiled at him again, tilting her head thoughtfully. "You obliged your fancy with Gaynelle, and now I'd like to oblige mine with you. Sounds fair, don'tcha think? Clay doesn't really need to know about any of it, though I'll be more inclined to keep your secret if I have one of my own."

Flush with power, Jessie quirked a triumphant eyebrow at him, waiting for his response. She savored the moment.

"I don't have much time, ma'am." Tommy floundered.

"It won't take much time, Tommy," she assured him, pushing him onto his back. Deftly, she unfastened his work trousers. As she lowered them and viewed the young man's nakedness, she gloated. He was becoming engorged, and her own body began to pulsate with feral desire.

Skipping unnecessary preliminaries, she slipped off her drawers. Straddling him, she began to gyrate, slowly at first and then faster and more intensely until at last she achieved a culmination of power quite different than any she had experienced before.

28 • Time with Julep

July 1922, Kingstree, SC

GAYNELLE WAS RELIEVED TO BE BACK IN KINGSTREE after the fashion tour. Since they'd arrived home, however, Anne's every waking hour had been spent in her workshop, and meanwhile Vivian had resumed assisting Dr. Connor at his office. Gaynelle didn't really mind. After the constant society of the fashion tour, she rather relished having a lull to read and spend time with Julep.

Aunt Anna's elegant house had quickly become home to Gaynelle, her bedroom more personalized than the old one in the farmhouse ever had been, thanks to the designer's thoughtful decorative touches and the old, cherished books on the shelves. Gaynelle would soak in the luxurious bathtub for hours on end with a novel, cooling off on particularly hot afternoons, and she felt welcome throughout the house, free to prepare food in the kitchen when she wished and go to the stables at any time of day.

Julep had been well-tended by the caretaker, Eddie, who made sure that the thoroughbred was exercised and groomed daily. Now that Gaynelle was home, however, she made up for time away by taking Julep just outside of town and its freshly-paved roads to where the thoroughfares were still just made of dirt. They'd stay for long spells at a large, open field Eddie had told her about, away from the rest of the world. She would ride Julep gently at first and then canter and even gallop for short distances. Gaynelle never pushed the old stallion, but he still enjoyed flying along on occasion, and during their joyrides, Gaynelle's own spirit soared along with his.

She would bring a blanket, a book, and a picnic—including oats and pears for Julep—for after their rides, allowing Julep time to graze and wander. Now and then, he'd meander back over to where she was, and his warmth would tickle her shoulder as he nudged her. She'd kiss his velvety nose and talk with him about the story she was reading, about the weather, about the flowers, about anything. It was her tone of voice that told Julep that she loved him.

Julep seemed as devoted to Gaynelle as she liked to imagine that he had been to her mother before her—and apparently to an uncle before that. His caretakers had changed with Julep as he aged. According to Anne, an uncle named Sam had bonded with him in his youth, when he was most dynamic and energetic. Sam's kindness and strength had helped form Julep's temperament. At his peak he had been passed on to Caroline, as dynamic but with a softer nature. While Julep couldn't possibly understand how her mother had saved him, Gaynelle was sure he knew in his heart of her loyalty to him, and that he'd also seen this loyalty in Daddy, who had likewise cared for him for many years. As gray threads wove into his chestnut coat, Julep now had the gentlest master of all, and she hoped he sensed that his latest transition from the rural life he'd known for so long to this town abode was only because of her love for him. She was certain that her sweetest, most tender affections also reverberated in Julep's heart. He mirrored her feelings in a true and unpretentious way, as only infants and primal animals tend to do.

The long days with Julep were healing to her soul. When she wasn't with Julep or relaxing with a book, she spent her time in Anne's studio, ever impressed at how much there was to learn.

Anne's old habits had returned. Her life was once more an endless blur of work on her designs, and she seemed to think of little else. When Gaynelle wanted to see her beyond mealtimes, she would have to join her in her workshop. There, Anne would look up hazily from her designs, blink a few times, and then offer sewing or fashion lessons, thereby making the girl's education for now something of an informal apprenticeship. The designer seemed to enjoy giving her the lessons, and Gaynelle thrived on spending time with Anne as well as Julep. She liked the subject matter well enough but was primarily sustained by the maternal love that Anne had shelved for so long.

Gaynelle bloomed under Anne's and Julep's constant affections, and her heartache subsided.

29 • Jessie's Bliss

Jessie had availed herself of the young farmhand frequently through the rest of the spring and into the summer—until certain that her monthlies had ceased, at which point she discontinued their encounters as abruptly as she had started them. The experience had been invigorating, but it was a hazardous means to an end—and Jessie always planned towards the future.

Tommy had come to perversely enjoy their sessions. Her lack of attachment was as unsettling as the risk they'd been taking, and it was all oddly exciting. She'd otherwise remained as cordial with him as she had always been, and the illicit sex had begun to seem just another facet of his job on the farm. Then she had suddenly and inexplicably halted her attentions. At first he worried that Clayton had caught on to their shenanigans, but the farmer's friendliness never seemed to waver. Perplexed, Tommy began to purposely make himself available, but she shooed him away as if she had no inkling of their recent pastime.

When at last Tommy made a direct overture, Jessie merely shook her head, replying with amused annoyance, "I'll let you know when I require your services again. Now stop dallyin'. You have work to do."

Baffled, Tommy let it go, none the wiser as to the gestation of his offspring in her womb, much less his paternal link to baby Ginny.

Jessie kept the pregnancy secret until after Tommy left the farm for the winter. She had quietly progressed to her fifth month, and she was hopeful for success this time.

With bated breath, the couple waited for the final months of the pregnancy to pass. Wanting to help its success in any way possible, Clayton chose to spend the winter caring for Ginny and helping around the house, in lieu of his typical winter expansion of the farm. Jessie noted the shift in his attitude with satisfaction. His regard for her had increased the moment he became aware that she was with child again, and he grew more affectionate and solicitous of her well-being as the pregnancy went on.

Jessie didn't realize that her own satisfaction in pregnancy and impending motherhood was the pivotal reason for Clayton's change of behavior. Truly, her increasing displeasure with her lot had been the crux of their marital discord. While it was true that Clayton was excited about the expected child, he was also relieved at seeing her more content than she had been since the early years of their marriage, before multiple miscarriages had embittered her.

At last, a baby girl was born. Jessie's regret over the baby's gender was overshadowed by her immense relief. She'd truly become a mother at last, and now she wouldn't have to worry about a boy growing up to look exactly like Tommy. This time she claimed the name 'Anne' for her daughter without argument from her husband, and in Anne she found her bliss.

Vivian, Gaynelle, and Ginny had been mere practice for this exquisite bundle of self-manifestation. Jessie rejoiced in breastfeeding the child as she had not been able to do for the other children. She spent hours rocking and whispering to the babe, believing her lessons to be almost magically absorbed as they were spoken aloud, like incantations. Secrets of influence and advantage, secrets of survival were shared. A peculiar delight was to be had in the murmuring of what others in their ignorance might deem to be 'sins', knowing that such confessions were safe with the worthy babe. As she crooned of these mysteries, she was oblivious to the presence of an older child, a child with keen ears, a quiet tongue, and a penchant for lingering behind the rocking chair, where so many bizarre and instructional tales could be heard.

Thus were the powers of self-discipline and secrecy, of the well-timed sacrifice for the greater good of one's future, revealed to Ginny. Indeed, she found Mama's reckonings to be fascinating, and the small girl absorbed the Machiavellian principles in bits, stealthily versed in the hidden nature of things and slowly assimilating Jessie's pragmatic and self-serving view of the world. The small child could no more repeat or remember the lessons she learned than she could recount the details of her own conception, but the effects were as real and enduring.

30 • Ginny Talks to her Granny

Almost two years later
July 1925, Greeleyville, SC

GINNY CLUNG WITH ONE HAND TO THE SIDEWALL as she perched on the tail end of the open wagon. Her legs swung freely. The dirt road rolled by underneath as they headed to her granny's to deliver newly-picked summer vegetables—tomatoes and peppers, okra and squash. It had been Ginny's job to stop the two watermelons from rolling around in the bed of the wagon, but she'd long since pushed them behind Annie's basket, wedging them up under the seat. The bushel baskets were neatly organized in the wagon bed, where two-year-old Annie was taking her afternoon nap, curled up in her own wicker basket. Mama drove up front.

Now Ginny stretched her left leg down as far as it would go, seeing if she could brush the grass with her toes. She never could quite reach and once had actually fallen out of the wagon. She'd sat on the side of the road and cried as Mama continued on without her. When she'd finally come back, she'd first examined Ginny for injuries and then whipped her soundly, scolding her carelessness. Despite all that, Ginny again stretched her leg as far as possible towards the rolling ground, enjoying the occasional wispy brush of dogfennel against her foot.

When they arrived, she slid off the wagon end and ran up the stairs of the little ramshackle cabin. Only a dirty tint of its former blue still graced the exterior. She pounced into the arms of her granny and hurried to share her news before they had to leave. Mama rarely stayed very long.

Glancing around to make sure Mama was still busy with toting vegetables inside, Ginny announced, "I got a spinning top for my birthday."

"You did? I never did have one o' dem." Amarintha caught the girl's enthusiasm. "Not in my whole, long life."

"Oh, it's red and blue and has elephants painted on it. It's all shiny." Ginny's face shone just as brightly as her recollection, but then it fell. "I wanted to bring it to show you, but Mama said no." She pouted for a moment and then looked up at Jessie's approaching footsteps.

"How've you been, Aunt Amarintha?" asked Jessie. "Where's Uncle Simms?"

"Out at the still, prob'ly."

Jessie shook her head. "Is that girl botherin' you?"

"Nah, honey, she sure ain't. I'm enjoyin' chattin' wid her."

"Well, don't you let her pester you. She will, you know." Jessie glared at the youngster on the old woman's lap.

"Ain't no bother," assured Amarintha, patting Ginny's head for emphasis.

"Humph!" Jessie snorted but the tension in her shoulders relaxed a bit. "Thank heavens for that. Land sakes, she's like to drive *me* crazy." Though she rarely indulged in pointless chatter, Jessie occasionally appreciated the novel feeling of camaraderie it gave her to vent to the old woman. There were few folks that she felt comfortable enough around to do so. Besides, it was expected on such visits.

"Sounds like you could use an extra hand wid de chillun again." In truth, Amarintha thought the two small girls could benefit from a gentler touch. Chuckling to herself, she wondered if it was the first time she had ever considered her own hand to be 'gentle'.

Jessie waved dismissively. "Oh, I've got it under control. I expect she'll be able to start helpin' out more pretty soon here. I ain't gonna stand for a lazy youngun. She's four now, you—"

Suddenly, an ear-piercing shriek disrupted their conversation. They ran to the door and saw Annie thrashing on the ground near the rear of the wagon.

Jessie dashed towards the tot, deftly lifting her into the front seat of the wagon. She anxiously climbed up beside her, then shouted to Amarintha, "I've gotta take Annie to the doctor in town. Can you keep Ginny?"

"You go on," Amarintha called back. "I've got her."

"I declare," Amarintha muttered, horrified at the sight of Annie's unnaturally bent arm. Her head shook back and forth as she watched them leave, tongue clucking for added emphasis.

Ginny had watched the scene unfold wordlessly. Now she turned and buried her head in her granny's bosom, uncertain of what exactly had happened. The words sounded right, though, so she passionately repeated, "I declare! I declare!"

Stroking the child's curly hair, Amarintha smiled. "You sure is gettin' big. Wish I got to see more o' you deze days."

Ginny clung to the old woman. "Is Annie gonna be alright?"

"Yeah, she'll have dat arm set back straight and wear a splint fer a while."

"I don't wanna see her arm all bent up like that." Ginny cuddled her granny, feeling better.

Agitated from the commotion, Amarintha pulled out her corncob pipe to settle her nerves. She let Ginny pour in the tobacco and hold it for her while she lit it, ignoring the spatters of tobacco that Ginny dropped all over them. Jessie might have a hard time comprehending it, but Amarintha never minded the child hanging onto her. In fact, she enjoyed spoiling the girl a bit. She always made sure Ginny received extra portions of her favorite dishes, and whenever they came by, Amarintha tried to remember to open a jar of fruit preserves. After a while, perhaps she'd get up from the rocking chair and let Ginny help her in the kitchen. Today it looked like they'd have time to satisfy Ginny's sweet tooth. Poor thing had been forbidden from the kitchen in her own home—Jessie couldn't stand her getting underfoot, but that sounded as though it might be changing all too soon.

Ginny snuggled comfortably against her rocking, smoking granny, who never fussed, no matter how messy she was. "Can you come live with us?"

"Ain't room for an ole lady at your house, chile."

"Is, too! Please!" Ginny tugged at the pipe.

Amarintha puffed on it, relishing being so earnestly begged. Not many people were solicitous of her company these days, and the loving little girl warmed her heart.

"Mama's gonna need your help extra a lot to take care of Annie an' me now. Annie's gonna be a whole lotta trouble with her arm like that."

"Ain't no place fer me to sleep."

"Mm-hmm. You can sleep on the couch."

"I need more room dan dat."

"It's big enough! Mama and Tommy fit it jus' fine."

"I can't lay down on dat thing. It ain't big enough fer the likes of me."

"Mm-hmmm," Ginny argued, nodding her head. "Mama and Tommy can lay down on it jus' fine. They jus' have to bend their legs some—but it fits 'em both at the same time."

"When was dis?" Amarintha scowled. She clasped the girl's arm. "What you blabberin' on about?"

"You'd fit it all by yourself!" Ginny insisted. "You can sleep on the couch, Granny. It's big enough for you."

"Your mama and dat helper was layin' down on dat couch together?"

Ginny squirmed uncomfortably at the accusatory tone. She'd been naughty for peeking when she was supposed to stay in her room, but she hadn't expected Granny to know that she'd been breaking the rules—and Granny was never angry with her. This was an unprecedented situation.

"Don't tell Mama. Let's keep it secret, Granny," Ginny pleaded, tears welling in her eyes. Mama was sure to beat her for disobeying.

Amarintha's expression softened at once. She nodded slowly, murmuring as she began to stroke the girl's back, "Dat's right. You can tell Granny anythin'. I won't tell on ya, chile."

By the time that Jessie returned for Ginny, the old cabin was quiet. When she walked in, Simms was sitting alone, sipping on a bottle of moonshine. Glancing around the empty rooms, she asked, "Where's Ginny?"

Simms sighed. "Rintha done took her to yore house. They was all ready to leave by da time I got here."

"Alright. Thanks, Uncle Simms."

Jessie was already turning to leave when he added, "Yup... sure gonna miss my sis's cookin'."

Surprised, she paused. "What do you mean?"

"You don't know? Well, she done decided to move back in wid y'all to help look after da chillun." The abandoned man sighed again as he brought the bottle back to his lips. "Said somethin' 'bout you needin' extra help fer a while."

"Oh," Jessie replied. That was all she needed—an old woman again in addition to two youngsters to tend. "Alright, well, I guess we'll see. I'll head on home, then. 'Bye, Uncle Simms."

As Jessie directed the wagon towards her house, she was grateful that Annie was asleep again, tuckered out from her visit with the doctor—and from all that blessed screaming. It gave Jessie time to ponder how she would convince Amarintha to return to live with Simms once more.

As she approached the house, she was greeted by Clayton hailing her from the field. Running to meet her, he called, "How is she?"

"Oh, she's fine. Just gotta leave that arm alone for a few weeks. We're gonna have to put up with some whinin', I expect."

Clayton looked relieved. "Well, thank goodness Mama is here to help you with the younguns. I tell you what, sure is a relief to have her back here. I been missin' her. You know, I've often thought it'd be nice for her to jus' be sittin' on the porch while Ginny's playin' outside, jus' to keep an eye on her while you're gettin' your work done."

"See now, Clay, I wanna talk with you 'bout that. I just don't think we've got room for her here." Jessie furrowed her eyebrows and shook her head. "We never did, really."

"I already got that worked out," he said brightly. "She can sleep with Ginny for now, and meanwhile we can add on a room. Annie can go back to sleepin' with us for the time bein'. Or in her cradle. It'd be nice to have another room, wouldn't it? I wasn't plannin' on clearin' another field this winter, nohow."

Jessie stifled a sigh. His mind was clearly made up. There was no sense arguing—at least not right now. To placate him, she said, "I suppose it might be nice to have the help."

When she arrived at the house, Ginny and Amarintha were already setting the table for supper. Amarintha nodded at her. "Cookin' up some summer squash an' onions to go wid deze fried taters. Dem's my boy's favorites."

Jessie blinked, surprised she didn't know this after all her years with Clayton. Sinking uncertainly on the sofa, she reflected that perhaps she *could* glean more useful knowledge from the old hag— and it was nice not to have to cook. She could use more time to relax. Propping her feet up, Jessie mused, *Might as well make the best of it while she's still here.*

Clayton continued in fine spirits that evening, talking between each and every bite, asking all about Annie's experiences at the doctor's office.

Meanwhile, Tommy ate silently. He observed the newcomer with curiosity. She used more pepper in her cooking than Jessie did, which he rather liked. He jumped with each cackle, though, and stared at the twisted, black stumps jutting from her gums. It took him half the meal to realize they were just the decayed remnants of teeth. Smiling to himself, he wondered if they might be the real reason all the food was cooked down to a mush.

Amarintha's conversation dominated the table, despite Clayton's chatter. At his idea for an extra room for her, she smacked with delight.

After supper, Tommy gathered his things to leave. As he washed his hands at the hand pump in the yard, the strange old woman approached him, a determined gleam in her eye.

Her tone was matter-of-fact. "I'm thinkin' you ought not to come back here tomorrow."

Confused, Tommy stopped pumping. "What?"

"You been helpin' out a bit too much 'round here. Best make yourself scarce." She handed him a towel, transmitting her censure with an implacable stare.

"But I'm s'posed to work the whole summer. Mr. Clay done hired me through most o' the fall—"

"I ain't got da patience fer dis, young man. Ain't havin' no shenanigans goin' on under my son's nose."

Tommy's stomach plummeted. He busied himself with straightening the towel.

"Get yore things an' git. If I see that face o' your'n again, I'm gonna tell Clay what I know, an' you won't be such a pretty boy no more."

Tommy could hardly catch his breath. How the old woman had learned about the illicit trysts was beyond him. Jessie wouldn't have told her. Their behavior at dinner couldn't have given them away. They were only ever cordial, whether or not they were engaging in intimate behaviors on the side. Jessie had indeed taken a fancy to him again that spring after not paying him any attention at all the previous year. He hadn't really minded the lapse. Made sense that a mother would be preoccupied with her new baby. Besides, he'd known for a while that women were unpredictable. It was a mystery how a man could stay married to one. So much easier to just roll with things, to be unattached. Women were like the seasons, he'd decided. They only wanted to be pleasured for a time before turning cold, but eventually they warmed back up again. He tried to be understanding, but he was starting to think that there was an easier answer to this dilemma. It made sense that there might be a woman who was in the season for wanting pleasure when another was not; it was just a matter of figuring out who was where on that spectrum. Why worry about their moods when they inevitably changed? When they wanted him, he was obliging; when they weren't in the mood, he wasn't demanding. No, he prided himself on being an understanding and obliging fellow— and discreet to boot. He liked to think that he brightened their lives for a while, like a summer breeze. In return, he enjoyed them unconditionally. They were all so different and interesting.

After his initial shock, even the affair with Jessie had been to his taste, more provocative and thrilling than most of his liaisons. Some part of him had been relieved when their trysts had ended the first time, though he'd been ready and willing when she'd resumed their dalliance. Yet now that it was time for it to end again, he found the thought not unwelcome. Maybe he'd go somewhere new this time, see who else he might meet without old relationships complicating the mix.

Tommy met the old woman's intractable stare and sighed. "I'll jus' let Mr. Clay know that I gotta leave, alright? You should know that I have really enjoyed workin' with your son, Ms. Bell. He's a good man. I didn't mean him no harm."

Amarintha nodded a grudging acknowledgment. She had seen the seedy side of life far too often to feel any malice towards the boy. Not for this. She saw only a situation in need of correction.

31 • A Date to Remember

A few months later
December 1925, Kingstree, SC

GAYNELLE GAZED IN THE MIRROR and slid the bobby pin in place. She had resisted Vivian's insistence that she keep her hair short, never having come to terms with having it shorn that time at the farm. Smoothing hair lotion over the remaining blond strands, she spun the final neat pincurl in the row below her barrette, framing her face.

Slipping into a gray, Art-Deco-inspired model gown from the past season, Gaynelle adjusted the shoulder straps and admired the geometric designs of white-and-black beadwork. The complex patterns finished in a beaded fringe just above her knees. Adding a bit of ivory powder and an extra coating of plum lipstick, Gaynelle nodded approval at her image before pulling on her cross-strap gray Louis heels.

She was going out with Vivian to see *The Big Parade*. Afterwards they planned to dance with her sister's fun-loving friends at the pavilion of the new Wee Nee Beach Swimming Club. Vivian had somehow amassed quite a social circle in Kingstree in this past year while Gaynelle was still in Charleston finishing her time at Ashley Hall. Aunt Anna had finally been persuaded to send her there, compliments of Vivian's tenacity, and meanwhile Vivian had returned to finish her degree at the College of Charleston. So the sisters had traipsed off to Charleston together, but Gaynelle had been relegated to admiring her sister's escapades from within the sheltered confines of Ashley Hall. She'd enjoyed it, though. There she had made her own friends, one of whom wrote her weekly.

On their breaks and after her graduation, Vivian had continued to assist Dr. Connor in his clinic; when not on fashion tours both young women continued to work as mannequins during long summers and holiday tours. Soon, however, Vivian developed friendships with newspaper journalists at *The County Journal* and began writing freelance articles. Before long, she was assistant to the copy editor. Her new income allowed her to rent a studio apartment alone, an act that gratified her fierce independent streak.

I wonder where <u>my</u> independent streak is? Gaynelle thought with a small frown. *I couldn't wait to come back home, even though Vivian begged me to stay in Charleston to go to college. But maybe I'll do like her and go back after a while. Perhaps I'll be there for the next presidential election.* As Gaynelle slipped on a pair of silver drop earrings, she recalled how her sister had swung by Ashley Hall to dance wildly with her friends outside Gaynelle's classroom window after participating in the election of the previous year—the very first election to permit women the vote. The teacher had recognized her, too, opening the window to chide 'Miss Bell', who merely laughed and called into the room, "We voted! We did it!" before traipsing off with her posse.

A horn honked, interrupting Gaynelle's reminiscences, and she rushed out of her bedroom, through the Queen Anne home, and down the stairs with a bell-sleeve coat tucked over her arm. A moment later, she was scooting into the backseat of a covered Oldsmobile Touring Sedan next to Vivian. "I should have known you wouldn't come alone to pick me up," she laughed. "Hey Frank. Good to see you."

A young man with a thin moustache glanced back from the front seat at the newcomer. He tipped his hat. "Hey, doll! Nice to see you, too. This here is Jimmy." Frank gestured towards the pale blond man to his right, who nodded in greeting.

Vivian, cloaked mysteriously in an Egyptian Assuit stole, greeted Gaynelle with a resounding kiss on her cheek.

Gaynelle leaned back in her seat, relaxing against her sister, trying to get herself in the mood for an evening of fun. Attitude was everything, she'd been told—and she truly had become more accustomed to the fast pace of the chic, urban social scene. Her sister never lost a chance to go out dancing and always wanted her along. In fact, Vivian had called from the newspaper office only that morning, suggesting they 'take some exercise' together that evening after a movie, despite having gone out just two nights before. She rarely went out with the same fellow more than a few times, and Gaynelle guessed that she'd already dated half the eligible men at the paper. Gaynelle glanced at Frank again, noting that she did cycle back through the regulars—and Frank certainly seemed to be becoming a regular.

Vivian had a penchant for taking leave of their male escorts at some point during the evenings—when she was with Gaynelle, at least. She'd wave a hand, insisting that the men were too blind with drink to care, despite their protests. They'd go make merry for a while on their own before Vivian took her back to Anne's. Gaynelle suspected, however, that she sometimes rejoined the men after her little sister was safe and sound at home. Despite Vivian's push to get Gaynelle to socialize, she tended to be protective and never liked when Gaynelle's dates took an interest in necking her. She'd interrupt, scolding laughingly, "Bank's closed, mister. I need sissy to come dance with me."

On this particular evening, the town was bedecked in bright holiday trim. The doors of the Academy Theatre were covered in garland, and the snack vendors wore Santa hats. It was a cheerful time of year for everyone, and Gaynelle delighted in trying to navigate through the cacophonous small crowd with her companions. She and Vivian soon found their seats in the theatre; before the lights dimmed and the pianist's overture began, Jimmy had settled into the seat next to her with a Coca-Cola for each of them and popcorn to share.

To her amusement, the protagonist of the film was also named Jim. Unlike her companion, however, the movie star had smooth dark hair. Soon Gaynelle was carried away with emotion, wiping tears at the young man's return to his beloved after a prolonged separation. The lyrical piano accompaniment only made her tears worse, and Jimmy good-naturedly proffered his pocket handkerchief.

The group had a grilled supper at the club where a band played, and soon Vivian was dancing the Charleston with Frank. She was a well-known favorite, and fellow revelers whistled and called out, "Get hot, Vivian!"

After polishing off a smuggled drink, Gaynelle accepted Jimmy's invitation to dance. She merrily tried to keep up with the fast-paced steps, stumbling through them in good humor. As soon as she finished dancing the Charleston with Jimmy, she was fox-trotting with Frank, then shimmying with Vivian. Wickedly fast dances were the entire point of wearing the fringed dresses, and Gaynelle loved how the beads shook, accentuating her gyrations to the music.

Overheated and out of breath, she grabbed some punch and carried it off the pavilion, heading towards the bank of the Black River for some fresh air—to cool off and escape her sister's incredible endurance. She leaned against a sweetgum tree, wondering if she should put her feet in the river—and then hoping she wasn't getting any ticks on her. She hesitated, looking back towards the pavilion. From this more peaceful vantage point, she could appreciate the entire scene better. Laughter and jazz music drifted down to her. Flashes of Vivian's dress could be seen from amidst a circle of admirers. Gaynelle's gaze wandered across the Main Street Bridge and back to the pavilion, where a young man was exiting the side steps, pulling off his apron. He carried a wool overcoat and seemed preoccupied.

She watched him curiously, smiling at the smooth dark hair, styled like the movie star. Then she gasped in shock. "Tommy? Tommy Salters?"

He glanced up, somehow hearing his name despite the music and the distance between them. Turning in her direction, he stared for a long moment before finally coming towards her.

Gaynelle remained as still as an egret before it takes flight, waiting to see him more clearly, but she knew that saunter, that lithe form.

His head cocked at an angle as he made out the sylvan statue before him. Then he inhaled sharply. "Good Lord! It can't be."

He beheld an elegant young woman so unlike the girl he had known, but the sweet face was the same. Those lush lips were now painted brightly into a Cupid's bow, and her large blue eyes were accentuated with heavy makeup. He drew closer and whispered, "Gaynelle?"

The young woman was still frozen, overcome with shock. It had been five years, years during which she had given birth to his child and had gone away to school. She had *grown up* in those five years, yet as she saw the same stilted smile blossom on his face, she felt fifteen again.

"Still the prettiest girl I know, even with all the face paint," he murmured, touching her arm. His fingertips met with gooseflesh. "Hey, are you cold?"

A moment later, she gratefully shrugged into his woolen coat, but she still couldn't find words to say to him, only gazed on his face in wonderment as he buttoned the coat.

"I just finished my shift," Tommy said. "Wanna go somewhere and talk? I'm rentin' a room at Ms. Nelson's boarding house—it'd be quiet there."

Her quivering insides went upside-down. Nodding faintly, she smiled back at his earnest face. It was like a dream come true.

Taking her elbow, Tommy started to lead the way when Gaynelle finally managed to speak. "Hold on, I have to tell Vivian."

She left Tommy waiting near the street as she ran back inside the pavilion. There she collected her own coat and reticule before finding Vivian among the crowd. "I'm taking off now. Just wanted to let you know."

"What's the matter? Are you ill?"

"Maybe a bit." Gaynelle's face was flushed, her averted eyes brilliant.

"Let me grab my things. We'll go home right now." Vivian hurried to collect her own mesh bag and stole. "I'll tell Frank, and he'll drive us."

"No, wait." Gaynelle clutched at Vivian's arm before she could hail their escort. "I met someone I know, and we wanna talk privately. I'm meetin' them outside."

"Them?" Vivian eyed her suspiciously, her face still registering concern as she teased, "Gaynelle, you big sneak. May I know who 'them' is?"

"Ginny's father," whispered Gaynelle.

"Oh, no." Vivian's smile faded. "Sure this is wise?"

The question was futile. She could no more stop Gaynelle than she could stop a steam engine. Trying to ignore the sick feeling in her gut, Vivian fished out some money from her mesh bag and thrust the purse at her sister. "Take this with you."

At her puzzled expression, Vivian heaved an exasperated sigh. "There are condoms in there. If you want some nookie, use them." Vivian punctuated her suggestion by shrugging and attempting a lighthearted laugh—though her eyebrows refused to be drawn apart. She couldn't stop Gaynelle, but she prayed that she might prevent a repeat of the devastation wrought once already.

Gaynelle clutched the bag, searching for the argument that should have been on the tip of her tongue. Finally she just nodded in embarrassed acknowledgment.

Vivian threw her arms around her younger sister before shooing her off. "Go on, then, go! I'll make your excuses to the boys."

She whirled back onto the dance floor and shimmied towards her circle of friends.

32 • Ecstasy & Revelations

GAYNELLE BLINKED AS THE MORNING LIGHT BROKE THROUGH the small window of the simple room, dappling the far wall.

Contentment welled in her heart. She lay nestled in Tommy's arms, her happiness almost complete. Despite the years she'd spent feeling reproachful of Tommy and rationalizing away their future, she had always, deep down, hoped that somehow, someday, they would be together again. Now all that was missing was Ginny.

She'd never accepted the need to give up their daughter, remaining convinced that Tommy had deserved to know about the pregnancy and should have been given a chance to do right by them. Daddy had only insisted she give up the child out of love, but it had seemed all wrong. It still did.

Now, though, she was a grown woman. The father of her child embraced her in his arms, and they lay as a man and wife should, at last. Despite Vivian's good intentions and bold efforts, Gaynelle had not bothered with the protection her sister had thrust upon her. This time she and Tommy were more mature and could make their own decisions. They were old enough to be wed.

Gaynelle considered the practicalities, wondering if she could live in such meager conditions. She looked around the barren room and knew that she could. After all, her own mother had made a similar choice. Daddy had regretted that Caroline hadn't had *things*, that she'd had to do with less, but Gaynelle was sure her mother hadn't felt that way. Caroline had been fortunate to wed Daddy, and Gaynelle would, in turn, be likewise fortunate in having the man she loved for a husband.

She sighed with contentment, and Tommy stirred. Pressing her lips together, Gaynelle stilled herself, afraid this magical reunion might disintegrate when he opened his eyes. She wanted to prolong the ecstasy of being held in his arms, but as all good things must come to an end, he eventually awoke and, shifting his arm from under her, rose to a sitting position to stretch.

"Good morning, Tommy." Gaynelle slid her hand onto his smooth chest. She loved the supple feel of his warm skin against her fingertips and the round, rich sound of his name actually emerging from her lips.

He leaned over her, smiling warmly. "Good morning, darlin'."

"I love you." Gaynelle said it because it felt right—pure and true.

"I love you, too." Tommy bent to kiss her soft lips, but his feelings were more ambiguous than hers. There was a sense of happiness, but another, stranger feeling lay over it like a thick quilt. He wasn't used to analyzing his feelings, but Tommy pondered on them as they kissed. Finally, he decided that the feeling had to do with going to work. He wanted to stay with Gaynelle instead. Of course… but no, it wasn't just that he wanted to stay with her. He was afraid of leaving her. The last time he'd left her, he'd lost her. Gaynelle hadn't been there when he'd finally returned. The possibility had never even occurred to him. He'd always assumed she'd be there at her own home when he got back, and he'd returned just as soon as Clayton would hire him again. Then his strange relationship with Jessie had so confounded him. Ever after he hadn't been able to think straight on it, shoving it from his mind. He'd been too ashamed to wonder on Gaynelle after that. There'd been other women since then, but now it seemed that they'd been there just to get by, that the one he'd wanted and needed most was in his arms once more at last.

Having made this realization, his heart swelled with hope. Surely they could overcome their difficulties. They'd done a swimming job of it so far. Her beautiful, trusting eyes made him feel trusting as well, as though all things were possible through their love.

Smiling, he admitted, "I don't wanna leave you today."

"Me, neither." Gaynelle sighed again, sneaking her arms securely around him as if to keep him there.

"I have to go to work," he reminded her. "There's a train arrivin' at the depot. I gotta be there."

Gaynelle ignored him, kissing his jaw line in small pecks. It didn't take much persuasion to keep Tommy in bed, and the couple remained happily occupied for some time. At last, however, Tommy slipped from between the sheets and began getting dressed.

Gaynelle stretched luxuriously. "This is nice, Tommy. Can we do this every day?"

He laughed. "I'd get fired if I came in to work late every day, sweetheart." Then he turned to her in sudden seriousness. "Don't go. Why don't you just stay here?"

She considered this. Aunt Anna had just departed on another brief trip. She wouldn't be back for a fortnight. No one was policing her. It sounded perfect.

She cast him an ecstatic smile. "I'd love to, Tommy."

Thus were the next two weeks spent, excepting brief excursions to the market and to Aunt Anna's house to peek in on Julep, take wonderful hot baths, and retrieve clean clothes. She sent a message to Vivian to let her know where to find her in case of emergency, and then she told Aunt Anna's household staff to contact Vivian if they needed her for any reason. She felt inordinately pleased with her cleverness at coming up with this round-about.

Unfortunately, she ended up having to make an appointment with Dr. Connor for what he called a urinary tract infection, but soon it didn't burn when she peed anymore—and otherwise she had never been so happy. The days flew by in a blur, a haze of lovemaking and talks about everything and nothing—except for the single most important, critical topic of all.

On the last evening before Aunt Anna's return, Gaynelle set the compact wooden table in Tommy's room with candlelight and a simple supper. A sense of dread hung over her, given the news that she was determined to finally share with him. She couldn't let this time together end without telling him about Ginny. It would only become more difficult and awkward—and unforgivable—to wait any longer.

Just before they sat down together, Gaynelle ladled watery potato soup over bowls of rice, unusually silent as they began to eat.

Tommy attempted to chat about his day at work, but she hardly seemed to notice, merely nodding and making absent-minded 'mm-hmm' sounds or saying 'really?' while gazing distractedly about the room. He regarded her with mild consternation but finally decided that she was just bothered about going back to her aunt's house. Trying to comfort her, he said, "Don't worry, sweetheart. I'm not goin' nowhere. We'll still be together, no matter what. We'll figure it out."

Biting her lip, she looked into his loving gaze and knew the moment had come. She could procrastinate no longer. Taking a deep breath, she blurted out, "I have to tell you somethin' important." Immediately, her hands covered her face.

"What is it?"

The kind tone of his voice reminded her of how gentle he'd been after her hair had been shorn. Taking heart, she mumbled through spread fingers, "You're a father."

"Already? How could you possibly know already? You can't be certain!"

At this unexpected reaction, she lowered her hands to stare at him.

His jaw hung open, and he blinked at her.

She repressed a giggle. "No, silly. You've been a father for years."

"What do you mean?" Agitated fingers ran through his hair.

Reaching forward to clasp his other hand, she said simply, "Ginny is our daughter."

He sat in stunned silence. The idea had never entered his mind. He didn't feel ready to be a father. "Wow," he managed.

Gaynelle sat in anticipation, waiting fruitlessly for more of a response. Dismayed, she told him the rest in a garbled rush, "But Mama and Daddy adopted her. I'm sorry, Tommy, but you were away at that automobile factory, and Mama said there was no way to reach you. Daddy thought it was for the best if I was to go on to school. He said I'd be ruint by a baby... but it just didn't seem right."

He shook his head. "Automobile factory? What are you talkin' about?"

"That's where you were workin' when she was born. Leastways, that's what Mama told me."

"I ain't never worked at no car factory. I told you, I worked right there in Manning at that general store the whole time before I went back to work for your pa again." Grasping at the discrepancy, he was still trying to make sense of the situation.

She absorbed his words in disbelief. He'd been so close. If he had only known about the pregnancy, they could have married long ago, been united as a family for all these years.

Noticing her expression at last, he stroked her hand. Trying to bring the conversation back to its subject, he asked, "What can we do about Ginny?"

"Nothing, I guess." Her voice was full of pain as she realized he held no more sway than she did. "Mama made me swear never to contact them again. I signed adoption papers, and they sent me away for good. I see Daddy sometimes, when he comes into town, but that's it."

"I'll be damned." Tommy sat back in his chair, watching helplessly as her tears began to fall. After a while, she retreated to the bed, curling into a ball and weeping bitterly. Tentatively, he began to rub her back, and at last she fell asleep.

At a complete loss and mercilessly wide awake, Tommy left the apartment to find an aid for his overwhelmed, floundering mind—forgetfulness in a bottle.

33 • The Deputy

The music stopped, and Tommy was being asked to leave Howle's restaurant, an out-of-the-way joint located behind the old drugstore. In a stupor from the hooch he had scored, he stumbled outside, down an alley, and then began to wander the streets. It was past midnight, and the town was quiet, but he wasn't yet ready to face Gaynelle. He didn't want to think about children and consequences. He didn't want to think about Mrs. Bell, either—about what they'd done together. He didn't know how he could ever come to terms with having been intimate with both Gaynelle and her mama. He'd avoided unnecessary worries up until now, happily relinquishing such thoughts. As the unprecedented alcohol levels in his circulation began to dwindle, however, they insistently rapped upon his consciousness like a crying babe.

Tommy had never paid much attention to Ginny. He could only recollect a fuzzy image of the child. She had curly hair, maybe blue eyes? Her indistinct image had haunted him all night, but the music and company of the club had helped to diminish her persistent presence in his mind.

The quiet of the street seemed to pierce his thoughts, bringing with it Ginny's small voice. Coming to a standstill, he gave in, allowing himself to say the words aloud. "I have a daughter…"

Swallowing, he again tried to remember Ginny, to allow her image to crystallize. As he did so, a far less welcome image arose, this one dark and sinister.

Jessie's distinct, foreboding visage obfuscated his already hazy recollection of the small girl. Ominous, well-remembered eyes penetrated straight through him, and he found himself running. Her mocking laughter seemed to trail after him.

When the splashing of a fountain filtered through his waking nightmare, Tommy ran towards the sound, the soothing sound of water. Collapsing at the base of the fountain, Tommy clung to its hard rim as though it were a ship, a vessel that could carry him away. At first he clung with all his might, but soon he was fumbling for his liquor bottle, washing away the unremitting thoughts, at length falling asleep there.

"Wake up!"

Tommy winced as someone prodded his ribs, but the light shining through his eyelids made him pinch them fast shut.

"Wake up, boy!"

Tommy sat up and blinked. The blinding light was right in his face. He could make out a deputy sheriff's hat.

"What are you doin' out here?"

"Nothin', sir. Just fell asleep." Slowly, Tommy realized where he was.

"You're drunk." The officer's voice reverberated with disgust. He picked up the empty moonshine bottle and sniffed at it. "Bein' a public nuisance, that's what you're doin'."

Tommy tried to rise but found himself leaning over the fountain. The world spun as though he were on a carousel.

"Alright, you're comin' to the station." The deputy pulled him up, hauling the unwilling young man on foot to the sheriff's office.

Soon cell bars were clanking closed behind Tommy, despite his protests that he needed to get back home.

"Didn't seem in too much of a hurry to me," was the only response.

He was confined to one of three empty cells separated from the main office by a solid wall that effectively blocked his objections. Eventually realizing that his pleas were futile, Tommy miserably availed himself of the cell's woolen blanket and hard cot.

Gaynelle awoke in Tommy's small apartment to find herself alone, yet Tommy's work apron still hung on its peg. Worriedly, she dressed in a knee-length linen dress and pulled her hair back into a simple bun—or a chignon, as Anne had taught her to call it. With only a light coating of powder and an application of lipstick, she slipped on her pumps and coat then left the room to walk down Main Street, eyes peeled for any sign of Tommy.

Might've forgotten his apron, she told herself as she headed towards the pavilion. Beyond it, a group of children played knee-deep in the cold river, not quite daring to swim in it as they did all summer long. A burly, bald fellow was cleaning the pavilion itself; he scowled so fiercely at the sound of Tommy's name that she hurried away, jumping off the pavilion rather than going round to the steps. Wincing as she landed wrong in her pumps, she limped away, hoping she hadn't just made things worse for Tommy. No help was to be had there, clearly—nor, as it turned out, at the empty train depot, drugstores, or any other shops that she could recall him mentioning in their time together.

As she passed by the courthouse, the tap of her heels on the pavement slowed and then came to a halt. She gazed at the Doric columns towering above her, remembering how she'd visited the place once before when she was with her daddy. Her great-uncle's office had been inside, and as far as she knew, he was still sheriff. He might be able to point her in the right direction. She had little idea where to go next, otherwise.

Taking a deep breath, she found her way into the vast structure, and within a few moments she'd located the sheriff's office. A tinkling bell sounded as she opened the door, and an unfamiliar officer not many years older than herself looked up from a crossword puzzle. He quickly tucked it away. "Yes, ma'am. How can I help you?"

"Umm, is Sheriff Bell here?"

"Not yet. Anythin' I do for you?"

"I'm—I'm lookin' for someone who's gone missing."

Without ceremony, the deputy waved at a chair across from his desk. "Alright. Why don't you have a seat here, and we'll fill out a missing person's report."

As she gratefully sank onto the edge of the chair, she noted the aroma of coffee pervading the room.

"First I need your name, ma'am."

"Gaynelle Bell."

He looked up. "Mr. Clay's daughter?"

Startled, she replied, "Yes, I am. Do you know him?"

"He sells vegetables to my uncle." The officer leaned back in his chair with a pleased grin. "Leastways he used to when I worked at the grocery store. I gave you your first marshmallow. Remember?"

Gaynelle peered at the man in surprise. His golden brown eyes were twinkling. She laughed. "We ran from the Chinaman together, didn't we?"

"That's right. I'm Chief Deputy Hammond now, but you can jus' call me Joel, since we're old friends." He was struck by the pretty young woman, amazed by how she had changed. Finally remembering the reason for her visit, he asked with concern, "Who's missing, Gaynelle?"

"Tommy Salters."

Recording the name on his form, Joel inquired, "What's your relationship to the missing person?"

Without batting an eyelash, Gaynelle replied, "He's my fiancé." Anticipating Joel's next question, she rapidly explained, "I gave him some upsetting news last night, and he seems to have left and never come back."

Setting down his pen, Joel shook his head. "Sounds like a normal lover's quarrel to me. Maybe he just went over to his folks'."

"They don't live around here… but maybe."

"I'm sure he'll come back home soon. We see this all the time. Why don't you go on home? Give him a couple o' days. If you don't hear from him within 48 hours, then come back here and we can file a report, check things out for you. I'll call the station wherever his folks live, and they can go see if he's there. But this kind of thing is so common that it's actually our policy to wait a bit to submit an official report."

Joel's kind eyes soothed her fraught nerves. *Of course he's right. Tommy had a shock last night. He just needs some time to sort things out for himself.* Sighing reluctantly, she thanked Joel and rose to leave.

As she headed towards Anne's house, she realized that while there was little she could do for Tommy, it would be best if she got home before her aunt returned, rather than be found frantically searching for a missing lover, a lover Anne had never even met. She'd only been gone for two weeks. Gaynelle bit her lip. *She'd be just so proud at findin' out that I've been shackin' up with him this entire time.*

Hurrying home, she willed herself to calm down. No need to cause Anne unnecessary disappointment and worry. Gaynelle would just have to trust that she would hear from Tommy soon.

34 • Sheriff Bell

D EPUTY JOEL HAMMOND LEANED BACK IN HIS CHAIR, reflecting on the young woman. Her case was not particularly intriguing, but he was tickled to make her acquaintance once more. She still had that same sweet energy that he remembered, and she'd grown up well—she had a right pleasing appearance. It was too bad that she was already engaged. He sighed. *To be expected. Just my luck.*

The town clock chimed the hour, reminding Joel to check on the lollygagger from the night before, for all that he'd rather just pretend the fellow didn't exist. Joel had little patience for drunkards and loiterers when so many citizens worked so hard to make their town a beautiful place, but they generally didn't hold first-time offenders. Nevertheless, as distasteful as it was to interact with the county's sorriest elements, he'd chosen this career, and he needed to get the boy's information before the sheriff showed up.

Hauling open the reinforced metal door that divided the jail from the main office area, he entered to find the loiterer perched on the edge of his cot, already awake. By the time Joel reached the cell, the fellow was gripping the bars that separated them.

Joel gave him a hard look. "I need to get your identification, young man. We don't take kindly to folks loiterin' around our town, especially not with illegal booze."

Tommy stammered, "Yes, sir. I—I apologize, sir. I made unwise decisions last night, and I won't do it again."

"Just give me your name," Joel said, but he was somewhat mollified. He reached for the cell keys hanging from his belt, reflecting that he'd rather not have to do unnecessary paperwork.

"Thomas Salters."

Joel snorted in disgust. *This* was Gaynelle's fiancé? "What brought you to public drunkenness, Thomas?"

"I'm sorry, sir. I just found out I have a kid. I didn't even know."

Head shaking, Joel wondered with surprise if Gaynelle was a mother already and how she had kept it a secret. "Sounds pretty irresponsible of you. Sure ain't no reason to go makin' a nuisance of yourself."

"You're right, sir. I swear I won't let it happen again."

Joel paused. *Sheriff Bell is kin to Gaynelle. Perhaps I should relay these goings-on to him first, just to keep him in the loop.* He would certainly appreciate the same consideration regarding his own family. Sighing, he let go of the keys. But perhaps he'd wait on the paperwork anyhow. The sheriff might prefer to avoid putting his family's private business on the books. So instead of releasing Tommy or getting any more information from him, he simply acquired some breakfast for the young derelict then settled back in the main office to await the sheriff.

The old sheriff arrived at the office shortly after ten o'clock. He'd held the same position since before his deputies were born and had gradually transferred most of his duties into their capable hands. He now kept a somewhat reduced schedule at the office, but he still tried to stay abreast of the town's happenings.

"Hello, Joel." Sheriff Bell greeted his chief deputy with a hearty clap on the shoulder. Joel was not only his most reliable and trusted officer, but the most likeable, too.

"Hey, Sheriff. I have a situation that might be of interest to you." Joel quickly recounted the events of the night and morning.

"Where's the write-up?" the sheriff asked as he grabbed the jail key.

"I was waitin' on that. Wasn't sure you'd want me to write it up."

The old man nodded then made his way back to the cell holding the young man, making sure the dividing door clicked closed behind him.

Three hours later, a rather shell-shocked sheriff re-entered the main office. His many years of inquisitorial experience had allowed him to glean more from the scared young man than he'd first expected—but had in no way prepared him to cope with what he'd learned.

Initially, he'd only meant to meet the young man and to validate Joel's assessment of him, but he'd been intrigued by the gaps in Salter's story. Each time he learned more, he'd felt it necessary to delve a bit deeper, until at last he'd ruthlessly scoured the boy for all of his personal associations with Clayton's family. The old sheriff had been jarred to hear the boy admit to an affair with Jessie. He'd only guessed it in half-jest due to a suspicious, repetitive eye aversion when her name was mentioned. He'd actually assumed the eye movements were a mere indication of the boy's fear of Jessie, a natural-enough reaction to his niece, but the moment he suggested the affair, he'd recognized the truth of it in Salter's abashed face.

Sheriff Bell wiped his brow then sank into a chair, muttering invectives to himself.

Joel observed the generally unflappable old man with concern, thinking about his heart troubles. Happenings in their relatively quiet town rarely seemed to provoke him that way, but you never knew.

"Have some water, sir." Joel handed the sheriff a glass and sat down across from him. "What's going on, sir?"

Sheriff Bell regarded him with stony eyes. Determined to resolve his family's scandal without airing their knickers any more than necessary, he merely said, "I'm gonna go see some o' my kinfolk today, an' that boy's comin' with me."

Jessie pulled onto the main road and turned right. She was headed to drop off their weekly delivery of vegetables and eggs with Uncle

Simms. It was Clayton's idea to continue taking the produce over there, even after Amarintha had moved back in with them.

Amarintha usually accompanied her—had in fact become her rather constant companion—but this time she had stayed home with Ginny and Annie, quite amiably shooing Jessie out the door. "Go on, git! You need a break from all dis catterwallin'."

Rushing off without an argument, Jessie was relieved to get away for a while. Tension eased from her shoulders as she listened to the rhythmic squeak of the wagon and the plodding steps of the mule.

Just past the gate to the New Market Cemetery, a motorcar could be heard approaching. She soon made out the Ford police wagon with its familiar figure inside, a cloud of dust trailing behind. The vehicle slowed as it approached, pulling over to the side of the road just after passing her.

Jessie reined in the mule. She climbed down, curious as to what her uncle was doing out in Greeleyville. Still in an unusually amiable mood, Jessie greeted her childhood guardian near the rear of her wagon. "Good afternoon, Uncle Joe. What brings you out this way?"

He opened his mouth then closed it, seeming perplexed.

"We weren't expectin' you, were we?" At his head shake, she asked, "Everythin' alright?"

"Afternoon, Jessie," he finally said, his expression serious. "I actually came out here to see you, honey."

"What's goin' on?" As the question fell from her lips, Jessie spied a backseat passenger in the police wagon. Tommy had turned in his seat to look at them, and a flicker of unease shot through her.

Sheriff Bell sucked in his breath then slowly blew it out. "I been talkin' to this boy, an' turns out there's been some real objectionable goings-on at your place."

Jessie frowned. "What do you mean?"

The old man looked her straight in the eye. "I mean that you been cheatin' on Clay. You know I can't jus' allow this to go on."

After a long moment of silence, Jessie matched his solemn gaze with one of irritation. "That's ridiculous."

"I don't think so. It was mighty curious when you had a baby after all that time, an' it all fits together now that I done heard the story. Makes me sick to my stomach. The boy's scared to death, but I brought him along. He's gotta face repercussions."

Jessie scowled. "For what, aside from makin' up some cockamamie story? Maybe he's mad at me for some reason, but don't you dare repeat that to Clay."

Sheriff Bell folded his arms. "I'm gonna tell Clay myself, then let 'im do what he wants with the boy. That's what I'd want if I were in his shoes."

Even as he spoke, the sheriff felt his resolve wavering. Her point was well taken that the boy could be holding a grudge. Jessie had a knack for getting under folks' skin. He'd hate to ruin her current situation. She'd settled so nicely with Clayton. The thought spurred an increasingly familiar spasm of angina to shoot through his chest. He caught his breath, realizing what a shame it would be to disrupt their stability, for his own sake as much as anyone's. He might be responsible for her again—her and her ill-begotten children. He couldn't imagine having to take them all in.

Meanwhile, as the sheriff tried to breathe through his chest pain, Jessie's mind whirred. *Uncle Joe's a no-nonsense man, but he looks miserable. Always tryin', in that pathetic, idealistic way of his, to do the right thing. But now that overzealous sense of justice is takin' such a hold of him that it's threatenin' my family's well-being. Threatenin' our future.*

"Uncle Joe," Jessie said evenly, smoothing her skirt and trying to sound reasonable. "Ain't wise to go upsettin' everyone like this. The boy's confused—he had a bit of a hankerin' for me, and sometimes he tried to tell me his fantasies, but I didn't pay him no mind. I sure didn't repeat that nonsense to Clay. He was real good help to Clay, and good help's hard to find."

"Good help?" her uncle gasped. "I'd hardly want that kinda help around my own place."

"Oh gracious. He didn't usually talk that way. Of course not. I wouldn't have put up with too much foolishness. You know me better than that." Jessie raised her brows so convincingly that he nodded. "Was he drunk or somethin' when he told you those things? Can't you just let it go?"

Studying her face as he struggled to take regular, deep breaths, he decided that she seemed open and guileless, as open and guileless as Jessie had ever seemed in his experience with her. Increasingly torn, he truly wanted to believe her explanation. It was far preferable to the scenario he'd ferreted from the young stranger. The old man's expression softened and his breathing eased as he gratefully reconsidered. "Well, you know, it is kinda far-fetched, I guess. I'm sorry, darlin'. I think I just get carried away sometimes."

"I hate that this upset you so much, but it's good the way you look out for us, Uncle Joe. I don't know what woulda happened to me if you hadn't taken me in so long ago, after my stepdad booted me out. You always did pay attention to what needed takin' care of, and I love you for it, even if this time it wasn't what you thought."

She punctuated her words with a well-timed hug. To her surprise, as she leaned her head against her uncle's shoulder, a surge of real affection washed over her. The bay rum of his aftershave filled her nostrils, and her shoulders began to relax. It was a bit unsettling to realize how much he had done for her—and how gullible he could be.

"Aww, now, I gotta look after my family," he said gruffly, beaming at the unaccustomed warmth from his niece, grateful that this was all working itself out.

Lifting her cheek from his uniform shirt, she suggested, "Y'all headed back to town, then? I'd invite you over, but Clay is in the middle of a mighty messy construction project right now. He's puttin' a new room on the house."

Patting her back, the sheriff answered thoughtfully, "Well, now, I think I'll jus' mosey on up to your house anyway if that's alright with you. I got some other business 'bout this boy to discuss with him."

"What business is that?"

He looked at her for a long moment and then nodded. "Seems Salters is plannin' on marryin' Gaynelle, and I just don't think he's a fit match fer that girl."

Jessie stiffened. Tommy was going to *marry* Gaynelle? Wisps of alarm coiled around her mind. They'd try to take Ginny. He might figure out about Annie, too.

Sheriff Bell noticed her change in demeanor. "Yeah, I know. We need to put a stop to this. Can't have Gaynelle ruinin' all that schoolin' and wastin' that sacrifice y'all made 'bout Ginny on this boy."

Startled, Jessie glanced up in surprise, and Uncle Joe said with chagrin, "Oh, yeah, he told me about that, too, an' I believed it. Is that part true?"

Jessie's carefully constructed life was about to unravel. She had safeguarded the secret of Ginny's parentage so well that not even the child knew. Tommy hadn't known, either, she was sure, before his reunion with Gaynelle. Now it was apparent that Uncle Joe was determined to sort things out. He didn't have the foresight nor the worldliness to understand the sacrifices she'd made. He didn't know or value her lifetime's work to assemble the family that she craved. He was a threat to her marriage, to her entire life plan, and as such had little useful future value that she could clearly see. Swallowing, Jessie steeled herself. The time had come to make yet another sacrifice for her future, for Clayton's future, for her family's future. Uncle Joe would want it that way if he really understood—he valued his family that much. Unbidden tears rose in her eyes, then a pathetic pang of remorse racked her body, a sensation she wasn't at all used to. Her shoulders began to shake.

"Aw, honey, it'll be alright." The old man hugged her to him again, and she clung there for a brief moment, accepting his comfort before pulling away, drawing his pistol from his shoulder holster as she did so.

Jessie stepped back from him, allowing the tears to just slide down her cheeks. They were entirely pointless, but they didn't really hinder her so long as she could see to shoot straight. She cocked the hammer, leveling it at his head. He only had the slightest moment of alarmed confusion before she pulled the trigger of the Smith & Wesson .38 special, dropping him to the ground in a lifeless heap.

If only Sheriff Joseph Bell hadn't been so determined to straighten out his family members' messy lives, he could have been peacefully eating dinner with his wife just then. If only he had retired from service years before, as many had suggested and pleaded with him to do, he could have avoided this catastrophe. There were so many 'if only's' that could have made the difference for the unfortunate old man, but it seemed that he had been destined to follow this course, that fate had meant for his life to end on a dusty road on the outskirts of Greeleyville.

The value of his sacrifice can only be perceived in hindsight, in how it affected the other participants of the brutal scene—for young Tommy, a boy who ill-understood malice, had witnessed the atrocity. The trauma of the crime and its fallout were to scar him for life, his resilience no match for the cold-bloodedness of the encounter. It was to influence all future generations of the family.

After wrapping Sheriff Bell's jacket around his bloody head, Jessie tried in vain to pick up her uncle's body. At last she thought of Tommy, now absent from the patrol car's backseat window.

Approaching the car, she found him quaking in the floorboard. She breathed a sigh of relief, understanding at last why he was there. It was divine providence. She needed the assistance. This spontaneous incident had not had the proper planning and preparation that she typically preferred, but God always looked after her.

Opening the car door, she said calmly, "Come on out here. I need your help."

The young man kept shaking and refused to look up.

Rolling her eyes, she cocked the pistol. "Move it, Tommy."

He scrambled out of the vehicle, and she could see that he had wet himself.

"Put him in the back of the wagon," she instructed. Jessie didn't help their former farm laborer as he struggled with the large man. It seemed wisest to keep the revolver leveled at Tommy.

Once he had finished hoisting the figure into the wagon, Jessie directed him to guide the mule into the cemetery, where she scanned the plots. Triumphantly, she pointed at a fresh grave. "Over there."

Exploring the wagon for some sort of digging tool, Jessie rejoiced at finding the long-handled shovel. It was there for getting them out of ruts in the road but was often forgotten at home, especially in summertime after a farmhand used it. She'd been stuck more than once without it. Keeping the firearm on Tommy, she said, "Break up the earth and dig with this."

As he worked, she wondered what to do with the young man. It was foolhardy to even consider letting him go free. She liked Tommy. He had pleasured her and had provided hope for a son. He had given her Annie. Nevertheless, this was clearly not a time for feeblemindedness. God was calling her to make an oblation in gratitude for her relationship with Clayton, and she would do so. Despite the onset of aging that she couldn't deny, she still adored her husband with all of her heart. She had to remember that her affair with Tommy had been for Clayton all along, to produce a son for him. Tommy was an expendable tool—once useful, now a risk. Jessie gazed at his handsome face while he worked, determined to savor these last moments with her beautiful offering.

He quickly cleared the loose earth down to the recently-interred coffin. Wiping his forehead with a shaky hand, he looked up questioningly.

"Pull the body from the wagon and throw it in." Jessie bit her lip as he followed her instructions. The penultimate sacrifice of her uncle had not been easier than this one would be. He was so young.

Once the body was in the grave, Tommy picked up the shovel and began to toss the dirt back in.

It was at this critical moment that Jessie made her mistake. She stepped closer to her quarry, and a twig snapped.

His nerves were already on edge when she cocked the revolver. He bolted around as she cracked a shot. The bullet narrowly missed his head. Instinctively, he swung the shovel with all his might, knocking her to the ground.

He took to his heels. Shots rained after him as he sprinted out of the cemetery. Once on the road, he looked about desperately. The police wagon was still sitting on the shoulder. He dashed to the automobile and began frantically spinning the crank, fear fueling his speed and agility. The motor of the well-tuned police vehicle sprang to life, and he jumped into the driver's seat. Jessie was running towards him with the shovel when he pulled the vehicle onto the road. He floored the gas pedal, hurtling away from the site with filthy, blood-tainted hands.

35• Keeping Family Secrets

TWO LONG DAYS HAD PASSED since Sheriff Bell had left with the Salters boy, and there was still no sign of them. Deputy Joel Hammond had been out to see Clayton and Jessie Bell himself, but they had merely expressed surprise at his inquiry. The pipe-smoking old woman and little girls had clearly not seen the men, either.

When Gaynelle came back into the office to file the missing person's report, Joel admitted the gist of what had transpired and told her that both the sheriff and Tommy were missing. A report had already been filed.

Joel felt overwhelming concern for the sad young woman, who accepted his words with a surreal calmness.

Since Tommy's departure, Gaynelle had been painfully reminded that this had been the consequence of loving Tommy before. Their love was simply too good and pure for the universe to allow, a universe that was now counterbalancing that exquisite joy. As Tommy had filled her with warmth and happiness, so would the bliss now be ripped from her heart, her soul trampled. She accepted her fate with resignation, glad enough to pay the price for the brief time they had together, praying for the opportunity to do so again, no matter the outcome.

Though she had dreamt of their future together and had exclusively known happiness while with him, when he'd left the brutal realities of life had hit—and they did so with an intensity that left her weary and war-torn, physically as well as emotionally. As she considered this, she shifted uncomfortably. An itch had started to bother her in the last day or so. There seemed to be some kind of rash in her private area, and she didn't even want to think about what the strange discharge might mean. It was all too much.

Joel treated her kindly but asked her to the station for routine questioning. It couldn't be helped. He was hoping for some clue, for any information she might be able to share about Tommy, who was, of course, the primary suspect.

During the course of their interview, Joel learned about the heartbreaking adoption of their daughter, Ginny. Wishing to be of service to the bereft young woman, Joel grasped hold of a slim possibility for assisting Gaynelle, completely aside from the investigation, and suggested that he could accompany her to see her child.

"Perhaps with an officer of the law supporting you, they'll be more willing to allow some form of visitation. You'd be surprised at how people will bend if they think the law's involved, regardless of what the word of law actually says." Joel shrugged. "Heck, half the police officers in this state don't care what the law says, nohow. They think badges like these make *them* the law."

Gaynelle smiled wanly. Joel was a solid man, a comforting, warm-hearted person—someone she could trust and rely upon—and his suggestion to see Ginny was unexpected but welcome, even if her heart was at that moment in the process of fracturing.

When the deputy's Model T Touring motorcar drove into her yard yet again, Jessie swore and braced herself. She should have known that she could never have more than a moment's peace to herself.

Strangely enough, she'd finally been relishing another rare quiet moment, this one at the house, as Clayton and Amarintha had taken the girls with them to the lumber mill.

It took a few moments for Jessie to identify Gaynelle, but when she did, her heart slowed to a crawl.

Seconds later, the classy young woman had ascended the porch steps. She approached Jessie and gave her a hug as if she weren't in direct defiance of their agreement, saying, "Hey, Mama. I've missed you. Your camellias are lookin' real pretty."

Jessie looked over her shoulder at the deputy sheriff as she returned the hug.

"What brings you out here?" Jessie asked without a trace of a smile. "I thought we'd agreed that you were gonna stay in Kingstree with your fine relations there."

"Well, Mama." Gaynelle swallowed hard. "I am a grown woman now. Haven't you missed me at all?"

Jessie sighed. "That has nothin' to do with it, and you know it."

"Yes, ma'am, I know. But I would… I'd like to talk with you about spendin' some time with my daughter."

"*Your* daughter?" Jessie scoffed. She shook her head, crossing her arms. "No, honey. Thank the Lord they ain't home right now. All our work to give her a stable upbringin', and you wanna confuse her like that? How selfish, Gaynelle. For shame."

"Please, Mama. Let's talk about it."

Tossing her hands up in exasperation, Jessie nodded towards the house. "Ain't nothin' to talk about, but if you insist, I'll let you have your say just this once, since you're already here."

"Thank you, Mama."

"This can't become a habit," Jessie sharply reminded her as they climbed the porch steps. "Can't go ruinin' all the sacrifices we've made to cover *your* mistakes. I'm just glad Clay's gone out with the girls right now."

"Well now, maybe there didn't have to be any sacrifice, ma'am," interjected Joel as the screen door clattered behind him.

Jessie's withering glance was enough to send his own gaze to the wooden floor. She asked, "Did y'all ever find Tommy or my uncle?"

He shook his head.

"You think a teenage girl could've raised a child on her own?"

"I coulda married Tommy!" Gaynelle cried. "He loves me!"

"Neither o' you chillun was in any condition to be gettin' married."

"He was workin'. And I know now that you lied about him," Gaynelle added in an accusing tone, then bit her tongue. *We could have married*, she thought furiously, trying not to glare at Jessie. *He never, ever worked in an automobile factory.*

"Lied?"

"I know everythin'—Tommy told me."

Jessie took a step back, daunted. She'd never have suspected in a thousand harvests that the boy would wag his tongue so much about their affair. He'd seemed such a discreet youth. She'd never had a clue that he had been the one to impregnate Gaynelle until the girl told her later. That's why Jessie had picked him. She'd deemed their secret safe, but it seemed he had not only told the old sheriff but Gaynelle, too. Jessie could only assume that this other officer knew as well. "Sounds like we have a lot to talk about. Let me get y'all some tea, and we'll sit down."

Backing into her kitchen, Jessie's hand shook as she slid open a drawer filled with knives. In the rear of the drawer, she had erected a false wooden back, behind which lay the revolver. Cursing herself for not yet buying more bullets, she took out the sharpest, longest, thinnest blade they had and, wrapping a handtowel loosely around it, slipped it into her apron. She could bring the tea up from behind the deputy and then take him out with a quick slice to the throat. After that, it would be a simple matter to eliminate Gaynelle with the officer's own gun. Yes, that would be the wisest course of action. She couldn't allow them to disrupt her family, to tell Clayton of her affair, the affair she'd had for his sake.

As she pushed the drawer shut, the rumble of wagon wheels sounded in the lane. She closed her eyes, grateful they hadn't returned just a few minutes later. She couldn't possibly have cleared the bodies before being discovered. *What was I thinkin'?* Jessie heaved a sigh of relief at being spared the life-ruining situation. *But what am I gonna do now?* Her mind continued to churn, fueled by fear. She was in a precarious position, but there was still something Gaynelle wanted: the adoption papers plainly stated that she had given up her rights to the child.

"Alright, Gaynelle." Jessie clasped her shaking hands behind her as she stepped into the living room again. "Seems we both have secrets we'd like to be kept quiet. You know my main desire is for Ginny to feel secure, right?" Jessie adopted her most caring expression.

The young woman nodded slowly.

"So, if you wanna spend time with her," Jessie continued, trying to contain her urgency, "I'm gonna ask that you do so as her sister. Can you keep our secrets, Gaynelle?" Jessie forced her hands to unclench. In mere seconds the little girl and Clayton would be bursting in.

Gaynelle's face lit up. Hardly daring to believe the offer, she clarified, "So, you mean that I *can* have time with Ginny? I can take her to town and show her around?"

"So long as you are only ever her *sister*, and keep our family secrets. You shall *never* talk to anyone about our family secrets, understood?" Jessie's hands clasped back together so tightly that her knuckles grew white. She was taking a great risk, but it seemed her only option at this point.

Nodding, Gaynelle pressed her lips together, suppressing the shout of joy that threatened to erupt. She needed to seem as contained as humanly possible for Mama, but her heart leapt as footsteps clambered onto the porch. She raced to the door to embrace her daddy and take a peek at her girl—her *sister*.

Clayton was dumbfounded at Gaynelle's hug, which he heartily returned. Despite having been to visit the young woman a handful of times while in Kingstree delivering produce, he certainly never expected to see her here at the house again. He was speechless at her presence, *especially* with an escort from the sheriff's department.

He was still trying to gather himself when Gaynelle bent to greet the curly-headed girl who was gazing at her with such curiosity. In fact, Gaynelle had first mistaken Annie for Ginny—before the curly-headed girl had run into the house after the others. In fact, she still didn't quite recognize Ginny. This child's hair was several shades darker than the blond baby she remembered. "Hello, what's your name?"

The girl hid behind Clayton's legs but peeked out to answer. "I'm Ginny."

"I'm your sister Gaynelle. Would you like to come to town with me sometime? We could go to a movie and get ice cream." Gaynelle smiled broadly at the child.

"Really?" Ginny's eyes grew wide, and she turned for approval from her mama. "I can go with the fancy lady?"

"Yes, Ginny. Your sister is quite the grown-up now, isn't she?" The hint of a smile played around the corners of Jessie's own mouth, despite herself. She was fairly melting with relief. Gaynelle appeared to have no intention, at least for the time being, of causing any serious trouble for her. Strolling over to Clayton, Jessie leaned against him rather uncharacteristically.

He put an arm around her and viewed his family with satisfaction. Noticing the young man again, Clayton addressed him. "Thanks for bringing her by, Deputy Hammond. Was there any more official business that you were needin' to take care of?"

Joel shook his head. "No sir, Mr. Clay. I'm just here in the capacity of a friend."

Clayton tilted his head with pleased interest. He recalled the young man from years of dealing with him at the grocer's. He'd been a nice boy. "Alright, then I'm glad she has you fer a friend, Joel. This reunion needed to happen." His tone dropped as he added, "On that note, has there been any word on Uncle Joe or Tommy?"

The officer shook his head again. "We'll let you know if we find out anything."

36 • An Outing with Ginny

Almost three months later
March 1926, en route between Kingstree and Greeleyville

THE DAY OF GAYNELLE'S FIRST OUTING WITH GINNY arrived at last. Jessie had managed to push it off for a while, but Clayton and Joel had, between them, finally hammered out a set date. Meanwhile, Anne had created a pair of matching, floral-print frocks for them. Gaynelle was wearing hers, and Ginny's was in a satchel on the floorboard of Joel's motorcar.

Joel was there for a myriad of reasons. Firstly, he was interested in helping Gaynelle reunite with her daughter for purely joyful, philanthropic reasons. Secondly, he had little better to do on a Saturday, so he was happy to spend it with the attractive young woman. The most pressing reason, however, had to do with the sense of foreboding he'd had when they'd met with Jessie on the previous trip. The small hairs on the back of his neck had tingled almost the entire time they were in the clapboard house, the same curious reaction he had when he escorted violent prisoners to court. Maybe it wasn't much of a reason, but Joel felt an otherwise-inexplicable concern for Gaynelle's safety.

This was one of those uncharacteristically warm days in March. They wore hats to keep the sun from their eyes, hers a bright orange hat with an extra-wide brim, tied on to keep it from flying off, and his a typical Homberg. He had donned a Bryan's classic suit, wanting to keep some hint of respectful formality for the occasion, and Anne had nodded approvingly when he came by to pick up Gaynelle.

Gaynelle's pensive mood had lightened for a moment. She'd draped her arm around Anne's shoulders and said in a teasing manner, "Aunt Anna has a thing for Bryan Fashions."

Anne smiled mysteriously. "I do sometimes buy their designs."

"Ready made!" Gaynelle exclaimed, as if that were contraband.

"Not illegal," Joel laughed.

"I told you I'm sentimental," Anne said.

"Vivian's pegged her as a romantic." Gaynelle turned to Joel. "What do you think?"

"Maybe." He shrugged awkwardly. "Ready to head out?"

On the way to pick up Ginny, Joel regained his element, fondly recalling the chicanery of his youth, picking up his tales where they'd left off so many years before. He'd been something of a town rascal, he informed her, operating in cahoots with a whole band of miscreants who all turned out in the end to be pillars of the community—each working off the various debts to society accrued in his youth, such as that time they'd set off a Civil War cannon during a commemorative celebration. They'd done it intentionally but hadn't actually believed the cannon would work. "Golly, were we lucky that nobody got hurt that day."

Gaynelle smiled gratefully at the distraction, otherwise still preoccupied with her worries about Tommy and nervous about the day with her daughter. *I hope Tommy's alright. I wonder if Ginny will like the dress? Does he have a warm place to sleep? I wonder if she'll like me? Will she be scared? Is he scared? I wish he could be with us today.*

A decent judge of human nature, Joel could sense Gaynelle's mood and eventually fell silent, turning his attention instead to the drooping lavender wisteria and bright yellow jasmine blooms that graced patches of the woods alongside the fields they passed.

When they arrived at the farmhouse, Ginny ran out to meet them. She jumped up and down in the yard next to their vehicle and burst out excitedly, "You came! You came!"

"Of course," laughed Gaynelle as she climbed out holding the parcel. "And I brought you a new dress to wear today that matches mine. It was made by someone very special to me."

Ginny held her breath, nodding excitedly. She seized the satchel and ran inside to change clothes, calling out as she disappeared, "I'll be right back!"

Jessie was coming out of the house as Ginny was going in, and Gaynelle heard her mutter in a tone of irritable resignation, "Mind you take care of that. Might be the only frivolous getup you ever get."

Then she was outside, reluctantly greeting the visitors. "Would y'all like to come in for some tea?"

Before Gaynelle could answer, Joel said, "Thank you, ma'am, but we're anxious to make it on time for the matinee, so we'll be off as soon as Ginny's ready to go."

Gaynelle glanced at him in surprise but didn't argue. "Will it be alright if Ginny doesn't come home until late? We have a lot planned for today."

Jessie nodded, seeming about to speak when Ginny dashed past her, back to the vehicle.

"Bye, Mama!" the girl yelled, clambering in the middle of the bench seat, full of excitement about her new adventure.

"You behave," Jessie called. She watched pensively as they situated themselves inside the motorcar.

Once they were back on the road, Ginny turned to Gaynelle and asked, "Is the policeman going with us to see the movie?" Not so much as casting a glance his way, the girl thrust her lower lip out.

"Oh…" Gaynelle was dismayed at the remark, but Joel laughed easily.

He had been most concerned about their safety for the trip and had no pressing desire to see *Felix the Cat*. He could have watched the new Mary Pickford action-adventure flick again---her husband, Douglas Fairbanks, had made a swashbuckling 'black pirate'—but he'd do better to get some work done instead. "Don't worry, Curly-top. How about I let you and your m—ouch!—*sister* have the day to yourselves once we get to town? I can drop you two off at Mrs. Sanders' house and pick you up there about seven to take you back home, how about that?"

Ginny nodded, snuggling contentedly against Gaynelle. She was convinced that this was going to be the best day ever—even when Gaynelle laughed aloud and pointed out that her new dress was situated backwards.

Gaynelle helped turn the wayward dress around as Joel continued to drive. While they fussed with it, she managed to forget her worries. Ginny brought her fully into the moment—a state of awareness that only a child's presence can bring about for long.

"Ginny, meet Julep. Julep, meet Ginny." Gaynelle made the introductions with a flourish. "Julep belonged to my mother. Then our daddy took care of him until he let me bring him to Kingstree with me. Eddie takes care of him here, but I try to see him as much as I can. He's gettin' quite old."

Patting the thoroughbred's smooth neck, Ginny asked hopefully, "Can I ride him?"

"Maybe next time. You'll hafta ride with me, and I'll need different clothes. But here, you can feed him." Gaynelle felt responsible and motherly as she dealt the young girl a handful of oats and showed her how to hold her palm out flat.

"It tickles!" Ginny giggled.

Gaynelle laughed, too, her heart full. She would have to plan out all the things she wanted to share with Ginny—*and there is plenty of time for that*, she told herself with more conviction than she felt. *This visit is just one of many to come.*

"Okay." Ginny turned abruptly. "Can I see your house?"

"It's Aunt Anna's house, not mine, but you can see it."

The girl gasped in amazement as Gaynelle led her into the spacious home. The Queen Anne edifice seemed as much a mansion to her as it first had to Gaynelle.

When Ginny saw the restroom, complete with a porcelain, claw-footed tub, actual running hot water, and its octagonal stained-glass window, she lingered there until Gaynelle managed to coax her out to see the tapestry in the hallway.

"I've always loved this fairytale scene," she called.

"What's a fairytale?" Ginny poked her head out of the bathroom door.

Gaynelle gestured towards the thickly-woven rendering of the well-known fable, recalling a similar conversation with Aunt Anna so many years ago. In this case, however, Ginny was too young to read her own stories—but *her mother* could read aloud to her. She caught her breath at the notion.

Ginny was already regarding the tapestry intently. Bending to Ginny's eye level, Gaynelle answered her question with great solemnity. "Well, a fairytale is a story about magic and make-believe people from long ago. Sometimes they're princes and princesses. This tapestry is about one called Rapunzel. I have it in a beautiful storybook full of fairytales. Would you like me to read the story of Rapunzel to you?"

At Ginny's eager nod, Gaynelle directed the girl into her own room, where she pulled down Anne's old leather-bound, gilded copy of the Grimm's fairytales from the ornate bookcase. Nearly giddy with anticipation, she opened the worn volume to the tale of *Rapunzel* and began to read aloud. As she read, she showed Ginny the beautiful illustrations, delighting when Ginny grew excited over the depiction of Rapunzel's hair tumbling from the tower towards the prince, "Just like in the tapestry!"

As Ginny grabbed the storybook to examine the art more closely, Gaynelle found herself musing about the original, darker tale, also on her shelves, in which Rapunzel's romance was only found out by the old sorceress due to a pregnancy of which Rapunzel was unaware, much as had happened in Gaynelle's own life. She sighed and wrapped an arm more firmly around Ginny.

This later version that Ginny now held was somewhat apropos as well. Rapunzel's prince was discovered due to a slip of the girl's tongue about her hair, which was then viciously hacked off by the angry sorceress. In both tales, Rapunzel was forced to leave her home in the tower and wander alone in the wilderness, until at last she found her prince and traveled to his kingdom to live happily ever after.

Little did Gaynelle know quite how well the story really did fit her own situation, for Tommy, like the prince, had been tormented by the young woman's caretaker, who had also taken his beloved when she was yet a babe from her real mother. He, too, had been wandering aimlessly through the wilderness after the assault by the old sorceress's likeness. Now, in the steps of the prince, he was very close to reuniting with his beloved, and bliss was very nearly within their grasp—if only life were as predictable as a fairytale.

Whrough Ginny and Gaynelle had their afternoon alone, Joel made his way to the courthouse, where he planned to spend the hours clearing up paperwork. It had mounted significantly since the disappearance of the sheriff. As he settled in to work at his desk, however, he received a call that the sheriff's Ford wagon had surfaced far down the Santee River. No bodies had yet been found.

He glanced at the clock, determining whether or not he had enough time to drive down to the site to confirm the identification of the vehicle and scan for evidence. He pulled on his coat and Homberg, deciding at last to stop by Mrs. Sanders' house to let Gaynelle know about the situation, in case he took longer than expected.

When he rang the doorbell, Gaynelle and her miniature floral-chiffon replica answered in high spirits.

Joel smiled at the picture they presented, then reluctantly shared, "I've just received word regarding the sheriff and Tommy."

Gaynelle's eyes lit up, and she threw her arms around him. "I knew you'd find them. Where are they?"

Startled at her response, Joel realized that she had misunderstood, but he waited a moment to correct himself, enjoying the feel of the young woman's supple arms around him. Distractedly, he breathed in her rose perfume. Finally, however, he recentered himself and relayed what he knew of the wagon's discovery, of the urgency of surveying the find.

Her face furrowed with concern as she drew away from him. "So, if there are no bodies, then they weren't in the vehicle, right? They weren't in the river?"

"I'm afraid we just don't know yet," Joel shook his head. "The wagon top was open, and their bodies would likely have at least partially decomposed by now. Gators and other river critters may have already eliminated any possibility of finding them."

At this, Gaynelle's eyes widened with the unwilling admission, "So, you think Tommy's dead?"

"I'm sorry, but that's how it seems." Joel patted her arm sympathetically. "Unless… I been thinkin'. Maybe he's got nothin' to do with the sheriff and that accident. Could be the sheriff let him go, and he just hopped a train to skip on out of town. You said he worked some at the depot, isn't that right?"

Gaynelle sniffed, then nodded. "He was awfully upset even before he got arrested. So you think maybe he'd simply had enough trouble, just wanted to get away from it all?"

A wave of dizziness came over her, and she put her hand towards Joel to steady herself. He took her elbow and led her into the house.

Even as Joel and Gaynelle discussed him, a tattered, filthy young man stood across the street, observing them. He had arrived only moments before and had been trying to build up the nerve to approach the house when the familiar officer had appeared in plainclothes. The young vagrant had lost all capacity for movement when he saw Gaynelle and Ginny together, looking like a picture in their identical outfits. His fleeting happiness at the sight of them dispersed instantly, however, when Gaynelle embraced the man. Tommy's heart sank as they all went inside the house.

They make a beautiful family, he admitted. His own prospects for providing a decent lifestyle were ever dwindling, given his probable status as a fugitive. With a bitter taste in his mouth, Tommy turned and began to walk away—away from the life he now realized was never meant to be his, no matter how lovely and possible it had seemed for a brief time.

While directing his Ford out of town, Joel spied a disheveled figure dashing towards an alley. The deputy sighed with exasperation and pulled over to check it out. As the vagabond entered the alley, Joel called for him to stop.

He continued to sprint away—and might have escaped if a stray brick hadn't tripped him up.

The next moment, Joel was looming over the runaway. He leveled his revolver. "Stay down! Don't move!"

The young man stilled when he heard the cock of the pistol. At Joel's command for him to get up slowly with his hands raised high, he protested half-heartedly, "I ain't done nothin'!"

It was then that the officer recognized the lollygagger, who looked even worse for wear than he had in the jail. "Well, I'll be damned."

"I ain't done nothin'," Tommy repeated, climbing to his feet.

Joel steadied the gun again. "Where's Sheriff Bell?"

"He's dead. But I didn't kill him, no matter what Mrs. Bell says."

"How do you mean?"

"Mrs. Bell shot him dead. Then she tried to shoot me, too, but I ran." Given the loaded pistol aimed at his head, it seemed important to be as succinct as possible. Being alone in a deserted alley with the sheriff's deputy made him nervous as anything, but even if he made it through this, the legal penalty for a sheriff's murder was likely more severe than that for most murders. Tommy's chest constricted with fright.

"Jessie Bell was at home and at her Uncle Simms' on the day you two disappeared. She's got folks to vouch for her whereabouts."

"We passed her on the road," Tommy protested. "That's where it happened."

"If your story's true, then what did she do with the sheriff?" Joel demanded, not sure what to make of the situation. Despite having encountered many a deceitful woman in the county, he'd never dealt with a truly violent female—and Jessie had already been accounted for that day. The young man was their major suspect, of course, having no alibi of his own of which to speak. Nonetheless, Joel remembered all too well the unaccountable chill that Jessie's mere presence evoked.

"She used the sheriff's gun to shoot him on the road, and then she made me bury him right there in the cemetery, in someone else's fresh-dug plot. She tried to shoot me, too, but I knocked her down with the shovel. Then I ran and drove off in the sheriff's car to get away from her," explained Tommy.

The story was sounding less and less plausible. "So what did you do with the car?"

Tommy ventured to turn around and face Joel. He spoke earnestly and openly, aware he had nothing to lose by sharing the truth. "I pushed it off the bridge into the Santee River, just a day or so after I got away from her."

"That's somethin' a guilty man would do."

"I did take the car. I was scared of gettin' in trouble."

"Why on earth didn't you go for help right off?"

"I was afraid of gettin' in trouble," he repeated.

Joel weighed the situation. Tommy was obviously frightened and seemed harmless enough. *What if he's lying?* Then Joel would be put in the unfavorable position of charging Gaynelle's fiancé with a crime, thus ruining his own chances with the young woman. *And if he's telling the truth?* Joel considered this possibility, once more recalling the hair-raising effect Jessie had upon him. Again he'd be in the same situation with Gaynelle—he'd be charging her family, and Tommy would be back in her life once more.

Having been chief deputy for a long time, Joel was no newcomer to the realities of the world. Cases were often complicated, and he'd learned to draw the line with certain investigations. This was the first time, however, that Joel found it in his own personal interest to turn a blind eye. He had become smitten with the young woman over the past couple of months, and venturing down this path with Tommy promised nothing but an empty future for himself.

"Listen, Tommy. You're a suspect right now in the murder of Sheriff Bell. No one is gonna believe Jessie did it. She's a woman. She has an alibi."

Tommy peered at Joel. "But you believe me?"

"Maybe I do." Joel lifted an eyebrow. "Or maybe I just don't wanna deal with you bein' 'round here no more. I can make all this go away, but you've gotta make yourself scarce, gotta get out o' Williamsburg County. They just now found that police wagon in the river, and everyone knows that Sheriff Bell had issues with chest pain. I can report it as an accident, probable cause 'heart attack while driving.' Everyone will buy it, lock, stock, and barrel. I'll keep your name out of the report, and in a few years, no one will remember you had any association whatsoever with the case. For now, though, the whole sheriff's department is on the lookout for you."

"I—I just need to talk with Gaynelle 'fore I go."

Laughing derisively, Joel scoffed, "No, boy. That's part of the deal. You don't need to be sullyin' up her life no more. She deserves way better than you. If I find out that she's so much as seen a hair of your hide, the deal's off. You'll be in the slammer 'fore you can sneeze."

Tommy gaped, finally understanding the officer's motivation. He had no choice. He had no means and no power. If he listened to this officer of the law, however, he could probably cross county lines and get safely away. He could head back over to Clarendon County, maybe even find a job again at that same store in Manning. Those were good folks, and it had been a while since Tommy had had a comfortable place to stay. He'd been so afraid of being arrested for the murder that he'd been hiding out for weeks in flea-ridden barns and tick-infested thickets. It was a relief to think of going back to Manning, to a life with a warm bed and regular meals. Tommy nodded and answered gravely, "Yes sir, I understand."

37 • Manning

WHEN TOMMY ARRIVED IN MANNING, dirty and disheveled, he stopped by the Morris's first. Shirley answered the door, her almond-shaped eyes blinking at him. "You need somethin'?"

"It's me, Tommy." He waved a hand at himself.

Her eyes grew round. "Tommy? What in da world?"

"Can I come in?"

"I s'pose." She moved grudgingly out of the way, just enough for him to pass.

"Is Barney here?"

Shirley gestured for him to have a seat at the little table and began pouring him a glass of sweet tea. "Barney got married last year. He done moved clear across town."

"Your folks here?"

"Dey workin' at da store, like dey usually is." She peered at him curiously. "You ain't yo'self at all. Ain't even said hello. Usually you'd be tryin' to flatter me by now."

"Sorry 'bout that. You look real good. I like your hair like that, in just two braids." He sipped on the tea, grateful for how the sweet taste refreshed his mouth. He swished it around. "How you doin'?"

She stuck out her lower lip. "Been better. Leroy found hisself another girl on da side, so I had to get rid o' his sorry behind."

Tommy nodded tiredly. "My girl has herself a new fella, too. Don't think there's nothin' I can do 'bout it."

Shirley laughed. "Did ya try takin' a bath? Wanna borrow a razor?"

He put a hand up to his hair, trying to smooth it. "I was hopin' I might be able to let out a space from y'all again. My old room still free?"

She shook her head. "It's my sewin' room now. I started takin' in mendin' and alterations and even sometimes some dressmakin'. Ladies from da store bring me patterns, and I sew 'em. I like it heaps better dan cleanin' houses."

He sighed. "I don't got money nohow. I was hopin' I could get my old job back at the store, that I could jus' pay y'all later." He buried his head in his hands. "I don't know what I'm gonna do."

"Hey," she patted his shoulder. "Don't you worry none. We'll figgur it out. Barney's room is open now. Maybe you can rent it. It's a sight bigger dan your old one."

Tommy blinked up at her. "You think?"

"I'm sure my folks won't mind you stayin' a li'l while, anyway."

"I'd sure appreciate it."

"'Cept… you better take a bath before dey see you, or dey might not let you stay, after all."

Eight months later

Tommy let himself into the house as quietly as he could, trying not to disturb the Morrises. He'd have to return Barney's car in the morning, but he needed to get some sleep first.

As the door to his upstairs bedroom creaked open, Shirley peeked her head out of the sewing room. "You out late." She projected her whisper down the hall.

He nodded. "You're up late, too."

"But I ain't traipsin' all over da country. Where'dya go?" She squinted at him suspiciously.

"You know."

"Gaynelle again? She still wid dat other man?"

He nodded.

"She didn't see you?"

He shook his head, and Shirley laughed.

"Dat a sweet girl, but you gotta move on."

"Move on to what?" Tommy rubbed his face.

"You used to go 'round wid all da girls. Remember how you even used to flirt wid me?"

Tommy smiled wanly. "And you put me in my place every time."

"Dat's cuz I was wid Leroy, and you know it."

Tommy shook his head. "Even before then."

"Dat was cuz… o' Gaynelle's family, really. I told you 'bout dat."

"How they bought y'all's place from under you," he said hesitantly.

"All cuz we hung out wid dat li'l white girl. So when you talked to me, course I was scared to death we'd get run outta town again. Least Mr. Bell found us dis nice place to stay here and got my pa a job at da general store."

He nodded. "This place is bigger than his own house."

"Still upset us."

"But you ain't scared no more?"

"Of goin' out wid you?" She laughed. "Tommy, you done been livin' wid us fer ages now. And you been spendin' most all da rest of your time wid us, too, when you not off tryin' to figgur out what Li'l Miss Gaynelle be up to. I think dey'd have run us off by now if dey was gonna."

He shrugged sheepishly. "I still think you're awfully pretty. Wanna go on a date sometime?"

Shirley tilted her head as if she were only considering, but a broad smile lit up her face. "Hmm… I don't know. You a single man?"

He considered for a moment. "I don't wanna be."

She laughed. "Now dat's an answer." Growing more serious, she shrugged. "If you date me and it don't work out, you gonna hafta live somewhere else."

"Then it better work out."

She smiled, but then her smile hardened. "And if I find you chasin' after Miss Gaynelle, I swear I'm gonna run you over wid Barney's car. I ain't puttin' up wid dat."

His jaw dropped. "Shirley, we ain't even been on a first date yet!"

She crossed her arms. "Jus' lettin' you know how it's gonna be. You date me, you betta treat me right."

"I would. I—I will. And… I'm not chasin' after her. I ain't even tryin' to speak to her. I jus' wanna know she's alright. I don't like that fella she's with." Tommy shuddered.

Shirley sighed. "Goodnight, Mr. Salters."

Tommy swiftly closed the distance between them. "Can I have a goodnight kiss?"

"No." She scowled at him a moment, then held out her hand. "But I s'pose you can kiss my hand goodnight, if you like."

He dropped to one knee and took her hand as if it were the most precious and delicate in the world, grazing it with a kiss. He looked up. "Like that?"

"Dat will do."

"Will you still go on a date with me?"

"Maybe. Maybe not." She was having a hard time not smiling again, though, and he knew it.

He cast her one of his charming, lopsided grins. "I really hope you will. Goodnight, Miss Morris."

38 • The Road Ahead

Four years later
November 1931, Greeleyville, SC

BLOND CURLS TOSSING IN THE WIND, Gaynelle laughed gaily. The nippy breeze blew her scarf behind her, a flapping silken banner. She pulled their new Ford Standard up to the farmhouse, slamming on the brakes and honking the horn. Ever since Joel had taught her how to handle his motorcar, she'd insisted upon driving to pick up the girls, much to his chagrin.

Crunching through a layer of brittle brown and scarlet leaves, Ginny and Annie came running out to meet them. Joel picked up the younger brunette child, twirling her about in the air. Annie was a remarkably happy girl, showing little predilection for secrecy or deceit. She basked in the warmth of her mother's love and had turned out to be a most amiable child.

Gaynelle had been surprised at Joel's ongoing insistence about accompanying her to see Ginny, each and every visit. She didn't mind, even if it was a touch over-protective. Once Annie had joined them, she'd been especially glad of his company; it allowed her more time to devote to Ginny. Her daughter was growing at a rate that left Gaynelle continually stunned. Ginny's hair continued to darken and was ash brown now, but it was still curly like hers.

Pulling Ginny to the side of the car, she surreptitiously handed her a wrapped package. The increasingly self-contained girl nodded slyly and ran to stash it in the cubbyhole in the stable. This time Gaynelle had brought her *1001 Arabian Nights*, and she happily accepted back *Anne of Green Gables* for safe-keeping. Sharing these books filled Gaynelle with nostalgia.

Ginny exchanged the books with conspiratorial elation, delighted to outwit Mama in some small way. She wasn't literary at all, however, nor even what might be called dreamy. Most of the time she barely scanned through the volumes, but she loved sharing this secret, adored smuggling books with Gaynelle.

Mama would always favor Annie, and Ginny would never, could never truly please her. It wasn't Annie's fault. No, Annie adored her big sister and seemed blind to their mother's contempt for Ginny. The sisters formed a tightly-knit team, with the older girl blatantly responsible for most household duties and the younger voluntarily pitching in to help her, if a bit sporadically.

By the time Ginny returned from the stables, Clayton had joined them outside. His hair had grown whiter and his brow more lined, but he still posed an intimidating figure.

He broke into a jovial smile. "Hello, Sheriff. Hey Gaynelle." He nodded at the Ford. "You drive that thing here again yourself?"

"If Amelia Earhart can fly a plane across the ocean, then I should be able to drive a motorcar," she laughed. "Least that's what Vivian says."

"I reckon maybe she's got a point."

Rushing to give him a hug, Gaynelle joyously announced, "Joel and I have some good news, Daddy!"

Clayton raised an eyebrow. Good news was an unceasing onslaught with this couple. As Jessie came outside, he guessed, "Did you finish your new house?"

"No..." Gaynelle smiled, waiting for another guess. Over his shoulder, she called, "Hey, Mama."

"Did you manage to stud Julep out successfully?" he proposed.

"Why, we did indeed. Queen Blue is expected to have her colt in late spring, or so Dr. Connor says." Gaynelle paused, biting her lip, then threw up her hands. "But not before me!"

"You don't say!" Clayton burst out, laughing with delight. "Congratulations!" he enthused, clapping hugs on each of them once more. His gratitude at her finding a husband as stable as Joel swelled yet again. Joel would make a wonderful father. Their happiness was and would continue to be affirmation of the best sort—confirming his and Jessie's decision to adopt Ginny, to give Gaynelle a fresh start on a life together with the right man. A child, any child—not necessarily Ginny in particular—could have ruint Gaynelle's chances. Instead, Clayton now had the pleasure of seeing his daughter's newly formed, successful family blossom and grow, despite the ever-worsening depression that now held the country in its grip.

Turning to the girls, Gaynelle declared, "You're gonna be aunts!"

Ginny's mouth dropped. "You're havin' a baby?"

"What? A baby?" Annie stared at Gaynelle's still-flat stomach then squealed.

Jessie stepped forward, pressing her lips together as the din continued. Joel was swinging Annie around, and Ginny was trying to make Gaynelle sit down, but Jessie didn't begrudge Gaynelle the attention. Such a well-established family played perfectly into Jessie's desire for her own stability. Joel's position and competence were an ever-present threat, in a way, but he'd as yet given no substantial indication that he suspected her with regards to the sheriff's death. There had been certain sideways glances, but if he hadn't brought it up thus far, she doubted he ever would. Stepping forward, she begrudgingly smiled at him, surprised at the sincere rush of satisfaction their news gave her. This new sheriff was a sensible and discreet man, and while he might not be as tall or broad as Clayton— few men were—he seemed just as sturdy, rooted to the ground even more firmly, if anything, securing their future in his own self-interest. Jessie could be glad of this pregnancy cementing their bond. Maybe they'd turn their focus towards their own child, once it was born. Not that she cared if they wanted to continue going on these little outings with Ginny, especially since Annie had begun joining them. Let them play the doting relatives and give her some much-needed peace and quiet as long as they liked.

A few minutes later, the attractive young family was roaring off towards Kingstree, this time with Joel driving. Ginny and Annie had to shout from the backseat of the Ford as they discussed the film they were headed to see. Then they all debated the merits of the new talkie movies against the old silent films.

"The pianist's accompaniment set the mood so wonderfully," Gaynelle insisted, full of nostalgia for the silent films, "makin' each showing unique, no matter how many times you watch the same film. And the intertitles between shots tell you what's going on, so you still have all the words."

"I don't like having to read so fast," Annie explained, almost apologetically.

"Me neither," Joel agreed.

"Well, I just like hearing what they're saying," Ginny stated, no-nonsense as always.

"Fine! Y'all win." Gaynelle gave an exaggerated sigh. "Talkies *aren't* as grand musically, but seems as though they have it. Apparently I'm just an old '20's gal." Turning further in her seat, she drank in Ginny's smug, self-contented expression. Annie's lips were set in pudgy thoughtfulness, her collar turned up in the breeze. Joel's hand settled on Gaynelle's knee, protective in its warmth. She wanted to remember them all just as they were at that moment. No matter how much she might wish for things to stay the same—regarding the movies, or Ginny's youth, or even those occasional glimpses of Tommy she used to imagine—life kept rolling forward. A flutter low within her abdomen reminded her that, indeed, time was a beautiful thing. Gaynelle rested her fingers lightly over the spot. Smiling with contentment, she turned back around, clasping her husband's hand as she looked forward to the road ahead.

Acknowledgments

I AM ONCE MORE IMMENSELY THANKFUL for my support network, especially my husband Michael. I couldn't have done it without him.

Laura Landstrom not only edited this novel, but she unfailingly cheered me on throughout the entire process, always encouraging.

Many thanks to Linda Brown on a number of levels: for providing inspiration with local anecdotes through both her book publications and her *Royal Town Rambles* blog; for improving the authenticity of the locale descriptions; and for catching typos. Beyond all that, I was blown away when she recently unearthed the only photograph I've ever seen of the very Caroline this entire fictional trilogy began with—a lovely image I never, ever expected to see. Linda has influenced these stories from the very beginning, and I am profoundly grateful to her for her passion for local history, for her dedicated scholarship, and for her support.

My sister and parents were early, solicitous readers. More recently, my cousin Jennifer Durham lent her critical eye to save me

Acknowledgments

from a few awkward sentences and consistency blunders; her editorial skills are so sharp that I like to fancy that it runs in the family!

My daughter Fiona pushed me to get the novel polished enough to submit, while my entrepreneurial son Alex insisted I actually do it—that I get this trilogy out there to readers at last.

It's impossible to recall everyone who helped me on this novel's journey over the years, but I'd like to send warm hugs to the members of my writing groups. I miss not only their feedback but their friendship, as we've been on hiatus ever since the coronavirus pandemic hit. They certainly helped shape at least a few chapters of this novel. Whether or not we ever reconvene, I am indebted for all their help.

Oddly enough, the pandemic itself gave me the opportunity to regroup instead of continually trying to produce new work. Instead, I've been able to focus more on getting my work published, though I'll stop short of being grateful for the cause of this occasion. Still, there's a silver lining in almost every situation, and perhaps this is it for me. Of course, it might also have something to do with my kids having flown the nest. It's so strange having them both off at university. Between their absence and the pandemic, I suppose I've had the chance to finally wrap up a few things. So here you are, and I really hope you've enjoyed the story—for readers like you are the entire point of all such grand endeavors, of course!

Keep reading for a preview of the third and last volume of the Silk Trilogy:

Homespun

SOPHIA ALEXANDER

ONALEX BOOKS

Savannah, GA

1• Zingle's Family

October 1917, Greeleyville, SC

RENNIE DIDN'T KNOW SHE'D JUST FINISHED HER LAST DANCE with her unborn child. Breathlessly, she sank into a chair and smiled at Ben. Her five-year-old was perched on his grandma Epsie's lap, bouncing to the rhythm of guitar music. His eyes twinkled in the light of the flickering bonfire; they watched her expectantly, waiting for her to resume the dance.

"Mommy's tuckered right now—but check out your pa." Her face squinched as she indicated the lanky man. He continued their exuberant dance alone, like some sort of great blue heron strutting in their midst. Absently holding her swollen abdomen, she turned her attention back towards him.

Despite their years of marriage, she still marveled at Zingle Caddell's coordination. No matter how much he drank, his reflexes remained unusually quick. His sharp movements and impeccable timing made him a pleasure to watch, especially now with the fiery haze of smoke silhouetting him and Epsie yipping encouragement. Rennie clapped enthusiastically when the music ended.

Grinning, Zingle scooped up his tattered old Fedora, discarded at some point during the dance. He flicked it onto his head at its characteristic jaunty angle, then joined his brother-in-law. Accepting a jug from Tink, he straddled the bench, eyes closing gratefully as he swigged the moonshine, savoring its burn down his throat.

The teenager strummed a languid chord. "Them bones gettin' a bit creaky, ain't they, Zingle? Your feet barely left the ground."

Zingle snorted. "Ah, you just sittin' there behind that guitar cuz you ain't got a hope o' movin' like me."

Tink only smiled, saying easily, "I'm sittin' here cuz I'm the only one that can play."

Roaring with laughter, Ben slid off Epsie's lap. "Uncle Tink can play the guitar and you can't, Pa!"

"You don't think so?" Cocking an eyebrow, Zingle reached for the instrument. "Jus' hand it over, Injun. I'll show y'all what I can do with it."

Tink hesitated for a moment then shrugged, passing it to him.

Rennie's smile faded. She rose awkwardly to her feet, recognizing the steely flash in Zingle's gray eyes. Then she rushed towards them. "Don't give it to him. Stop it, Zingle."

Her words were wasted. Zingle was already lifting the guitar over his head. The next moment he was swinging downwards. She threw herself forward to try to catch it, hoping to halt the destruction of her younger brother's beloved instrument. The guitar slammed against her outstretched arms, taking her to the ground with it. She lay there for a moment, gasping, then caught at her abdomen and moaned.

"Damn it, Rennie!" Zingle yelled. "God blast, I ain't cracked! I wasn't really gonna mess it up. Stupid woman."

As Tink tried to help her up, Zingle scowled, pushing him away. "Leave her be. She don't need none o' your help, neither."

Picking up his guitar, Tink backed away, eyeing Zingle warily. "You okay, Rennie?"

Grimacing, she clambered to her feet. Her face contorted as she began to examine and then clutch at a widening damp patch on her skirt. "Oh, no."

"Her water's done broke." Epsie rushed forward to steady her.

Rennie looked up in alarm. "Lord have mercy, I ain't due for at least two more months."

"Jus' go clean yourself up," Zingle growled. "You womenfolk always gotta get so excited over every little thing." He took another swig of moonshine. A moment later, he was coughing and sputtering. Epsie had just landed a smack to the backside of his head.

"You the sorriest excuse for a husband I ever did see!" She spat on the ground in front of him before helping Rennie into the house.

Zingle stared after them for a moment and then back at Tink, who bent his head to tune his guitar. A silken cascade of ebony hair hid his expression.

Picking up his jug with a snort, Zingle strolled over to a chair and sank into it, muttering, "A man can't do nothin' right no more." Soon he was fast asleep in front of the dwindling fire.

A little over an hour later, Rennie clasped her stillborn tightly to her chest. Epsie disposed of the afterbirth, chanting prayers she'd learned in the Santee-Indian native tongue of her mother. She no longer remembered exactly what the words meant, just what they were for. The sacred prayers spilled by rote from her lips, keeping her from succumbing to grief as she continued to tend her daughter, pressing towels into place against the birth canal.

Rennie ignored the chant, refusing to be shielded from the death of her own child. Instead, she stared intently at the lifeless form in her arms, her misery punctuated by afterpains, each slow contraction like her womb being stabbed.

"Can I see my new baby?" Ben appeared at Rennie's elbow and tugged at her arm.

Epsie abruptly ceased her chant and caught the boy's arm. She'd failed to notice the child entering the house. Swearing under her breath, she pulled him directly towards the back door. "Get on outta here. Your mama needs to rest."

She hoped he hadn't noticed his mother's hollow-eyed gaze. There was no need for him to see her like this—none at all.

"Rosa! Come get Ben," she shouted, maintaining a grip on the child's arm. When her youngest daughter approached—her brow furrowed with concern—Epsie told her matter-of-factly, "It was too early. She'll need a little time to get over this. I need you to watch Ben, alright?"

Rosa nodded. She took Ben's hand in hers, unconsciously mimicking her mother's show of strength—her own emotion betrayed only by the glistening of her eyes. She turned to the boy. "You jus' come with Aunt Rosa, sugar. Maybe we can get Uncle Tink to play again, and this time *you* can dance for me."

Closing weary eyes for a long moment, Epsie went back into the house and latched the door. Making her way to the couch, she lay a hand against Rennie's strangely cold cheek, murmuring, "You're gonna be alright, honey. You'll get through this."

Her own chest heaved. After a deep breath, she resumed her chanting, finishing the prayers for sending a child's soul on its way.

Feeling a nudge, Zingle swatted. "Leave me alone."

"You need to wake up." Tink shook him again.

Zingle pushed the hand off his shoulder and grunted, settling back down into his chair.

"Wake up, you no-good piece o' crap."

Zingle's eyes flew open. He bared his teeth and wondered whether it was worth the bother to slug the insolence out of the youth. "Whadya call me?"

"You need to go check on Rennie. She done lost that baby."

Zingle glared, but uneasiness was swiftly replacing his anger. "Shouldn'ta done what she did. Nothin' I can do 'bout it now."

"'Cept go on in there and check to see if there *is* somethin' you can do fer her."

Slowly rising to his feet, Zingle gave an exasperated sigh and shuffled towards the house. He pulled on the creaky screen door only to find it latched. Before he could knock, however, his diminutive mother-in-law was already there, unlatching the door. She continued to block his way, however, eyeing him reproachfully.

"Rennie alright?" Zingle's gaze flicked over his mother-in-law's taut expression to stare past her.

"She's sleepin' now. Don't go wakin' her up." Epsie folded her arms across her chest. Her feet remained firmly planted in the doorway.

"I'm awake," Rennie called.

Peering into the gloom, Zingle spied her lying in the next room on the threadbare couch. He pushed past the older woman and into the kitchen, cringing as he noted the bundle in Rennie's arms. "Shame 'bout earlier."

"You didn't know it was gonna happen." She managed a forlorn smile.

"Well, it's just too bad. You should take it easy tomorrow," Zingle said charitably. He turned to Epsie. "Think you can stay with her, Ma?"

"I was plannin' on it." Her mouth puckered as though she'd just bitten into a lemon. "You got a lot to take care of."

He shrugged. "Yes'm, sure do. Gettin' up early to go fishin' with Tink, and I ain't got nothin' together yet. We'll be down at the Santee River if you need us."

Epsie shook a spatula at him. "You gotta go make them funeral arrangements, boy."

"Funeral? That baby weren't even born yet." Zingle raised an eyebrow.

She smacked him on the arm with the spatula. "I ain't got the patience for any more foolishness outta you, Zingle. You best go make them arrangements—no more backtalk. And you better not go breathin' vapors all over them good folks, neither."

Backing away from Epsie, he grinned at her indignant glare. As he turned and headed off the porch, he shot out, "You a right mean Injun, Ma."

"Ain't got a lick o' common decency," she murmured, glaring at Zingle's tall profile as he swung his arms down the lane and began to whistle. Clutching at the protective amulet she wore around her neck, she struggled to quell the rising angst she felt towards her son-in-law—an angst only just beginning to take form.

About the Author

I, Sophia Alexander, am the mother of a college-age son and daughter in addition to a number of manuscripts. A naturopathic-doctor-turned-writer, I used to feel sheepish about the huge swing in my career; recently, however, I've realized that some of my favorite novelists also have science backgrounds, so I'm in outstanding company that way. We live on the outskirts of the beautiful city of Savannah, GA, where my husband was born, and studied at the College of Charleston in the even-more-beautiful city where I was born, then at Bastyr University for grad school in the Pacific Northwest. Savannah and Charleston are 'sister cities' full of historic buildings and trees—majestic live oaks especially—but beware visiting, as you might then feel compelled to relocate here. Many do. I now divide my time between Savannah and my grandparents' old home in rural South Carolina, near my folks. There, most of my hours are spent in a big writing study that was once a parlor that I was forbidden from entering as a child (I sometimes wonder what they would think of this, and if I'm actually being ornery...). The Silk Trilogy is my debut work, aside from a few award-winning short stories in local anthologies. I hope you enjoy reading it. If so, you can hear my musings and receive updates on my publications by signing up for my newsletter at authorsophiaalexander.blogspot.com and by following me on social media:

www.facebook.com/authorsophiaalexander
Instagram: authorsophiaalexander
Twitter: @authorsophiaa